Lady Georgiana Fullerton

The Life of Mère Marie de la Providence

Foundress of the Helpers of the Holy Souls

Lady Georgiana Fullerton

The Life of Mère Marie de la Providence
Foundress of the Helpers of the Holy Souls

ISBN/EAN: 9783337053956

Printed in Europe, USA, Canada, Australia, Japan

Cover: Foto ©Raphael Reischuk / pixelio.de

More available books at **www.hansebooks.com**

THE LIFE

OF

MÈRE MARIE DE LA PROVIDENCE

Foundress of the 'Helpers of the Holy Souls'

BY

LADY GEORGIANA FULLERTON

THIRD EDITION, WITH PREFACE AND APPENDIX

BY THE

Rev. SYDNEY F. SMITH, S.J.

LONDON: BURNS & OATES, LIMITED

NEW YORK, CINCINNATI, CHICAGO: BENZIGER BROTHERS

1896

PREFACE.

Devotion to the souls departed is a feeling natural to all Christians. Even those outside the Church experience an instinctive emotion at the thought of prayers for the dead, although they do not believe in their efficacy; the sentiment is universal, but even when it is founded on faith it does not always bear the fruits it ought to produce. Few there are who steadily, fervently, and perseveringly act on their convictions in this respect. The dead are too often neglected, even by those who fondly loved them on earth. So thought the chosen soul whom God inspired, some thirty years ago, to found the Congregation of the Helpers of the Holy Souls. The following pages will present a sketch of her life and of her work.

Should this simple record of what one valiant woman effected during a brief period of years, in our own times, and without any other resources than an ardent faith, a strong will, and a devoted heart, inspire even one reader with the thought of treading in her footsteps, and working like her for the salvation of souls, the end of the writer will be abundantly fulfilled.

PREFACE TO THE THIRD EDITION.

I HAVE been asked to bring up to date the account of the works carried on by the Helpers of the Holy Souls, and this I have done in the Second Appendix. I have also been asked to introduce this new edition with a few words of preface. Perhaps this latter office is superfluous, for the name of the authoress still lives in the reverence of English Catholics, and her recommendation is still a sufficient guarantee of the excellence of any work to which it has been given. At the same time I am glad to bear testimony to the great good done by these nuns, in this city of London, in so quiet and unostentatious a way, as likewise to the solid character of their religious training. In particular, I am sure all who know them must be struck by the fulness with which they have inherited their Foundress's simple reliance on the Providence of God, and the manifest response from on high with which it is justified. Their work is well deserving of the notice of English Catholics, and may the same Providence which has hitherto supported them inspire some generous young hearts to reinforce their ranks.

I may take this opportunity to mention, for the sake of those who would like to learn something more about the Helpers and their work, that with the Commemoration of All Souls, each year, an octave of special devotions with daily sermons commences in the Chapel at 1 Gloucester Road, and that Leo XIII. has recently granted a plenary indulgence on the usual conditions to all who have attended these services five times.

SYDNEY F. SMITH, S.J.

31 FARM STREET.
Feast of the Maternity of the Blessed Virgin, 1896.

CONTENTS.

APPENDIX.

THE LIFE

OF

MÈRE MARIE DE LA PROVIDENCE.

CHAPTER I.

EUGÉNIE'S CHILDHOOD.

EUGÉNIE SMET was born at Lille, in France, on the Feast of the Annunciation, 1825. Her father, M. Henry Smet, was a highly-respected citizen of that town; and her mother, Mdlle. Pauline de Mont d'Hiver, belonged to an ancient and noble family in Picardy.

The position, the ample means, as well as the moral and social qualities of her parents, combined to make her home as bright and happy a one as possible. She was beloved by her numerous relatives. The world smiled upon her from her infancy. She would not have exchanged her lot for any other upon earth. No sorrows, no ill-usage, no bereavement or disappointments clouded her early days. She was a strong, healthy, high-spirited, and highly-gifted girl, who enjoyed to the utmost the genial atmosphere of affection and kindness in which she lived, the society of loving friends, the beauties of Nature, and all the innocent pleasures of existence. But even in the gay hours of her happy childhood a Divine voice spoke to her heart of the sufferings which were to become the object of her lifelong solicitude.

She was scarcely more than an infant when the idea of Purgatory laid hold of her mind. She used to picture it to herself as a dark room, in which a little friend of hers who had lately died was perhaps shut up, whilst she was running about amongst the flowers in the bright sunshine; and she longed to open the door and to let her out.

When a little older, as she was bounding along one day at the head of a troop of young companions, in hot pursuit of butterflies, she suddenly stopped short, and remained pensive and motionless. The other children gathered around her, anxious to know what was occupying her. Roused from her fit of abstraction, she said, ' Do you know what I was thinking of?' As none of them guessed, she exclaimed, ' Tell me, if one of our playfellows were shut up in a fiery prison, and that by saying a few words we could let her out, should we not be sure to do it?' There was a pause: no one could understand what she was driving at. ' The

Holy Souls,' she went on to say, 'are shut up in a prison of fire : the good God would let them out if we prayed for them : why don't we pray for those poor souls ?'

Thus early did the thought haunt her mind which was to take hereafter a definite shape and influence her whole life. Even though the next bright-winged butterfly, darting by the little pleader for the Holy Souls, dispelled the solemn vision, and sent her scampering over the daisied field, we cannot but discover in this little incident the germ of a vocation, so strongly dawning amidst the wild glee of a childish heart.

Another trait of the future Foundress's early days suggests the same idea. Her hair had sometimes to be dressed in the complicated manner which was then in vogue. Every successive generation has to endure a certain amount of physical suffering, in compliance with the reigning absurdity of the moment, which, if it were practised as a penance, would excite in some cases compassion, and in others ridicule.

The intense discomfort we see persons going through in endeavouring to conform themselves to every successive freak of fashion makes one sometimes wonder how far this absolute submission might, under certain circumstances, extend, and whether sensible women would obey if, from those mysterious sources whence the word of command proceeds in such matters, an intimation were, for instance, given that the Chinese practice of compressing the feet—so as to make walking not difficult, but impossible—was to be, for a time, adopted.

At the time we are writing of, the head, it appears, was subjected to a painful ordeal ; and to an eager restless child the constraint of this elaborate process amounted to a real suffering, which sometimes drew tears from her eyes. Eugénie's nurse, concerned at the pain she was inflicting on her young charge, would say, ' Shall I leave off, my dear?' ' No, no,' the little girl answered, ' go on ;' and then was heard speaking to herself, and saying in a low voice. ' It is for the souls in Purgatory !'

Whence, but directly from God—who had chosen her as an instrument of mercy towards His loved and suffering creatures—could have arisen this spontaneous and abiding solicitude for the Holy Souls, so early evinced, so independent of personal feelings, so apparently at variance with the brightness of her early lot, and the joyous temperament with which Nature had endowed this child of prosperity?

Those who knew her in youth, as well as those who were intimately acquainted with her in after years, could not but feel that her vocation had all the marks of a Divine mission, so singularly out of keeping, if we may use that expression, did its solemn and mournful import appear with the tenor of her early life and the gaiety of her character.

When we hear of a vocation to a life of prayer, labour, and suffering in behalf of departed souls, the first thought which suggests itself is that of a heart broken by some agonising bereavement, or full of intense anxiety as to the fate of some beloved one, which can only find relief in continual appeals to God's merciful goodness—of one dead to all earthly joys, and following with yearning solicitude the spirit of a relative or a friend, dearer than life itself, to that mysterious region beyond the grave, over which it broods with impassioned tenderness.

True it is that some who have joined the Order Eugénie founded have been mourners of this description, who have sought and found in it what nothing on earth could have given them —patience for the weary length of a life they once trembled to contemplate.

But, much as the special devotion of this new family of religious souls adapts itself to the spiritual needs of mourners, there is something beautiful in the thought that she who was to lead the way in the path of heroic devotion to the Holy Souls gave no blighted, no aching heart to that new work of supernatural mercy which she conceived and achieved. We might borrow a line from one of her poets, and say that her bark was launched on the stream of life with

'Youth at the prow, and Pleasure at the helm.'
No personal affliction, but a wonderful love of
God and of His creatures, pointed to the place
of expiation, to that scene of devout suffering,
where, St. Catherine of Genoa tells us, the pain
is beyond human experience, but 'O! may she
be blessed for saying it, and most blessed be our
Father in heaven for permitting her to say it)
where there is likewise a joy beyond what we
can imagine. Our nearest, though still remote,
conception of that happiness and that suffering
is derived from what we know of the feelings of
the martyrs amidst excruciating torments. But
they had not seen God for one brief instant, and
then felt what it was to lose the bliss of that
vision.

When our Divine Lord has marked out a
soul for a special purpose, He confers upon it
certain gifts, which are the preludes, the tokens,
and usually the means by which it effects its
appointed work. The singular gift which enabled
Eugénie to fulfil her mission in its practical development was, like that mission itself, indicated
in her childhood. This gift was an unbounded,
firm, invariable, bold, faithful, daring reliance on
Divine Providence. Her whole course was a
visible illustration of, a perpetual homage to,
the existence of that sacred attribute of God—
scoffed and derided by infidels, lovingly adored
and proclaimed by the children of the Church.

The first time that she distinctly remembered having made an earnest appeal to Providence was at the age of eleven, when she was at the school of the Sacred Heart at Lille. She took the greatest delight at that time in all the ceremonies of Divine worship. From her seat in the convent chapel, which was close to the sanctuary, she could see the altar, and gaze on the Tabernacle to her heart's content. Great was her despair one day when the nun at the head of her class announced that on the occasion of an approaching festival those of the pupils who were not provided with white dresses would have to give up the front seats, and sit behind the others, in order not to spoil the general effect. Eugénie's heart sank within her. Of all the days of the year, that was the very one on which she cared most to have a full view of the sanctuary.

There seemed no help for it. Her parents were in the country. There was no time to write home for a white dress. It suddenly occurred to her that in this emergency her dear Divine Providence would come to her assistance.

No sooner had the thought entered her mind than she knelt down, clasped her hands together, and made her petition. 'O my dear Providence!' she cried, 'I do beg of You to send me a white dress. I will always love You, and ask You for everything I want, from the least thing to the greatest—for a pin or for heaven.' More than thirty years afterwards she vividly recalled the intense ardour and the entire confidence with which she put up this prayer. Never was there an engagement more faithfully adhered to than the bargain Eugénie made that day with her Divine Lord. What she promised in her childhood was performed to the letter.

God vouchsafed on that occasion to reward her faith, and to give her a pledge of His readiness to grant her prayers. On the eve of the feast she went up to the dormitory as certain as any girl in the school that she should find on her bed the coveted white dress. Others had asked their parents, or their friends, for what they wanted: she had applied directly to the good God. He was sure, she thought, not to disappoint her. And so it turned out. By some means which she never discovered, the white dress was forthcoming, and from that day forward Eugénie never hesitated to deal with God as a favourite child with a loving Father.

The little girl who prayed at school for a white frock was described by the martyred Père Olivaint, in after years, as 'that good Mère Marie, the spoilt child of Providence, who is exacting, capricious, dictatorial with Almighty God; who asks for everything she wants, and makes her own terms with the Divine Majesty.'

Purgatory on the one hand, Providence on the other, were the two devotions blended together, as it were, in Eugénie's soul. She kept thinking, 'How can I help God? He is my helper; He gives me everything. What can I give Him in return?'

As she was trying to solve that question, a sudden light came into her mind: 'Ah, I know what I will do. I see now how I can be the Providence of God. He loves the Holy Souls in Purgatory, and yet He cannot, on account of His justice, set them free. Well, I will give Him those souls He loves, and I will ask all my friends to join with me in saying prayers and making little sacrifices for their souls. I shall say to them, God is your Providence: will you refuse to be His Providence? He has given you everything: surely you will give Him something.'

The spirit of apostleship was already strongly apparent in this young disciple of the Sacred Heart. From her religious teachers she had learned lessons of self-devotion and zeal which were beginning to bear fruit, and her devotion to the Holy Souls was the form which that zeal was beginning to assume.

She was endowed with all the natural gifts which tend to give a personal influence over others. Her countenance and her manner were so winning, her affectionate frankness, her brightness and gaiety, so irresistible, that she was a general favourite with all her companions. Quick

and clever at learning, and always at the head of
her class, her liveliness and high spirits made her
equally the life and soul of the play-hours. The
moment she appeared on the playground all the
girls crowded around her; and it was at these
times that, with youthful eloquence, she pleaded
the cause of the Holy Souls, and obtained on
every side promises of prayers, and acts of mortification in their behalf.

These appeals were short and earnest, and
the transition rapid to an eager participation in
active games and childish sports. She, who in
a short space of years was to accomplish a great
work, was quick in all she did. It was her wont
then, and ever afterwards, to carry her point by
a few heartfelt words, which never failed in their
effect.

Eugénie's teachers were often struck by the
apparently opposite qualities they remarked in
her. One of them had noticed that, passionately
as she loved amusement, there was no day that
she did not spend part of her playtime in prayer;
and so she asked her, ' What prayers are you in
the habit of saying, my child, when you go into
the chapel during recreation?' ' Madam,' Eugénie answered, ' I say the Litany of the Holy
Ghost in order to be enlightened as to the vanity
of this world, and the *Veni Creator*, that I may
know what is my vocation.'

The Holy Spirit, to whose guidance she committed herself with so much faith, soon inspired her with a leaning towards the religious life. The thought of consecrating herself entirely to God began to fill her with new and delightful emotions. At the same time, there was a dark side to the picture. Her strong affection for her family and her home saddened a prevision which, if realised, would entail a separation she could hardly endure to contemplate.

One day when she had been musing on this subject, and suffering from the contradictory feelings it inspired, she went suddenly up to the nun who was in charge of the class, and said, 'Madam, will you be so kind as to tell me if one can have a vocation to the religious life without an attraction to it?' 'No doubt of it,' was the reply. 'Such vocations are, in one sense, the best, because there is then less danger of being deceived by imagination.'

'O, thank you, madam!' Eugénie exclaimed. 'I am very glad, then, to know that. A great sorrow at the idea of leaving home would be no proof that one had not a vocation; but it might be a proof, on the contrary, that it was a solid one.'

Eugénie's progress in all her studies kept pace with her growth; pursuit of knowledge was a pleasure, not a toil, to her active mind. She liked every branch of learning, but chiefly the natural sciences. Astronomy interested her to such a degree that at no time of her life could she look at a starry sky without emotion. In this she resembled St. Ignatius, one of the Saints towards whom she felt much devotion—he who used to stand on the roof of the Roman College gazing on the glowing vault of heaven, his soul raised to the highest contemplation of the Divine Creator, and earth vanishing to nothingness in his estimation. The tone, if we may so speak, of his sanctity was peculiarly congenial to Eugénie's mind. There was in her soul a singular union of strength which might almost be termed masculine, and a tenderness of devotion which delighted in the most simple and childlike acts of piety. The thought of the Guardian Angels —of her own, and those of her friends—was so constantly present to her, that one would have imagined she was personally acquainted with them.

Madame Desmarquets, the nun who had been her teacher, left Lille some time before Eugénie's school-days were over. This was a real sorrow to her, and, realising without the shadow of a doubt all that belongs to the spiritual world, she found consolation in sending this dear friend communications through their respective Guardian Angels. She never doubted that these celestial messengers delivered her messages.

We find her pious mistress writing to her on one occasion, ' You have every reason, my dearest child, to be satisfied with the faithfulness of your Guardian Angel. Mine did not fail to convey to me that I should pray for you in a very special manner on Easter Day, for I certainly felt moved to do so with singular fervour.'

Such are the reminiscences of Eugénie's childhood and early youth up to the time of her leaving school—such the promise she gave of future excellence. In the following chapter we shall follow her to her home, and see her extending by degrees the devout apostolate begun amongst her playmates.

CHAPTER II.

EUGÉNIE IN HER HOME.

ON the 4th of September, 1843. M. and Madame Smet welcomed their daughter home at their country house near the little town of Loos les Lille. Her education was completed, and she had now to begin life under a new aspect. The time was come for her to put in practice what she had learnt during the happy years spent at school. It might be said of her that 'she had a great heart, and knew how to will' (*corde magno et animo volenti*,—a knowledge and a power without which holiness can hardly exist. Neither herself nor her parents

could then foresee what were God's designs on
her soul ; but no one could be long with Eugénie
and not perceive that what she willed that she
would do, and that what she did would be well
done.

In taking possession of a pretty little room,
carefully furnished and arranged for her by a
mother's tender care, her first feeling was one of
joy that she could see from her window the spire
of the village church. 'God is there,' she felt ;
and that thought hallowed the quiet landscape,
and endeared to her the room which was to be
for several years her cell, her oratory, the place
of her rest, the scene of her fervent converse with
her dear Lord and His Blessed Mother.

It is always an epoch, and sometimes a turn-
ing-point, in a girl's life when she has first a
room of her own——one anxiously watched by her
Guardian Angel ; for on the employment of her
solitary hours often depends the happiness or
the misery, the usefulness or the worse than use-
lessness, of her future existence. The priceless
gift of time is then, in some measure, placed at
her own disposal, to be carefully invested or
recklessly squandered. O that the young could
know with what feelings the old gather up the
fragments that remain——the ebbing treasure they
make so little account of !

It is not often that at once a young creature
of Eugénie's age sets herself to regulate her life

as she did. From the first day she returned
from school she formed for herself a plan which
included prayer, active works of charity, and the
exact performance of social and domestic duties.
Charity was the passion of her heart, and all the
powers of her mind were soon directed to devise
means to assist the poor. Her purse, though
fairly supplied by her parents, was, alas! soon
exhausted, and then she invented all sorts of
expedients for the relief of her dear destitute
clients. Amongst other perquisites, she claimed
all the fallen fruit in her father's large orchard,
and had no scruple in 'helping the good God,'
as she used to say, by giving the trees some
vigorous shakes, and thus hastening the work of
Providence.

Generosity, in every sense of the word, was
the leading feature of her character; and we
may perhaps trace the origin of her ardent devotion to the Holy Souls, and the spirit of the
Society she founded in their behalf, to this special characteristic; for the Heroic Act of Charity,
by which the religious of her Order not only consecrate themselves and their whole time to the
relief and delivery of the sufferers in Purgatory,
but also make over to them the satisfactory
portion of their good works—a sacrifice which
cannot be made in favour of the living—is, no
doubt, the highest possible stretch of generous
self-devotion.

But as long as her solicitude for departed souls was only an aspiration—or, if we may so express it, a presentiment of her future vocation—her zeal found vent in a variety of good works. She was always casting about how to promote some useful undertaking or some special devotion.

One day, while praying before the image of Our Lady of Graces *Notre Dame des Graces*), which was held in great veneration by the inhabitants of Loos, a desire seized her to ornament the altar, and to make it more worthy of the dear image to which so many devout feelings were attached. She had not at that moment a penny in her purse; but it struck her that she might compose a Litany in honour of Our Lady of Graces, which would serve the double purpose of increasing the devotion of her clients and of raising a sum for the decoration of her altar. After a few minutes of prayer and meditation, she went home and wrote one, which met with the cordial approval of the Archbishop of Cambray. With his permission it was printed and sold. After all expenses were paid, one hundred francs remained—the very sum Eugénie had bargained with our Blessed Lady to secure her for the accomplishment of her scheme. Her Litany became the favourite prayer of the pilgrims who resorted to the little sanctuary of Loos les Lille.

She was one of the first believers in the miracle of La Salette. and, when she heard that funds were being raised to build a church on the spot of the Apparition, she entered into the project with all her heart and soul.

Her plan always was, to give to a pious work as much as she possibly could, and then boldly to beg of others the means of carrying it on. She used to say. ' It is a consolation to give oneself. but when we have nothing left there is a double merit in asking others to help us.' Some of the persons she applied to expressed doubts as to the truth of the Apparition: Eugénie thought it so likely, so natural, that miracles should take place, that she could hardly understand their hesitation.

One day as she was trying to persuade one of the nuns of the Sacred Heart, a former teacher of hers, to subscribe to the Church of La Salette, she found her by no means convinced on the subject. ' Well, madam,' Eugénie exclaimed, ' if you do not believe in the miracle, now do just make a novena for Mère Benoit, and let her drink every day some of this water from our Lady's fountain. If she is cured by the end of the novena, then I am sure you will subscribe to the church.'

Mère Benoit, one of the religious of that convent, had been laid up for years with a paralysed knee, and was pronounced incurable. But

Eugénie spoke in a tone that expressed such confidence, such earnest faith, that the good nun was struck with it, and agreed to her proposal.

On the last day of the novena a change was apparent. She was carried to the church, and, as usual, supported on her way to the altar, where she received Holy Communion: but as she returned to her place Mère Benoit felt herself perfectly able to walk, and said, ' I am cured.'   As the news spread through the chapel, great was the emotion of all those who were present. With one voice they intoned the *Te Deum*; and this miracle, confirmed by the most undoubted evidence, was one of the first series of supernatural graces which have revived in France the memory of the early days of the Church.

Love and zeal are great schemers.   Just as a miser adds one piece of gold to another, and a speculator embarks every day in some new enterprise, so a soul, consumed by a desire for the Divine glory, never rests satisfied with what it has achieved, but plans and strives and pleads—with God and with men—for the furtherance of holy works.   Every pious undertaking, whether at home or abroad, whether for the poor of her native place, or for the Chinese children, or for the persecuted Christians of the East, found in her an ever-ready advocate, an indefatigable promoter.   She had, as we have already said, a singular gift of winning others to second her efforts.

Her power in that way was quite remarkable, for the real secret of her success was her bold reliance on Providence. As a child, she had felt this unbounded confidence, and it went on increasing with her years.

She had pasted on the door of her room a little print of our Blessed Lord feeding with one hand the fowls of the air and with the other pointing to the lilies of the field. Above this picture was a scroll, with the words, 'Your Heavenly Father knoweth that you have need of these things. Take no thought for the morrow.' Each time that she went in and out, a glance at that picture reminded her to make an act of childlike faith in Divine Providence.

She organised at one time a very successful lottery for some charity, and wrote to a friend, ' We wanted 850 prizes ; we began with nothing but a shabby little doll, and a great trust in Providence. Prize number two proved tantamount to 845 prizes.'

This immense activity, this constant devotion to good works, served to sustain her desires for the religious life, which were every day acquiring fresh strength. Little as she mixed with the world, that little was all too much for a soul consumed by a thirst for self-sacrifice, and a closer union with God. Soon after her return home she had broached the subject to her parents, and found them decidedly averse to her wishes. The sufferings she was beginning to endure from neuralgic pains in the head, to which she was subject ever afterwards, had begun to affect her health, and she required an amount of care quite incompatible with the life of a Religious.

It was difficult not to admit the reasonableness of the argument, and yet Eugénie felt convinced that she was called to that life, and that God in His own time would remove the obstacles to her vocation. She had no distinct idea as to the Order she wished to join, and felt no attraction to any one in particular. She was haunted by the sense that our Blessed Lord claimed for Himself her whole heart, being, and existence; but when and where and how this consecration was to take place she did not discern.

In this state of mind it was hardly possible to urge her own convictions on her reluctant parents, and overcome their opposition. In the anxiety which this suspense was beginning to cause her, she found consolation in a sudden and marked increase of devotion to the Blessed Virgin. The love for that Divine Mother took a new form. She poured out to her in loving and fervent colloquies all the conflicting fears, hopes, joys, and sorrows of her heart.

During the month of May of the year 1853 her little room was turned into an oratory, where daily devotions were performed with more than ordinary splendour. Blue and white draperies ornamented the walls, and the image of the Mother of God was surrounded by lighted tapers and a variety of sweet flowers. That little image became Mère Marie de la Providence's companion through life. It had been solemnly consecrated by the prayers of the Church, and received the name of '*Notre Dame de la Providence*' (Our Lady of Providence). Later on it was to bear an additional title, that of '*Reine du Purgatoire*' (Queen of Purgatory). That double designation comprised the two leading characteristics of Eugénie's spiritual life.

From the month of May of that year she began to look on her Mother in heaven in a new light. She became her consolation in grief, her stay in hours of suffering, the source of every heroic resolution, the strength of her soul when desolation for a while overclouded its bright joyousness. The lips of the statue seemed to her to move, and a voice to proceed from them which said, 'One day I shall be in a chapel.'

Whatever was the origin of this impression, it stirred powerfully Eugénie's feelings. The intimation or the presentiment, whichever we consider it, was eventually realised, and the dear image before which she had so often offered herself to God, for any purpose or any work He might choose, was the silent witness of her vows when the day came that she consecrated herself and her sisters in religion to the holy vocation which we are now about to see revealed to her, who for years had said, like Mary, ' Behold the handmaid of the Lord. Be it done unto me according to Thy word.'

CHAPTER III.

THE FIRST WHISPERS OF GRACE.

IT was on the Feast of All Saints, 1853, that Eugénie Smet received the first intimation of her special vocation. The weather that year happened to be particularly fine; the brilliant sunshine, the cloudless sky, the merry peals of the church bells seemed to invite the children of the Church on earth to rejoice with their glorified brethren in heaven, and from the moment she awoke the heart of the future Helper of the Holy Souls was filled with a strange unutterable joy. During High Mass, and again at Benediction, her emotion seemed to presage some impending crisis in the life of her soul.

It was during the latter service that a kind of remorse came over her at the thought that the multiplicity of good works in which she had been engaged during the past year had prevented her from devoting herself in as special a manner as she intended to do to the relief of the Holy

Souls. A general and tacit desire to aid them had, indeed, never been absent from her mind ; but she now felt inwardly moved to something more positive, more specific, than she had as yet undertaken.

As she was praying with her head bowed down before our Blessed Lord in the Sacrament of His love, the idea of an association of prayers and good works in behalf of the dead was rising distinctly before her eyes. But then came the doubt—was it God who was inspiring her with this thought? or was it the result of her own fancy? In her unhesitating faith she determined to ask our Blessed Lord, by some unmistakable sign, to give her a token of His will. 'If You wish me to begin this work, my Lord,' she said, with the holy boldness of one accustomed to deal with God as a Father, 'make one of my friends think of the same thing, and let her speak to me about it as soon as I come out of church.'

She had taken the Gospel at its word, so to speak, and always acted upon the promise, ' Ask, and you shall receive.' In no case was her confidence deceived, and, as life went on, often and often might those other words have been addressed to her, 'O woman, great is thy faith ! be it done unto thee as thou wilt.'

On the Eve of All Souls, so memorable a day to herself and many others, it was indeed done to her as she had asked. She slowly descended the long flight of steps from the door of the church to the village square, anxiously thinking over the prayer she had made. Her heart sank within her when she reached the bottom of the stairs and no one had spoken to her. But just at that moment a young girl of her own age, a great friend of hers, came forward and said, 'Dear Eugénie, I am so glad to have met you! During the Benediction I had an inspiration. I thought of offering to join you in doing everything we can during November for the souls in Purgatory.' 'Have you indeed had that thought?' Eugénie exclaimed, with so much emotion that her friend seemed surprised, and looked at her inquiringly. Eugénie explained that what she had just said was the very proof she had herself asked of our Lord to give her, that the desire she had conceived whilst praying before the Blessed Sacrament was a true inspiration.

'O, how near God seemed to me at that moment!' she often used to say when speaking of this circumstance. The joy which had then filled her heart seemed to increase during the whole of the following day. It is a sad one to those who forget the dead all the year round, and only call them to mind when the Church puts on mourning, and reminds them in solemn accents to pray for the departed. But to Eugénie it was the most consoling of all festivals, the feast-day of her dear Holy Souls, the hour of release to many of them, the brief period during which they are held in special remembrance, the protest of their mother the Church against the heartless neglect of an unthinking world.

With the most lively faith and intense devotion Eugénie went to Communion, of course with the one intention uppermost in her mind. Just after receiving our Blessed Lord into her heart, and whilst she was renewing the consecration of her whole self and her whole life to the Divine Master whom she had deliberately chosen as the Spouse of her soul, a thought passed through her mind which was to give rise to a new Order in the Church. She said to herself, Religious communities exist which answer every need of the Church Militant on earth, but not a single one specially devoted to the relief of the suffering Church in Purgatory; was she called, perhaps, to fill up that void?

Startling are these first whispers of grace to a soul watching for God's leadings. The idea seemed too bold a one. She felt at once what it would involve, with that strange rapidity of thought which in an instant presents to the mind a whole series of consequences and considerations. She saw rising before her the old dread of a total separation from those she loved, the long array of obstacles, of oppositions, of reproaches, which meet even an ordinary vocation to the religious life; then the appearance of extravagance which the thought of founding a new Order would bear, the scorn and ridicule it would excite in worldly persons, and the contempt with which even the good and wise would treat it; then, more dimly, a consciousness that those who might pledge themselves by vows to be victims for the Holy Souls would have to bare their breast, as it were, to every kind of suffering, spiritual and temporal. No, no, she mentally exclaimed; this is going too far; it is not this that God wants of me.

Still the voice said, 'Is it not what He asks?' It seemed as if the Holy Souls were addressing to her the words of our Lord to His Apostles, 'Can you drink of the chalice we drink? Can you be baptised with the baptism of suffering that we are baptised with?' She did not venture to answer, 'I am able;' but no doubt she felt, like St. Paul, 'I can do all things through Him who strengthens me.'

From the church, that day, she went straight to the house of the Curé of the Parish, M. l'Abbé Lemaheu. He had known her from a child, and she had great confidence in his judgment. She told him simply and exactly how early and how unchanging had been her attraction to a special work for the Holy Souls, and the thoughts and desires which, that day and the previous one, had taken so strong a possession of her mind.

He listened attentively, took a little time to

reflect, and then gave his entire approbation to the plan of an Association of Prayer in behalf of the Holy Souls, and told her to put down his name in the list of associates. But, as to the idea of a Congregation specially consecrated to the same object, he at once and decidedly opposed it. In his opinion her vocation was to lead a pious life in the world, and so dedicate her time, her fortune, and her talents to active good works. The great success which had attended her various charitable undertakings he considered to be a proof that such was the will of God.

Eugénie was not discouraged by his answer ; she felt that time and patience would bring about what she herself believed to be a Divine inspiration, and that in the meantime her part must be to work, as St. Ignatius recommends, with as much earnestness as if the success of her efforts depended on herself, and to rely as entirely upon God as if she could do nothing at all.

And so she set about at once pushing on her Association, which in a very short time numbered many hundreds. She asked all those who joined it to say once a month either the ordinary beads, or a rosary composed of Acts of Faith, Hope, and Charity ; and once a year, during the Octave of All Souls, to recite five ' Our Fathers ' and five ' Hail Marys,' in honour of the Five Wounds of our Lord, and to offer up a Communion for the souls in Purgatory.

She advised the more fervent of the associates to go to Communion and make the Way of the Cross once a month, and to offer up one or more Masses in the course of the year for the same intention.

This devotion extended rapidly in all the neighbouring parishes. The priests were quite surprised at the number of Masses they were asked to say for the dead. Numbers of persons were seen in the churches devoutly performing the devotion of the Stations, and poor people received parcels of clothes with the words ‘ Pray for the Dead ’ inscribed upon them. Nor did the zealous promoter of these holy practices neglect any other means of doing good. She actively interested herself in the establishment of a Conference of the Society of St. Vincent de Paul at Loos, and devoted herself to a very peculiar and arduous apostolate amongst her poor neighbours.

One day the Curé of the church had been speaking with sorrowful indignation of the terrible manner in which the Holy Name of God is blasphemed in public-houses. And he had exclaimed, with a holy vehemence which made a strong impression on his hearers, ‘ Is there no one bold enough to speak in God’s behalf in those places where He is so deeply offended – one who will lift up his voice and protest against those insults to the Divine Majesty ? ’

One heart there was in his congregation consumed with the zeal of the house of God, and ready to dare anything for the sake of His glory. Eugénie had soon made up her mind, if M. le Curé thought it right, even though she felt in the inferior part of her nature the strongest reluctance to put herself forward in the matter : she would go round to all the public-houses in the parish, and ask leave of every landlord to affix to the walls of his tap-room a notice to the effect that no swearing was permitted there—'*On ne jure pas ici.*'

She made her offer to the Curé, frankly admitting that it would be a great relief to her if he did not accept it ; but he only smiled and said, '*My dear child, I do not know that I should have the courage myself to do what you propose ; but, as God has inspired you with the thought, I cannot say a word against it.' Upon this Eugénie set to work. It may be, perhaps, well to remark that what in a young lady in ordinary circumstances would hardly have been prudent or becoming, was in her case justified by the position she occupied in her native place. She was at that time twenty-seven years of age, and for years had been at the head of all the charitable works of the parish. Her family was so well known, her own character so much respected, that she had acquired a prescriptive right to advocate the cause of religion and de-

fend the interests of God : and so she went forth
on her crusade against oaths and blasphemy.

On a bitterly cold winter day, in the midst
of a heavy snow-storm, she called on the fourteen publicans of Loos, and received everywhere
the same answer, ' Mademoiselle might do as she
liked, provided all the others agreed to it also.'
It was, therefore, necessary to secure a general
assent : but, to her surprise, Eugénie met with
no refusals, though the consent given was not
particularly gracious.   As soon as the notices
were printed, she sallied forth again, armed with
hammer and nails, for she foresaw that no one
would help her to put them up, and, except in
one instance, her previsions were realised.

Some days afterwards her father received
an anonymous letter informing him of Mdlle.
Eugénie's round of visits, and turning it into the
utmost ridicule.   M. Smet was deeply annoyed.
It was very well to be pious and charitable, but
this was going rather too far, and he scolded his
daughter for what he termed her rash and in-
temperate zeal.   She tried to appease his anger,
and begged him not to attach importance to
anonymous comments on her conduct.   But he
would hear nothing in her defence, and ordered
her to go on the following day and remove all
the notices from the houses where she had placed
them.

Eugénie went straight to her room, knelt

down before her dear image of Our Lady of Providence, and said, with many tears, 'You know, my good Mother, that I cannot obey my father's commands : do, then, make him change his mind.' As usual, her prayer was heard, and the next morning the first thing M. Smet said, was that on second thoughts he did not care much for what the anonymous writer thought, and that she was to leave things as they were.

It would be well if persons under authority—wives, daughters, or others in a subordinate position—were sometimes to follow Eugénie's plan. They would often find a way, not only out of their difficulties, but also a strong confirmation in their faith, through the results which often follow from prayers thus simply offered up for special objects. It startles a person sometimes to find the simplest request immediately granted ; those are the moments in which, to use this devout woman's own expression, 'God seems very near to us.' Deliverance from a signal danger is not a greater proof of His omnipotence than the fulfilment of a little request ; both are equal signs of His fatherly love.

CHAPTER IV.

DAWN OF EUGÉNIE'S VOCATION.

EVERY year, for a few days, Eugénie withdrew from her domestic circle and her round of good works, to make a Retreat at the Convent of the Sacred Heart, where she was surrounded by all the holy associations of her happy childhood.

At one of these annual Retreats it was Monseigneur Chalendon who gave the spiritual exercises, and, as her own director was absent at the time, she went to confession to this holy prelate. The excellent advice he gave her, and the clear and definite answers to her questions relative to the religious life, induced her at the end of the Retreat to ask leave to write and consult him on her own vocation. The permission was kindly granted, and from that time forward a correspondence was carried on between Monseigneur and Mdlle. Smet. In that month of November, which proved an epoch in her life, she wrote and gave him an account of all that had passed through her mind during the Feasts of All Saints and of All Souls.

Like the Curé of Loos, his lordship strongly commended the pious association of intercessors for the Holy Souls. Like him, also, he hesitated to encourage the ultimate extent of her scheme.

'Your zeal,' he wrote, 'for the Souls in Purgatory I highly commend. The Church offers to the devotion of her children a variety of means to this end. You have obtained both prayers and alms for those poor souls. This is a good and beautiful work. As to your idea of an Order that would have for its object the redemption of the Holy Souls, even as the Order of Mercy was devoted to the redemption of captives, I do not deny that there is something new in it, and attractive to pious minds. But the realisation of this project would be a very difficult matter, unless God gave you extraordinary lights on the subject. The good Curé of Loos is quite right in advising you not to think of founding this new Order until you have exhausted other means of doing good.'

This answer was rather depressing than otherwise to Eugénie's hopes, and if it had been any ordinary good work—if the Holy Souls had not been interested in this question—she would have been tempted to give up all idea of carrying out her plan. She was disappointed to find that Monseigneur Chalandon, from whom she had expected a greater degree of sympathy, seemed to look upon her wishes as the work of imagination. But she fought against discouragement, and said to herself, 'This is, indeed, a trial : but if it is really God's will I shall attain my end in spite of every apparent obstacle.'

No one at that time seemed to think that she was called to the religious life, not even her friends and former teachers, the nuns of the Sacred Heart. One of them, Madame Giraud, a sister of the Cardinal of that name, says in a letter written on that subject :

'My dear Child, I do not tell you to be courageous,

know you have much more courage than strength. I am more
inclined to say, spare yourself, and do not attempt what you
cannot perform without excessive fatigue. Activity is, I know,
the very soul of your life, and, as your intentions are all holy,
our Lord will bless your efforts. I wonder, with such a mission as yours, that you venture to think of the religious life.
Your position seems so clearly indicated by Providence: do,
therefore, rest satisfied.'

Madame Desmarquets also wrote in the same
sense to her former pupil. It was only after she
had long resolved in her own mind, and, as we
have seen, mentioned her idea to a few confidential friends, that Eugénie at last spoke of it to
her confessor. When she had disclosed to him
all her thoughts on this subject, his answer quite
satisfied her, and filled her soul with a wonderful
peace.

'My child,' he said, 'I will pray and reflect
before God on what you have told me. Nothing
is impossible to Providence, and if It intends to
employ you for this work you will be provided
with the means of accomplishing it.'

From that time forward she lived in the anticipation of what was gradually engrossing all
the powers of her soul. On the 25th of January,
1854, with her confessor's permission, she made
an offering of her whole self to God for the Souls
in Purgatory, and at the same time, by her own
impulse, and as it were unconsciously, what is
called by the Church the heroic act of charity,
but only for six months in the first instance.
In her journal she wrote the following words :

'I thank Thee, my God, for the grace Thou hast vouchsafed to me this day. After Holy Communion this morning, I made a vow to perform all my actions with the intention of relieving the Souls in Purgatory. For six months only have I been permitted to make this vow: but I hope Thou wilt grant me the happiness of renewing it after that time, and then for ever.'

And accordingly, when the six months were over, with her confessor's permission, she did bind herself by a perpetual vow to that effect.

The Association of Prayers, begun by the two friends on the threshold of their parish church on the 1st of November, had marvellously succeeded, and at the end of three months fifteen hundred members were enrolled. This was in itself a great consolation to Eugénie, and also an earnest that the hope cherished in her inmost heart was destined likewise to be realised. She asked her confessor one day if he had lost sight of her project. 'No, my child,' he replied. 'I have both prayed and thought about it; and now want you to give me leave to speak of it to the Dean of St. Maurice.' 'With all my heart,' Eugénie answered, for she had the greatest veneration for that aged and saintly Curé. 'He has known me all my life, and we can place entire confidence in his prudence and piety. I know,' she added, 'that I cannot yet expect that you or he will be able to tell me positively what is God's will on this point, but I shall be satisfied if you think that I am not losing my time in useless projects.'

Some time afterwards her director wrote in a way which showed her how earnestly he was revolving in his own mind the subject of her vocation.

'I have seen the Dean of St. Maurice : we prayed before determining on the advice to give you. We are both of opinion that the desire which you so earnestly cherish is not the work of your imagination, but that you must wait patiently for the moment marked by God's Providence, and that if He really wills this foundation you will be provided with the means of accomplishing it. Now, then, in quietness and in hope meditate on your projects at the feet of our Lord. These cogitations are not useless, as they may one day lead to the promotion of His Divine glory.'

Happy in the sanction thus given to her devout aspirations, Eugénie continued the practical part of her work. One of her great objects was to popularise devotion to the Holy Souls, and she taught all the pious poor in her neighbourhood to say on their beads the Acts of Faith, Hope, and Charity with that intention. The constant use of these prayers had the twofold advantage of gaining numerous indulgences applicable to the dead, and of impressing on the minds of ignorant persons, many of them unable to read, the theological virtues contained in those acts. She printed, also, for distribution, many thousand copies of the heroic act of charity, and gave away an innumerable quantity of pictorial illustrations of the deliverance of the Holy Souls through the Holy Sacrifice of the Mass. On the back of the pictures were inscribed the words,

' O good and most sweet Jesus.' These pious publications are even now continually reprinted and disseminated in France.

We have dwelt on Eugénie Smet's peculiar attraction towards the work for the Holy Souls, and her tender love and intimate confidence in Her whom she always called the Queen of Purgatory. We will now say a few words on her ardent devotion to the Blessed Sacrament.

From a child she had felt this attraction, and her faith had suggested to her a number of pious practices connected with our Lord's sacramental presence on the altar. When the priest replaced the chalice in the Tabernacle after Benediction, she used to ask the Divine Prisoner to enclose her soul and those of her friends with Himself in that sacred captivity. And when the chalice was again withdrawn from its abode, to be removed to another altar, she followed our Lord in spirit with all those she mentally included in that spiritual procession. She had made when a child a little prayer for these occasions: ' My dear Lord,' she was wont to say, ' I desire to be shut up with Thee ; lock me up in Thy Divine Heart, and let my penance last for ever.' On one occasion at Loos she planned on a very magnificent scale a function in honour of the Feast of Corpus Christi. The banners, the garlands of flowers, the temporary altars exceeded in beauty and variety everything that had ever been seen in that part of the country. Amongst other things she erected an avenue of fir-trees on the way to the church, an enterprise which necessitated the removal of some of the paving-stones in the public road. It never occurred to her that this would offend the authorities of the place—a want of forethought somewhat extraordinary in France, where the fear of the mayor and the municipal council supplies the place of many other fears. She was denounced to the tribunal of the department, and informed that an accusation was lodged against her. The affair was, however, allowed to drop. The mayor and even the prefect may have felt afraid of engaging in the lists with Mdlle. Eugénie, whose popularity would have arrayed on her side almost all the inhabitants of Loos. The intended fête was, however, doomed to be an occasion of merit instead of a gratification to the pious zeal of the projector. The weather proved so unpropitious that it was impossible to carry out its details, and the procession could not even leave the church. Every one grieved, especially for Mdlle. Eugénie's great disappointment. 'To work so hard for weeks,' they said, 'and then no result after all!' They did not know that, in offering up this severe mortification with a contented heart, which readily acquiesced in the least, as in the greatest, trials ordained by Providence, the young girl whom they were sorry for was obtaining greater results than if her efforts to honour her Lord by a little outward token of love had been crowned with full success.

When, that year, the month of November arrived—that month which was the anniversary of the first dawn of her vocation—she made new efforts to spread her beloved devotion. A friend to whom she had spoken of her thoughts and hopes sent her at that time a little book called ' Month of the Souls in Purgatory' ; as she opened it great was her surprise to find in the prayer appointed for the 21st of November a petition which showed that the desire of her heart had already been felt and expressed by other pious souls. Those who know the kind of emotion which this sort of coincidences awakens when we are nursing some cherished projects in the secret depth of our hearts will read with interest the prayer in question. It ran thus :

' O God the Holy Ghost, Thou hast at different times inspired the foundation of a number of Religious Orders to supply the various needs of the Church Militant on earth. O Father of Lights, we implore You, out of zeal and compassion for the dead, to raise in behalf of the suffering portion of the Church an Order devoted to the relief and deliverance of the Souls in Purgatory. Thou alone, Creating Spirit, canst inspire the foundation of such a congregation —one so conducive to the greater glory of God, and for the establishment of which we shall never cease to pray.'

Strange sympathies these are which run through the hearts and the minds of the children of the Catholic Church ! Strange bonds of union which unite souls linked by no other ties than that glorious Faith which whispers to a simple nun in her convent, as in the case of the devotion to the Sacred Heart—nay, to a young girl at school, as in the case of the dedication of the month of July to the Precious Blood of our Saviour—first a thought, then a prayer, then a desire, then a hope, then a practice, which, when watered with tears, when sanctified by humiliations, when trampled under foot until such sweetness has exhaled from it that its Divine origin can no longer be mistaken, grows into a devotion, and blest by our Mother the Church, takes a place amongst the ever-old and ever-new ways of showing our love to Jesus.

Perhaps the writer of that prayer in the 'Month of the Holy Souls' and Eugénie Smet never knew each other by name in this world, but who can doubt that in heaven there will be a blessed recognition between those who on earth had been inspired with the same thought?

CHAPTER V.

SUCCESSIVE INDICATIONS OF GOD'S WILL.

SOME time was yet to elapse—years indeed—before Eugénie's path was made clear to her; her prayers were unceasing, and once during that interval she received an intimation that after devoting herself yet a while to her habitual works of charity she was to become a Religious, but that she would not be so until she was thirty-three years of age: and it did so happen that her final vows were not made till the year 1858.

Sometimes her heart sank within her, when good people said that to remain in the world was evidently her vocation. How she longed then for some one whom she could trust, to say to her, ' Go forward, my child ; it is God's will !' When was that voice to come? Where was the servant of God who was to speak thus in the name of his Master? When was the star to shine in the dark night of her perplexity, and clear away the doubts which were still besetting her eager and ardent soul, so long schooled by the discipline of restraint, and patient expectation, and humble dependence on the leadings of Providence? That long-desired moment arrived, and the voice—which was to be to her like that of our Lord calling His Apostles to delay no longer, but to leave their nets—true symbols of the worldly impediments so often thrown in the way of religious vocations—was that of the humble Saint and wonder of our age, the triumphant example of the power of faith and holiness, unaided by any earthly gifts or human prestige—the venerable Curé d'Ars.

It was in July, 1855, that Eugénie thought of

consulting that extraordinary man, whose sanctity was beginning to be spoken of, not only in France, but all over Europe. Pilgrims were flocking to the little insignificant town of Ars, seeking the advice and help of the poor Curé whose ascetic mode of life, spiritual discernment, heroic virtues, and miraculous gifts were becoming generally known, in spite of his strenuous efforts to conceal them.

We can hardly imagine, as we read this wonderful life, that in a country so near to us as France, and only a few years ago, a man was living—whom we might have easily seen and conversed with, and gone to confession to, and heard speak and preach and catechise—the details of whose supernatural existence equal the marvels we read of in the lives of the most eminent canonised Saints.

Eugénie felt persuaded that this holy priest was the instrument chosen by God to make her acquainted with His will, and was earnestly praying for an opportunity of entering into communication with him. She never thought of going herself to Ars. It seemed to her that, if by some other means she obtained an answer to the question she wished to put to M. Vianney, it would satisfy her more than if his decision were the result of a personal interview. She did not want to be tempted to say more than 'Such is my desire ; does it come from God ?'

With her mind full of this thought, she began a novena, and on the day it ended a friend of hers called on her and said that she was going to Ars had Eugénie any commission to give her? It was, indeed, an important one with which she was to be entrusted. With a heart full of gratitude, Eugénie thanked Mdlle. T ——, and gave her full explanations as to the question she was to ask, entreating her to obtain a clear and definite answer from the holy Curé. 'Was she, in the face of apparently insurmountable obstacles, to undertake the foundation of a religious Order devoted to the Souls in Purgatory; or was this project a mere illusion?'

Thus instructed, her friend left her. She did not then expect to be at Ars till two months later, but this Eugénie did not mind. After waiting so many years she could bear the delay of a few weeks.

On the 2nd of August she met her director, who knew of the question she had put to the Curé of Ars. He told her that he had felt prompted that morning to say Mass for her intention, and had begged our Lord to enlighten the holy man with regard to her vocation.

Great was Eugénie's surprise when soon afterwards she received a letter from her friend, dated from Ars, and written on that very 2nd of August. It was as follows:

'You will be very much surprised, my dear Eugénie, to hear

from me so soon ; the plan of our journey underwent a change. We have begun, instead of ending it, by a visit to Ars. I did not hear a single word of what M. le Curé said to me about myself, but I understood distinctly his answer to the question I put to him for you. " Tell her," he said, " that she may found an Order for the Souls in Purgatory as soon as she pleases." This is the reply I have to transmit to you, my dear friend : nothing more was said.'

When they met again Mdlle. T—— told the future foundress that, after speaking for some time in the confessional to M. Vianney of her own spiritual concerns, she came away much distressed, having found it impossible to catch what he said. It was only a little time afterwards that she recollected the important message which had been entrusted to her, and great was her remorse that it had escaped her memory ; for it was no easy matter to gain access a second time to the besieged confessional. She did, however, contrive it ; and no sooner had she briefly stated Eugénie's question, exactly in the way she had put it, than, quite distinctly, and without hesitation, M. Vianney gave her the above-mentioned answer.

When Eugénie read the few words that decided her vocation, her first impulse was to lift up her heart to God and to renew her vow of consecration to the service of the Souls in Purgatory. It was at that very moment that she became acquainted with the writings of St. Gertrude, and it was with wonder and emotion that she discovered the intense devotion of that sweet

Saint to the holy victims of the Divine justice. In the tenderness of her nature, in the ardour of her faith, in the brightness of her genius, St. Gertrude appeared to Eugénie at that time as an angel sent to guide and cheer her on her arduous course. She contracted with that holy Saint one of those intimacies, if we may venture so to speak, which unite saintly souls with the great servants of God of other days. She began to have recourse to her on all sorts of occasions, and many a proof she subsequently received of the interest which St. Gertrude took in her work, and of her powerful intercession in its behalf.

' Is there no religious order or society specially devoted to the Holy Souls? ' Such was the question Eugénie addressed over and over again to priests and holy persons, always with the latent hope that she might discover a path to follow, instead of having to open one amidst the thousand difficulties of a new foundation. But nowhere did any such society exist, and she was obliged to come to the conclusion that she was called to lay the first stone of that spiritual edifice.

Strong and energetic as was her nature, and fitted to cope with actual difficulties, she had a great dread of the unknown. The total ignorance she was in as to the form and the first steps of her undertaking often caused her severe anguish. In those moments she was wont to solicit with intense fervour the aid of the holy founders of religious Orders, and especially of St. Ignatius, for whom ever since her childhood she had felt a special devotion. The most important question relative to the future foundation, which was, of course, continually presenting itself to her mind, was the fundamental one of all —' Who would join it? Who would devote themselves with her to the Holy Souls, and embrace the cares, the suspense, the humiliations involved in these first beginnings of a religious institute?' It seemed at one moment as if everything was going to favour her project, and the road before her to become an unusually smooth one.

A young widow lady, belonging to one of the best families in Lille, and possessed of considerable wealth, came one day to visit Eugénie, and begged to be accepted as her first spiritual daughter. Three other requests of the same sort, from persons in easy circumstances, and well disposed to assist in the material part of the work, held out the prospect of a start unattended by the common difficulties of new foundations. But Eugénie's keen religious foresight was not deceived. 'No!' she exclaimed; 'this will never do. We should be far too well off. It is not in that way that God's works begin; they take their rise from a mere speck, and go on increasing.' She never faltered in that conviction, though at first her associates seemed full of zeal and ardour. In order to forestall, by a pious illusion, the result they aimed at, these young ladies, though they wore a secular dress, used between themselves to call each other Sister St. John, Sister St. Theresa, Sister Mary; and Eugénie Reverend Mother.

At the outset of her life of prayer and consecration to the Holy Souls, the future foundress had begged of our Lord to give her five indications of His will with regard to the end she had in view. What she asked for was that the Holy Father should approve in writing, and bestow his blessing on, the Association of Prayers set on foot on All Saints' Day, 1853. This was granted to her on the 1st July, 1854. Pius IX. on that day wrote with his own hand, at the bottom of the petition presented to him, *Benedicat vos Deus benedictione perpetua*—'May God bless you with an everlasting blessing.' Secondly, that a great number of Bishops should recommend the association. Thirdly, that it should rapidly extend. Fourthly, that many pious persons should join in active works connected with it in behalf of the Holy Souls.

During the last two years these four favours had been vouchsafed; her fifth petition was still unfulfilled at the time we are speaking of; it was, that she might meet with a priest who had himself previously formed a similar project.

This was about to happen, and God's merciful Providence, which always measures the number and the sort of trials He sends to His chosen instruments, had reserved this crowning sign of His approbation for the hour of, perhaps, her greatest cross.

The friends and companions who had gathered round her dropped off one by one, and with them all apparent means of carrying out her intentions. Humanly speaking, this seemed a token of the hopelessness of her undertaking. Forsaken by those who had shared her hopes, joined in her labours, sympathised with her efforts, she remained alone, with the consciousness of an apparently impossible vocation, the fulfilment of which her most sanguine expectations could hardly expect to see realised. But our Blessed Lord had not forgotten her bargain with Him. The time was at hand in which He was about to act Himself, and to say to her soul, ' Though all should forsake thee, I will not.'

It was during the Octave of All Souls that she obtained the fifth sign which she had asked for. It came in the form of a letter from a young lady with whom she had frequently corresponded on the subject of their common charities. That letter was as follows :

' My dear and kind Friend. —If your soul and heart were not as indulgent and as good as they are, I should feel afraid of

your resenting my long silence ; but I rely on that good heart
and dear soul of yours for a free and full pardon of my mis-
deeds. I am soon going back to Bourg to resume my accustomed mode of life. Pray for me, my dear friend, that I may
not find the resumption of it too bitter, and may turn it to
account for the glory of our good Master, the salvation of sinners, and the deliverance of our beloved Holy Souls. Whilst I
was in Paris I often saw a friend, and in some sort a connection of ours, who has been living there with her family for
more than a year. She must be about twenty-seven years of
age : she is very pious, very well informed, and in every respect
a superior person. One day, as we were conversing together
in the most intimate manner, she told me a secret which her
director had confided to her. It seems that he has been for
some time occupied with the thought of a work of suffrage for
the Souls in Purgatory, and has moreover formed the project of
a society for this object. Everything she said, and the plan she
described, seemed to me to tally exactly with your own aspirations, my dear friend. As I was certain of her discretion, I felt
myself justified in mentioning you, and imparting to her your
ideas, wishes, and hopes. She promised to keep to herself all
that I said, on condition that I should write and ask you, in
case you thought it well, and for the interest of the work you
have both in view, to write to her at once on the subject. On
account of family reasons this dear friend of mine does not
expect to be able herself to enter such a society, but she would
most willingly be your correspondent in Paris provided that
you give her leave to speak openly on the subject to her director, the Curé of St. Merry, who is endeavouring to organise
this association. Several persons in Paris express a wish to
form part of it. My friend has again written to urge me to
communicate all this to you, dear friend. You will judge
whether to act upon it or not. She is entirely to be trusted.
I can answer for her discretion as I would for my own. But
do not lose time ; her longing desire to aid the Holy Souls
makes her impatient of delay. I ought, however, to add that
her character and her imagination are less ardent than yours.
But she loves God, she is full of goodness and cleverness, and
would be, I think, of great use to you as a co-operator. Adieu,
dear friend. I shall employ myself very actively at Bourg about
our dear association.

Your little sister and friend,

PAULINE D'ESCRIMIEUX, Child of Mary.'

When Eugénie read this letter she felt that God was answering the question she had so long been asking, 'Lord, what wilt Thou have me do?' The crisis of her fate was approaching. The final sacrifice was at hand. None but those who have gone through a similar struggle before the consummation of an act of this sort probably know all it involves of joy and of suffering, the terrible fainting of the heart, if for a moment they let go the Divine Hand which is gently and forcibly drawing them on the thrilling consciousness that, in the total surrender of their souls to Him who has chosen them for His own, there are secrets of boundless happiness and depths of awful responsibility.

Eugénie experienced, all that time, the utmost amount of human reluctance to the sacrifice she was about to make, compatible with the ardent desire to offer it up. Let it not be said that, having long contemplated that hour and earnestly wished for its coming, it was no strange thing she was called upon to do, and that she had no business to shrink from what she had so often prayed might happen. Do not even ordinary persons, who have never dreamed of such struggles and such sacrifices as these, know how the young bride will weep as if her heart would break, on the threshold of her father's house, even whilst that heart beats with joy at the fulfilment of her vision of earthly bliss? how the soldier who has passionately longed for the summons to the battle-field, will look up with tearful eyes into his mother's face when on the day of his departure he kisses her for the last time? Even so those who have thirsted for a closer union with God, and for the free and sacred atmosphere of the religious life, will feel, when certainty takes the place of vague anticipations—when action is at hand—the intense pain which is compatible with a deep and holy joy.

Not only did Eugénie suffer—she had also to endure the temptations peculiar to such moments. It was not only the sweet thought of home—the tender yearning which feels almost like remorse at the prospect of soon having to abandon father and mother, the friends of her youth, the companions of her childhood, the familiar scenes where she had spent so many happy years—but the very good works in which she had been engaged, the pious associations she had so long directed in her native place, and all its neighbourhood, rose up, as it were, against her; and he who disguises himself as an angel of light found many an unconscious instrument who urged that she was forsaking certain good for uncertain results—the ordinary paths of Christian virtue for the visionary pursuit of a wild scheme which even the Church had not, as yet, marked with its approval. Sometimes she felt almost a regret that she had listened to the voice which, in those dark hours, she began to doubt was that of God. She almost wished to recall the day when the absence of any summons to a definite line of action left her free to muse on future possibilities, with no positive sacrifice to make of what nature holds most dear.

She had complained of uncertainty, and, now that events were pressing on, and the path before her no longer resembled the flashing but unreal road we gaze on in the waves at sunset, but the thorny rocky way by which strong souls ascend to the mountain summits, she would fain have drawn back. But grace fought with nature, and won a complete victory.

If we believe—and God knows that those who invoke them have reason for that belief— that the Holy Souls are conscious of the struggles of those who are their friends on earth, prayers must have been breathed during that hour in the regions of expiation, and joy felt amidst the flames of Purgatory, when she, who was to be the foundress of their Helpers, rose up from her knees, and, more convinced than ever that her vocation did not admit of a doubt, calmly resolved to follow, step by step, the indications vouchsafed by Providence, ready at any moment to begin the work she had now fully accepted as her own.

CHAPTER VI.

GRADUAL REMOVAL OF DIFFICULTIES.

EUGÉNIE had written to Mdlle. d'Escri-mieux's friend in Paris, but in very general terms, and without entering into particulars, with respect to the foundation both had in view. She soon received the following answer, which seemed to bring the matter to an issue :

' *Paris. October 29th*, 1855.

Mademoiselle. -Your letter gave me as much pleasure as Pauline's gave you. We rejoice in the hope that you are free, that you will perhaps come to us, and that by your means the work of the Holy Souls will be established. How earnestly we shall pray during the Octave of All Souls that our Lord may unite us still more closely to the new sister He has just given us !

We have never met, mademoiselle, but we are already friends in Christ. When two persons have the same ideas and the same feelings, it would be difficult for them not to care for one another. Love of God is the strongest bond of union between souls. It inspires humility, submissiveness, perseverance, and all the virtues necessary for those who wish to live in community.

When I spoke to Pauline of wishing to begin a correspondence with you, I was only thinking of the establishment of a religious community. We have in all the parishes, and in ours amongst the rest, the Confraternity of our Lady of Suffrage, on the same footing, or nearly so, as the one at Loos, and affiliated likewise to the central one at Rome. You see that we are already sisters in that respect. When I came here from Lyons, I was, at first, quite depressed at the small amount of faith and piety there seemed to be in Paris, but I was consoled by the existence of so many confraternities for the dead. Prayers for the dead must be the result of faith as well as love.

I cannot banish from my mind the thought that you will begin the establishment of such a community as we have in view by joining the persons already assembled in Paris for that purpose. All that Pauline tells me of you and of your great zeal leads me to believe that you have all the requisite qualities for such a work. I very much hope that you will find it possible to come here for a few days, in order to confer with the Abbé X. The Curé of our parish is forwarding the business at Rome, and we are quite certain of the Archbishop of Paris's protection.

I felt so much in need of help that it makes me very happy to recommend myself to your pious prayers, and, whether we are to become more intimately associated or not, I shall always be grateful to Pauline for having made us acquainted. It will be better in the interests of the work that you should now communicate directly with M. l'Abbé.

Good-bye, mademoiselle. I hope that our Blessed Lord will give you strength to bear all your sufferings, and that your health may improve so as to enable you to carry on our dear work. In a soul like yours sufferings are only fresh tokens of God's favour.

Yours devotedly in Christ.'

When Eugénie had read this letter, she reflected a moment, and then resolved not to write herself to the Vicaire of St. Merry, but to wait for a letter from him. We can observe from this how much she had even then laid to heart that great lesson which the saints so often inculcate—the practice of waiting for God's inspirations, for His hours, for the indications of His Providence—which is contrary to the natural impulse of an ardent character, and stamps a pious project with the mark of real sanctity. As Eugénie was making this resolution, and restoring to its envelope the letter she held in her hand, she discovered in it a thin sheet of folded paper which had escaped her notice. A glance at the signature showed her it was from the priest in question, and she read the following words :

'Mademoiselle,- I have read with the greatest pleasure your letter to Mdlle. — . I do not yet know you, but I understand you : all we have now to do is to come to some agreement. Our end is the same. There can be no difference between us except as to the means to that end. I should very much wish to converse with you on the subject, but I am unfortunately a prisoner here, and cannot for the present undertake the journey.

What I have done, mademoiselle, is nothing compared with what your zeal has accomplished. But my plan is not quite the same as yours. I have formed a little community of persons living in the world. In a month or six weeks, when the Curé of our parish returns from Rome, we shall think of taking a further step under the protection and auspices of the Archbishop of Paris, and under very advantageous spiritual conditions.

I do not venture to criticise in the least the zeal which leads you to embrace, as it were, the whole world in your scheme. The heart of a Christian, and yours in particular, has a craving for universality. But my proposal is that we should agree to constitute the centre of our work in Paris, where Monseigneur befriends our charitable undertaking. If you accept this as a basis, I will tell you my ideas as to your plan. I ask God every day to send us the humble but earnest and resolute person whom I should like to see at the head of our little community.

May it please Heaven to give you enough freedom to enable you, and sufficient abnegation of self to induce you, to change your sphere of action, and to come here for the purpose of interchanging ideas with us, and uniting together our efforts and our devotion to this holy work.

To conclude, then, mademoiselle, I ask, are you free to act ? Do you accept a fusion, and on what basis ? May I beg of you to give me an answer as soon as possible ? I shall pray for you as for a good sister in Christ, and I recommend myself to your good prayers. The Archconfraternity of Our Lady of Suffrage is established at St. Merry, and in every parish in Paris there are confraternities for the dead. But not a single community exists which devotes itself exclusively to the interest of departed souls. I shall anxiously await your answer, and remain.

Your very devoted servant.'

The decisive moment of Eugénie's life had arrived. That letter left no room for hesitation.

She wrote a clear and definite answer to it, and
stated her views as to the foundation of the
Order in question. M. l'Abbé's reply to her
communication opened before her a vista of
fresh perplexities and future sufferings. It was
easy to see that, though their original idea was
identical, they differed widely as to the manner
of carrying it out. But she was fully prepared
to meet with the cross at every stage of her
undertaking, and made up her mind to accept
everything that would not be evidently opposed
to God's will concerning her. She was confirmed
in that resolution by a letter from M. l'Abbé
Toccanier, vicar of the Curé d'Ars, which reached
her just at that moment. Not content with the
verbal answer which her friend had obtained
from M. Vianney, she had sent him, through
his Bishop, Monseigneur Chalandon, an earnest
entreaty that he would consider the subject of
her vocation before God in prayer, and then
acquaint her with the result. On the 11th
November the Abbé Toccanier, the holy priest's
assistant in his extensive correspondence, wrote
to her as follows :

' Your edifying letter reached me at Pont d'Ain, where our
worthy Bishop, Monseigneur Chalandon, was preaching a retreat.
This seemed providential, as it enabled me to speak to him of
you and your pious projects. On my return to Ars on All
Souls' Day, I mentioned your wishes to my holy Curé, begging
him to meditate on the subject in prayer before giving me an
answer. Three or four times since I have put to him the same

question and always received the same reply. He thinks that it is God who has inspired you with the thought of an heroic self-devotion, and that you will do well to found an Order in behalf of the Souls in Purgatory. Whether he speaks in consequence of a Divine enlightenment, or whether he only expresses his own opinion or his own wishes, which his tender devotion to the Holy Souls would naturally incline in favour of your project, neither I nor any of those most intimately associated with him would venture to affirm. But you may rest assured that he entirely believes in your vocation to the religious life, and quite approves of the foundation of this new Order, which he thinks will rapidly increase. This is surely enough to confirm you in your intention, which you will carry into effect whenever and wherever it will please God to open a way to it, and you will then be the faithful instrument of His Divine Providence.'

On the 25th of the same month M. Vianney sent a message to Eugénie in answer to a letter in which she had dwelt on the obstacles which she foresaw on the part of her family.

'If I have not written to you before, it is because you have particularly requested to have an answer after *special prayer*, and now here is that much-desired answer. The good Curé has been as explicit as possible. I told him that you were troubled at the thought of a separation from your family, rather on their account than your own, and also concerned about the many charitable works you carry on in your parish. He generally recommends young persons not to act against their parents' wishes, but patiently to await their consent. So I was greatly surprised that he did not hesitate in advising you to proceed. He says that your parents' tears will soon be dried up. Do not, then, be afraid of letting your heart burn with the love of Jesus: He will remove all the obstacles in your path : He will make you an angel of consolation to His holy spouses, the Souls in Purgatory. The moon has no light but that which she receives from the sun. This is truly my case with regard to our saintly priest. I will constantly remind him to pray for you, and will unite my unworthy prayers to his that, in the terrible struggle in your heart between nature and grace, grace may be victorious.'

By the time Eugénie received this letter the principal obstacle in her path was removed. She had felt some days before that the time had arrived when she could no longer delay to inform her family of the separation which her vocation was about to necessitate. It seemed, however, as if she could hardly find courage to broach this painful subject to her mother.

Who has not known the sinking of heart which precedes the moment when we are about to utter words which will inflict deep sorrow on those we devotedly love? She made up her mind that on the 21st November, the day of the Presentation of the Blessed Virgin in the Temple, she would make the effort, and try to obtain from her parents their consent to her own entrance into the sanctuary, and to the oblation she had determined to make of her whole self and her whole life to Him who had said to her from her earliest childhood, ' Daughter, give Me thy heart.'

She went to Communion in the morning, and earnestly begged for grace and strength not to falter in her resolution. The details of that important evening of her life give us a striking insight into the tenderness, almost amounting to weakness, of the heart which from that moment forward was to be so valiant and strong in its conflicts with nature.

Eugénie, her mother, and her sisters were

working and conversing together round the fireside in that easy and intimate manner with which the members of a family are wont to interchange the thoughts that come uppermost in their minds. None of them save Eugénie's mother probably noted the troubled expression of her countenance. It did not apparently escape the watchful eyes of that loving parent. As the minutes went by, and then the hours, she kept saying to herself, 'Now is the time to speak,' and yet it never seemed as if it was the right time. At last one of her sisters happened to mention that two of her friends had entered a convent, and dwelt on the grief of their parents, whom they had left without giving them notice of their intention. 'I do not understand how any one can act in that way,' Madame Smet said, fixing her eyes on her eldest daughter. 'If ever you thought of becoming a nun, my Eugénie, and we were to be so unhappy as to have to part with you, you would never leave us in that manner.' 'O, I should never have courage to do so!' Eugénie exclaimed, well aware that she was speaking ambiguously, but shrinking from uttering the words on her lips. No sooner had she made that answer than an inward voice reproved her; she felt as if our Lord was saying to her as He did to His Apostle, 'Lovest thou Me?' A moment afterwards her mother said, 'I do not think that you will die, my child, without having founded something that will last beyond your lifetime; your Association of Prayers has spread in so wonderful a manner that it seems as if it were meant to prepare the way for something more important.' 'That has nothing to do with a religious vocation,' Eugénie said, again failing in courage: she probably thought her mother was trying to reassure herself on a point which, up to that time, had been a constant subject of dread to her. Still more than the first time her conscience reproached her for this weakness, and, raising her heart to God, she prayed that her mother might revert again to the same topic, and that she might then have strength enough to make up for having twice so utterly failed in her resolution.

But the conversation had taken a different direction, and it seemed very unlikely that another opening would be afforded. In a few minutes, however, Madame Smet laid down her work, and, looking at Eugénie, said in a steady earnest manner, 'I think, my child, that God intends you to found a community in behalf of the Souls in Purgatory, and I may say I now wish it. Who knows but that I shall remain myself a shorter time in the place of expiation if you devote yourself entirely to that holy work?' 'O mother!' Eugénie exclaimed, thinking her ears must have misled her, 'is it possible? What have you been saying?' Madame Smet quietly repeated the words she had uttered. Her other daughters, who knew something of Eugénie's desires, all cried out, 'But that is exactly what she wants to do. Surely you will never agree to it?' 'What right have I to set myself against it, my children, if it is God's will?' Madame Smet answered. Eugénie was so overcome with emotion at discovering her mother's feelings about her vocation, that she could only shed tears of gratitude and joy. On the following day she enjoyed the happiness of opening her whole heart to this loved parent, and of relating to her every circumstance through which God's designs had been mercifully revealed to her.

The letters she received from every side all concurred to prove that it was indeed God's will that she should undertake the work which now at the last moment she shrank from with inexpressible dread. Not only did the effort of parting from her relations appear at moments beyond her strength, but the correspondence with M. l'Abbé made her foresee that in order to meet his views she would have to make many painful sacrifices. But, feeling convinced that it was God's will she should at any rate begin the undertaking in conjunction with this zealous priest, she begged him to come to Lille, in order to arrive at a decision on the subject.

They met at the beginning of December, and she found, as she had expected, that they differed in several respects, and especially on one important point—M. l'Abbé thought that the religious of his projected Order should teach as a means of support: the total absence of resources for the maintenance of a community necessitated, in his opinion, some such line of action. Eugénie, the child of Providence, accustomed from her earliest years to trust God without reserve or hesitation, could not admit this reasoning. According to her ideas, an Order devoted to the Holy Souls was to have nothing to do with means less absolutely directed to its end than works of mercy, and to rely upon Him who feeds the birds of the air and clothes the lilies of the field for the necessaries of life—of a life entirely devoted to poor sufferers on earth, and the poor sufferers on the other side of the grave.

The good Abbé told her that he had gathered together a few devout persons who lived at a small apartment at No. 22 Rue St. Martin, that they supported themselves by needlework, and followed a rule as nearly as possible similar to that of a religious house. 'I want some one who will train and direct them,' he said, 'and I reckon upon you for that purpose.' Eugénie's heart sank within her; there was nothing attractive or promising in the prospect placed before her: strangers to live with—a place to go to where she was not acquainted with a single

person —a coadjutor whose views did not altogether harmonise with hers. There was no
room for enthusiasm, or for the slightest natural
satisfaction in the undertaking thus presented
to her acceptance.

How often God tries and purifies the soul by
withdrawing all the brightness which had attended the anticipation of a cherished project,
and clothed it with glowing colours, leaving the
sad heart, the depressed spirits, and sometimes,
as in Eugénie's case, increasing feebleness of
body to accomplish what had been conceived in
days of exuberant sensible devotion, of high
health and natural activity! How frequently
does this change come over those who, before
they resolved to join the Catholic Church, were
full of delight in its worship; to whom its services were ecstasy; over whom a thrill of pleasure was wont to steal if its very name was
uttered before them; who had cried out, with
Dr. Newman in days of yore, 'O, that thy creed
were sound, thou Church of Rome!' but who,
when they have surrendered to the resistless
force of evidence, and have felt constrained to
act upon what had been heretofore a pleasant
dream, have seen the colouring of the picture
fade away, the light vanish like that of the
sunset clouds, leaving them face to face with
their convictions, alone with their new-born faith,
which supports but has ceased to cheer in those

last hours of final conflict, and of keenest human sorrow! Many have to go through a night of this sort, but daylight is at hand. More beautiful than the illusions of the sunset sky is the real sunshine of the morning. Fairer and stronger and more real than the romance of former years are the joys, the light, the strength of Catholic life, when the Sacraments have nourished the soul with their Divine sustenance, and the devotions of the Church have become part and parcel of our spiritual existence.

Disenchantment is often the test of the truth of our convictions. It is also the touchstone of a real vocation. Eugénie had to go through this ordeal. We see this in the letter which she wrote at that time to M. Toccanier, with a view of eliciting from the Curé d'Ars some further advice as to the circumstances in which she was placed :

'On the 5th of this month (of December) M. l'Abbé came to Lille for the purpose of seeing me : I cannot tell you how much I felt at that moment —of gratitude, on the one hand, for the liberal manner in which God had granted my prayer ; and, on the other, of terror at the prospect opening before me. The Curé of St Merry, who is greatly in favour of the projected community, had wished his vicaire, M. l'Abbé, to confer with me. He says he is convinced that it is the will of God I should undertake this work, and the first answers of your holy Curé which I read to him strengthened him in that belief. Eight persons at Paris made, on the day of the Immaculate Conception, the heroic vow in behalf of the Souls in Purgatory, and resolved to say every day the Little Office and the beads of the Immaculate Conception. Out of those eight persons five live together, and follow a rule of life which the Abbé has given them ; the others are at home with their parents, and look to joining their companions at some future time. There is no house or means of any kind secured for a first start. My parents will never give me leave to go to Paris as long as this is the case. M. l'Abbé, on the contrary, would like me to proceed there at once, and to begin the work with him and a lady who is only waiting for her father's consent to join us. Now, my opinion is that we must wait till Providence gives us the means of purchasing, or at any rate hiring, a house large enough to lodge the persons who may wish to join us, in order that they may be trained to the religious life, and each one exchange her own spirit for the Lord's Spirit which is to reign in their hearts. My idea, then, would be to remain here and collect means for this purpose, which I could not do at Paris, where I do not know a single soul. Tell me, my dear father, what I must do ; and, besides this first question, I want you also to put another to your holy Curé.

Will my health improve when I lead a community life ? I am praying that Providence may especially enlighten him on that point. Monseigneur de Belley wrote to me a month ago that, even supposing that everything were to go on smoothly, I should be obliged to wait till I got stronger. I have no organic disease, but, with the appearance of robust health, I am always ailing. I can go through a great deal of fatigue, and take long walks for my various works of charity : but I feel as if my strength were diminishing, and I often push my exertions to the utmost limits of possibility. The Curé d'Ars has cured a great many persons, and I think that Providence, which has brought me into communication with you, may intend to confer upon me that favour. I would not ask it supposing I were to remain as I am. I have often felt whilst praying that there is no greater grace than suffering ; but it seems to me that it will interfere with my vocation. You see, my dear father, what need I have of the decisions of your holy Curé. I entreat of you to submit to him those two questions. The matter is of course of the highest importance to me, and it is only since I have placed it in your hands that I feel at rest. Your answer will guide the course of my whole future life. O, I do beg your pardon for my great indiscretion. I open my heart to you entirely ; God will give me some day an opportunity of thanking you personally for all your kindness.'

On the 23rd of December the coadjutor of the Curé d'Ars wrote in answer to this letter :

'Divine Providence always acts with sweetness and with power. The consent of your good mother is an important step gained. The good Curé advises you not to go to Paris till you have some means wherewith to begin your work : you will do well to avail yourself of the interest you possess in your diocese to obtain some aid towards it. The Curé entirely approves of your becoming a religious ; it is quite possible that God may restore your health, and he advises you to make a novena to St. Philomena. The very day I received your letter, Monseigneur Chalandon, our worthy Bishop, came to Ars to call on my holy Curé ; I mentioned you to him, and he told me he had written to you. He persists in saying that you should not begin without some means and better health ; pray very hard that God may give you both. I think the Souls in Purgatory ought to seize on this opportunity to show they have influence with God. Their interest is concerned in the removal of these obstacles.'

Eugénie begged to make the proposed novena to St. Philomena conjointly with M. Vianney, and she received soon afterwards the following letter :

'It is to-day we begin (on the 9th of January). The Souls in Purgatory are interested in the re-establishment of your health. I am only the echo, you know, of our good and holy Curé. Your director's advice is excellent. You might, indeed, as soon as you have means enough of support for one year, go to Paris for a time, and come back again to Loos to forward the work in the same way you are now doing. You say that St. Vincent de Paul used to begin his works with nothing ; so he did ; but then, my good Curé observes, " St. Vincent de Paul was a great Saint."'

Eugénie's hesitations as to her journey to Paris, which the Vicaire of St. Merry and the lady who had been the first to invite her co-operation were continually urging her to make, were at last solved by an accidental circumstance which she looked upon as an indication of God's will.

Her purse was, as usual, at the lowest ebb; her habitual charities always forestalled her resources; and the future foundress had not enough money at that moment wherewith to pay the expenses of the proposed journey! She therefore asked our Lord, in case it was His will that she should go to Paris, to send her in some unexpected manner the sum she wanted for that purpose. A few days after, one of her friends who was about to take the habit in the Carmelite Convent of the Rue de Messine, at Paris, wrote to her as follows:

'My dear Eugénie, I have not given you a token of my existence since the 21st November, but I should feel my happiness incomplete if you were not to be present at my clothing on the 2nd of February. I know that, with all your charities, it would be difficult for you to find means for this journey. This will explain the meaning of the cheque for 400 francs enclosed in this letter.'

This providential solution of the difficulty left no doubt in Eugénie's mind as to the will of God in the matter, and she hastened to prepare for her departure.

CHAPTER VII.

FINAL DETERMINATION.

WHEN Eugénie took leave of her family no one but herself supposed that separation to be a final parting. Her parents thought she was going to Paris with no other object than to become practically acquainted with the details of the work which the Vicaire of St. Merry had brought under her notice. She gave, herself, to a friend the following account of that important moment of her life :

'I rose on the morning of the 19th of January with a terrible weight on my heart, went to Mass, and received Holy Communion in the church of Loos, and earnestly prayed for help to Our Lady of Grace. One of my sisters who was going with me was in the highest spirits at the thought of the journey. Nothing could be more different than my state of mind. I knew that I was on the road to Calvary. A great number of our friends met us at the station to bid us farewell : I told them all that I hoped soon to come back, but at the bottom of my heart I felt that I did not believe it. At last the whistle sounded, and away we went. The train seemed to me to clear the distance between Lille and Paris with the speed of lightning. My heart was breaking ; but there was no question then of turning back : indeed, I should never have forgiven myself if I had been so unfaithful to grace as to give up my resolution of seeing with my own eyes the little establishment in the Rue de St. Martin. My companions were all doing their best to raise my spirits, but my only consolation was to salute the spires of the churches as we swiftly flew past them, and to pray to our Lord, present in each of them, for strength and courage, for all my energy seemed to be ebbing away.'

It was in this depressed state of mind that the foundress of the Helpers of the Holy Souls arrived at that great city of Paris, the centre of so much good, the hotbed of so much evil, the battle-field where some of God's most faithful soldiers have been waging war for nearly a century with the most desperate and powerful of Satan's hosts. They have maintained their ground—these combatants; they occupy even now many a vantage-post: but the conflict is still raging: the sons of the Crusaders under the banner of Our Lady of Victories are still keeping at bay the sons of Voltaire, the evil genius of France. But will the *Te Deum* of their final triumph be sung with exulting joy in the walls of Notre Dame, or with tears over the smoking ruins of Paris? God only knows! We who love that fairest city on earth, not for its matchless beauty, nor for its old traditionary glories, but for its holy and great and noble sanctuaries, for its devout religious houses, its innumerable works of mercy, its recent martyrs, and its hidden Saints—we can but say from our hearts, ' May she know in this her day the things that belong to her peace !'

Some such thoughts as these may have been in Eugénie's mind twenty years ago, when she drove through the streets of Paris to the habitation of the infant community she had come to visit, and possibly to join.

A great disappointment awaited her. When the good Abbé —— had spoken of his foundation, and of a few persons leading together a community life, she had pictured to herself a very poor and simple abode, but one with some little resemblance to a religious house ; she was dismayed at finding that holy poverty had constrained the associates to accept the offer of a lady who had lent them a few rooms adjoining her own apartment.

Mdlle. N—— was a governess, a devout and generous person, who had some intention, it seemed, of joining the community at a future period, but in the meantime she had a great many pupils who came to her house to take lessons. The noise of the piano was incessant, and, as a door opened from her schoolroom into the rooms of the community, Mdlle. N—-— was continually going in and out : this must have been most trying to persons who naturally looked on the religious life as one of uninterrupted regularity and prayer.

Eugénie had been used to the sacrifices required by an active round of works of charity, but was not yet inured to that higher sort of abnegation practised in obscure, humiliating, trivial circumstances, which have nothing romantic or striking, or in any way gratifying to natural feeling. This form of self-devotion is an acquired taste, so to speak, which indicates the highest perfection of the religious spirit. Its growth is slow, and it is not to be wondered at that in the outset of her community life Eugénie, untrained as yet in the peculiar qualities requisite for her vocation, shrank with something like disgust from the particular form in which it was presented to her. The best proof of the reality of that vocation was given by the fact that she courageously set herself to overcome this distaste, and by her frankly acknowledging to the Vicaire de St. Merry how much the effort cost her. He did his best to reconcile her to what i was impossible to obviate at that moment, but which of course could only be a temporary state of things.

Eugénie wished to do nothing until she had obtained for the infant community the approval and blessing of the Archbishop of Paris. Her coadjutor would have liked to put off a little this decisive step; but after some hesitation he yielded the point, and offered to introduce her to the Abbé Gabriel, Curé of St. Merry, who was greatly in favour of the work, and would willingly give her a letter to Monseigneur Sibour.

As the name of the Abbé Gabriel is closely connected with the first beginnings of the Helpers of the Holy Souls, it will not be amiss to say a few words of the character, the talent, and the life of a man who may be reckoned amongst the most ardent and successful apostolic labourers of the last half-century in France. He had all the qualities requisite for a missioner as well as for a parish priest. His zeal and charity knew no bounds, and had that peculiar *élan* (we have no such word in English ; is it that what it expresses does not exist in our nature ?), that impulsive ardour which acts like magic on an impressionable people.

We find him at Pezénas, his first mission, forcing his way into the room of a man the very personification of the rabid revolutionary spirit of '93, who had never heard or uttered the word ' priest ' without blasphemy and cursing—who, when he saw him enter as he was lying on his death-bed, poured forth every expression of hatred and contempt that the vocabulary of the *sansculottes* could furnish, and fell back exhausted with rage, but still grinding his teeth at the Catholic who dared to darken his doors. But the young Abbé remained by his side, and when he was fainting raised him in his arms, and kissed the livid brow contracted with wild passion, and burst out into such a torrent of loving words and impassioned desires to aid and to save the dying sinner that the fierce heart was softened, and tears fell from those eyes which had perhaps never before been thus moistened. That man died believing, hoping, and loving. His last request was that the doors of his house might be thrown open, so that all his townsmen might see and know that he died a Christian and a Catholic. Again we meet the Abbé Gabriel preaching during Lent at Marseilles when the cholera was raging, falling ill himself of that disease, remounting the pulpit as soon as he could stir, and, with a boldness which took every one by surprise, exclaiming, ' Bring our Lord out of the Tabernacle! Carry the Blessed Sacrament in triumph through your streets and public places! Let every knee bend before Him, and every head be bowed down!' There was one difficulty which in his enthusiasm the preacher had forgotten. Since the Revolution of 1830, processions outside the churches were forbidden by the Government. The Préfet was in consternation, and the Bishop alarmed ; for the voice of the preacher had reached the hearts of the people, and the population of Marseilles rose like one man and claimed the right to do as their ancestors had done since the days of the holy Bishop Belzunce, a hundred years before, when the plague was stayed whilst the faithful walked in procession through the decimated city. The *vox populi* could not be withstood ; the authorities gave way ; twenty thousand persons marched out into the streets with lighted tapers in their hands. Women exclaimed in their native *patois*, as the image of the Blessed Virgin was seen once more in the light of the broad sunshine, ' *Viva bon choléra!* It has given us back our Mother !'

Every year since then the time-honoured procession has been renewed. The demagogues, for one moment in power during the last war, tried to forbid this popular manifestation of religious faith; but in vain. The true democracy, whose instincts are utterly at variance with that false and spurious counterfeit, modern Liberalism, won the day, as it had done at the voice of the Abbé Gabriel forty years ago, and asserted its highest right—' freedom to worship God.'

During the Revolution of '48 this zealous priest formed one of the devoted band who went about amongst the workmen and the mob, speaking of Christ and of religion in opposition to the wild theories of the street orators; ventured into the clubs to plead the cause of humanity, and stood on the barricades to assist the dying on both sides. His eloquence was sometimes compared to that of Lacordaire, yet he never was a popular preacher. His influence was immense, and yet his name is not famous; his labours were incessant, but little talked of; his simplicity, his total absence of vanity or ambition; the boldness of his language; his indifference to the esteem, and in some measure to the opinions, of others; something perhaps a little paradoxical in his expressions—inspired a sort of diffidence in those who were not intimately acquainted with him, and militated against his general popularity with persons of the world. But by the poor and by his friends he was all but worshipped. His death, in 1866, caused by an accident at sea, was mourned with an intensity of grief which showed the devoted love felt for this holy priest.

His character was peculiarly congenial to that of Eugénie Smet. On her first introduction to him she felt at once that she was conversing with a friend. The kindness of his manner, and the interest with which he entered into her views, was all she could have desired. He gave her a letter to the Archbishop.

We transcribe her own account of her visit to Monseigneur Sibour:

'On Tuesday, the 22nd of January,' she writes, 'I went to Mass at the church of St. Merry, and received Holy Communion. I felt very anxious about my visit to the Archbishop, and prayed that he might receive me in a fatherly manner, and with a gracious smile, because otherwise I knew I should not be able to utter a word. When I arrived at his palace the porter at the lodge stopped me, and said he was engaged, and could not see any one. I answered that I had brought a letter for him, and persisted in crossing the court to the front door. I rang the bell; no answer. I rang again; no one came. A third time I pulled the bell, and made a great noise; a servant appeared. "Have you been waiting, madame? I did not hear the bell. Monseigneur is busy; he is saying his Office." "Will you give him this letter?" In a few minutes he returned and said Monseigneur would see me as soon as he had finished his Office. It was time, indeed, to ejaculate my lifelong prayer, "Providence of God, directed by the Sacred Heart of Jesus, watch over me." I felt that my future destiny turned on the result of this interview. If the Archbishop sanctioned my undertaking, then my course would be plain. If he considered it impracticable, nothing would remain but to return to Loos and live at home as before; there was no other alternative. There I sat in that large drawing-room, my heart beating and my mind absorbed by that one thought—Was the Order of the Holy Souls to be or not to be? That question was about to be decided. At last I was informed that the Archbishop was ready to see me. I could not help saying to God, " Do make him smile." I went in, and there was Monseigneur standing before me, looking very benignant, and smiling upon me as kindly as possible. I knelt down to get his blessing, and he gave me his ring to kiss. " To what diocese do you belong, mademoiselle ? " he asked. " To the diocese of Cambray, monseigneur." " What has brought you to Paris ? " " The wish to establish a community, monseigneur, for the relief of the Souls in Purgatory—one whose good works would be all offered up for that intention." I then gave his Grace the history of my Association of Prayers, of the way in which the thought of the new Order had entered my mind, and of the providential circumstances which had brought about my journey to Paris. Monseigneur listened with great interest. " Yes," he said, when I ceased speaking : " it is exactly what the Abbé Gabriel has told me. Well, but, mademoiselle, what means have you to begin with ? " " Monseigneur, they are exceedingly small at present, but later on they will improve." " Have you a house ? " " No, monseigneur." " Then what will you do ? " " Why, monseigneur, would it be more extraordinary if Almighty God, to whom all the houses in Paris belong, helped me to find one, than that two persons who did not know of each other's existence –the Abbé and myself should have formed the same project ? " " Very well, my child," his Grace exclaimed ; " faith, which transplants mountains, can build houses. I give you leave to say openly in Paris that the Archbishop is heart and soul with you in this work ; and if you want advice and help come to me." I could hardly believe I had really heard those words from his Grace. I tried to express what I felt, and to tell him all the happiness they gave me.'

Eugénie came away from the archiepiscopal palace with that sort of joyful surprise at an unexpected blessing which is one of the sweetest emotions we can experience. Her heart was overflowing with gratitude. So complete an approval and so warm a sympathy from Monseigneur Sibour exceeded all her hopes. She kept saying to herself on her way home, ' God has done it all ! God has done it all ! '   She did not let the grass grow under her feet.   The next thing was to get the Archbishop's approval in writing.   She begged the Abbé Gabriel to forward to him at once the plan which his Vicaire had drawn up of the proposed institute.   This document was returned to her with the following words affixed to it :

' We approve of the establishment in our diocese of the above-mentioned work, reserving to ourselves a future consideration of the rules which will be submitted to our examination.

✠ M. E. AUGUSTE, Archbishop of Paris.'

Now that the spiritual foundation of her edifice was laid, it was time for Eugénie to look out for the means of providing a house for the new institute.   The fourth story of the house in the Rue St. Martin, shared with good Mdlle. N   , was insufficient even for the first attempt at a community life.   She had been hoping and waiting for a letter of introduction, which a friend at Lille had promised to send her, to a lady in Paris, well known for her zeal and piety, and whose ample means were devoted to good works.   Every day she had been disappointed. At last one morning, whilst hearing Mass at Notre Dame des Victoires, she begged our Blessed Lady very earnestly to obtain for her that very day this much-desired letter ; and the first thing she saw on her return home was a note on the table, which turned out to be the answer she had been so anxiously expecting. The few words it contained were satisfactory :

'Madame ⸺ had been informed of her arrival in Paris, and would be happy to see her between 10 and 12 the following day.'

Eugénie was not surprised she would have been much more astonished if her prayer had not been heard—but, falling on her knees, she poured out her thanks to her dear Mother in heaven, and looked forward with hope to the result of this interesting interview. Her own pen has described it. We copy from her letter :

'On Saturday, the 26th of January, I went to make Madame ⸺'s acquaintance. When I asked if she was at home, her maid, who had opened the door, answered shortly, " Madame is out." " Indeed ! " I said. " I am surprised at that, for this is the time madame had named, and I think she must have expected me." " O, then, you must be the person with whom madame had made an appointment ! she told me to remind her of it. Dear me ! she will be very much vexed. It is only a minute ago she went out." " I can wait for her," I said. " It would be wasting your time, I am afraid. I never can tell when madame will come home. She heard this morning that one of her uncles is very ill, and she is going into the country this evening to see him."

I felt thoroughly disappointed, and said how sorry I was not to have found Madame ⸺ at home. As I was getting into the cab the coachman asked where he was to drive. " Wherever the Blessed Sacrament is," I said. The poor man, not understanding his *direction*, stared at me. " I want to go to a church," I explained. " What church ? " he asked. " Any church," I said. " Find out a church the nearest you can." I was not better acquainted than he was with the churches in Paris. He got upon his box and drove down the Rue de Sèvres. When we passed the church of the Lazarists he stopped. "*Tenez*," he said, pointing to the steps: "that looks as if it might be a church." I went in and knelt down before the altar of the Blessed Sacrament, praying with all my heart, and repeating the same words—"My God, what must I do?" I felt strangely depressed, unreasonably discouraged, but continued to beg for light and guidance.

Suddenly I heard as it were a voice in my heart which said, "Go back to that lady's house." "Nonsense!" I said to myself; "it would be of no use." But, as I went on feeling the inward prompting, I could not resist it, and desired the coachman to drive me back to the house we had just left. When the servant opened the door she exclaimed, "O, there you are! How very lucky! Madame has come home. I will let her know you are here."

I was shown into the drawing-room, and found Madame — - with a child in her arms whom she seemed as fond of as if it had been her own. This was a little orphan girl she had adopted. All her means were devoted to works of charity, and her life was so pious and edifying that people looked upon her as a kind of nun. She received me in a very plain sort of fashion. "Good-morning, madame: sit down by me on this couch, and tell me all about yourself." I own that I felt rather dismayed at having to tell my story before the lady's maid; who did not offer to leave the room; but there was no help for it, and I was obliged to go through this ordeal. Madame listened very attentively, but all the time we were talking the baby was screaming, and she was rocking it and singing to it. In the midst of this hubbub I had to explain my plans, and all their important bearings. I felt almost as if I was dreaming, and kept thinking, "Will anything result from this?" "I have been advised, madame, to have recourse to you." "My child, you can rely upon me." "But what can I do, madame?" "Have you not heard what I have said, my child? It is our Lord who makes me tell you to rely upon me.' She spoke so positively that I was puzzled what next to say; she thought a moment, and then went on: "I may as well explain this to you. On New Year's Day I was walking along the Rue de Sèvres, and, just as I was coming to the end of it, all at once I thought of the Souls in Purgatory; and I said to myself, 'Every one to-day is receiving New Year's gifts except the Souls in Purgatory;' upon which I stopped at the house of the Lazarist Fathers and asked for two hundred Masses for those poor souls.

Then, as I was sitting before the Blessed Sacrament in the chapel, I heard a voice in my heart, which said, 'The Souls in Purgatory are a work of charity: you will soon know it.' (*Les âmes du Purgatoire c'est une œuvre. Tu le sauras bientôt.*) I remember that I said to myself, 'What! the Souls in Purgatory are a work of charity? What does that mean? It is not even good French.' I had almost forgotten all this, but since you have been talking to me, my child, it has come back to my recollection, and I felt what I mentioned to you just now—our Lord saying to me, 'That is the work I told thee of on the 1st of January.' Do not, therefore, be surprised at my saying that it is our Lord's will that you should count on my assistance." She then asked me where I lived, and promised to come and see me.'

After this extraordinary conversation Eugénie felt no doubt that she had met with the person whom God had appointed to be the first benefactress of her little Society; and it was not long before she had the proof of it. This kind friend often called at the Rue St. Martin, and found in the humble abode of the infant community ample opportunities of exercising her charitable zeal. The keen-sightedness of this pious lady likewise discovered that the future foundress, though surrounded with difficulties, had no adequate spiritual guide. Anxious to assist her in every possible way, she did not rest until she had made her acquainted with the Rev. Father Aussant, a religious of the Order of St. Dominic, and a most virtuous and experienced priest.

It was providential for the future of the Order and for Eugénie's own soul that she opened her mind to this servant of God, and revealed to him all the secrets of her conscience —the graces with which she had been favoured, the trials and struggles she had gone through; the temptations which were even then assailing her, and especially that of discouragement, almost amounting to despair, in the presence of obstacles which often seemed insurmountable. After he had heard her, and fully weighed in the light of the sanctuary the proofs of her vocation, no doubt remained in his mind that she was called to found this new institute, and that to draw back from it would be to fly in the face of God's manifest will. Therefore, when she told him that her intention was to begin nothing then, and to return to her home for an indefinite time, he assured her, with all the authority of one speaking in God's name, that her place was at Paris, and in the midst of all the difficulties of a foundation. Eugénie objected that her parents had suffered her to come to Paris only on condition of a speedy return. 'Never mind,' he answered. 'You cannot go away; you must ask our Lord to settle the matter with your parents. Later on you can go and see them for a few days, and then announce to them your final departure.'

Eugénie withdrew from the confessional full of sadness and perplexity, and, as usual, had recourse to the Blessed Virgin. 'My good Mother,' she said to her before leaving the church, 'if it is not our Lord's will that I should go home, make my parents change their minds about it, and let my mother write to me to stay on in Paris.' She felt more comfortable after having said this prayer, and that very night she received a letter from Madame Smet, which said :

'I do not think, my dear child, that you can have had time enough yet to acquire all the necessary information about the future foundation ; it will be better, then, to stay on longer.'

This answer to her prayer confirmed Eugénie's confidence in her director's advice and calmed her mind. As soon as it became possible she did go home, and broke to her family that it was for the last time. The agony she then endured exceeded anything she had felt before. In her grief she wrote to Father Aussant a letter, to which he made the following answer :

'GOD ALONE.

My dear daughter in Christ, It is rather late to thank you for your kind letter, but I am never up to the mark whether as to answering letters or as to loving our Lord as I ought to do. Contrive, my dear child, not to stay too long at Lille. You have at Paris a poor little community which calls for your return. Do not fancy that you can carry on every sort of good work both in Lille and in Paris. When you are as holy as St. Alphonsus Liguori you may bilocate ; but for the present learn to leave God for God, and, above all, to part with those you love for Him you ought to love far more. God asks for a great sacrifice. Make it without further delay—with generosity with good-will. There is no question now of asking for signs of God's will—for making conditions with our Lord. I abso-

lutely object to your offering any prayers of that sort, whatever
may be the result you wish to obtain. You have been hitherto
a spoiled and wilful child : now you must be an affianced bride,
and understand and practise at once the self-devotion and self-
renouncement that become a true spouse of our Divine Master.

You want a house—you want it very soon. Well, of course
you do. Does not God know it ? Is not that enough ? It is
His business to look out for it—to provide it. Let us do our
part, and leave to Providence Its own. Everything will get on
better in that way : for we always spoil God's work by insisting
on meddling with it, and He must have a wonderful amount of
patience to bear with us in this respect. as well as in many
others. Most probably God will wish you to come to Paris
without knowing where to lay your head, and thus constrain you
to appear a fool in the eyes of all your friends, even the best and
kindest of them. This comes of having made so many bargains
with Providence. and asked for so many proofs of your vocation.
You have now to pay for it by acts of blind faith. Leave, then,
all things save God. and God alone. Henceforward it is Him
alone whom you must love and serve.

Yours in that good Master.

P. L. Aussant, of the Order of St. Dominic.'

Eugénie's courage was revived by these heart-
stirring words, and she would have started at
once had not her bodily strength then given way
under the weight of mental suffering. She became positively ill ; and in writing to Madame
———, the friend in Paris who had done so much
for her, she poured forth her grief at this new
difficulty in her way. This true friend wrote to
her as follows :

' My dear Child,—You are in a good · a very good—state.
I do not wish you to be in a better one, because if you were
standing you might fall ; whereas, prostrate as you are, in utter
helplessness, and overcome by a sense of your wretchedness, you
have nothing to fear. When we feel ourselves raised above the
miseries of our nature, then we must be afraid of sinking ; but

when we are lying with our faces to the ground, as low as low can be, then we have only to thank God for keeping us in that humiliating position—free from the dangers which attend giddy heights, and secure against temptations of pride. You can do nothing just now for your work. Why should God give you graces which you do not need at this moment? He does not usually bestow such graces till they are wanted. Come, my child. Let us both thank Him that He keeps you in so humble, so helpless a state—that He takes from you even the power of making a sensible act of love; because, if afterwards His grace works in you and by you, the results must be evidently ascribed to Him, the Author of all good. Otherwise we should lose our time and our trouble; nothing we did would succeed and bring glory to God, our Master, our Love, our All. When you write to me again from Lille, and are very ill, say, my child, "I have devoted my time to the service and the glory of God; I have glorified Him by suffering lovingly for Him and by Him." Bravo! that is the language of a Christian soul—not that other sort of talk, "I lost my time entirely when I was last at Lille, because I was ill." The children of this world think and speak thus—not we who are the children of God, and on our way to heaven.'

Thus quieted, thus strengthened by two inestimable friends, and following the dictates of a heart which, though to the utmost degree sensible to all human affections, still loved God above all things, Eugénie made her final sacrifice, and left her home on the 25th of March, Feast of our Lady's Annunciation—that feast on which thousands of God's consecrated servants renew their vows, and Christian women in every state of life love to repeat the words with which their Mother in heaven accepted the stupendous message that Gabriel brought her from God—' Behold the handmaid of the Lord: be it done unto me according to thy word.' Blessed be the lips which made that prayer! Blessed be the lips which repeat it after her, whether along the steepest and highest paths leading to heaven, or in homes which faith brightens and hallows! Blessed be those words, whether on the lips of the bride of Christ on the threshold of the sanctuary, or the Christian bride of a Christian man at the foot of the altar! Blessed be those words when spoken in joy—yet more blessed when uttered in grief! Blessed be those words when they come from one who has just received some great temporal gift—more blessed when they are murmured by one on whom some great ruin has fallen, dashing to the ground every earthly hope! Blessed are they when said by the expectant mother, who places herself and her unborn treasure in the arms of her God's loving will—more blessed still when they rise from a broken heart beside the grave of a husband or an only child. They are the Christian woman's prayer. They sum up the teachings of her Mother from the day of the Annunciation to the hour of her great agony, and through the long patient years preceding her Assumption.

Eugénie had often said those words. She said them again as she left her home for ever. She will say them again twice in her life with a yet deeper meaning—on the day of her religious vows, and on her death-bed.

CHAPTER VIII.

THE HOUSE IN THE RUE DE LA BAROUILLÈRE.

THE work was started. Eugénie had joined her spiritual daughters in the wretched little apartment of the Rue St. Martin, and begun a life of privations, of labour, and of something beyond poverty, for at times it approached to positive destitution. She was afraid of letting her family know the position of the infant community: they would, no doubt, have sent her immediate assistance, but coupled with it such melancholy forebodings and renewed opposition that she did not venture to apprise them of the real state of the case. She experienced what always happens to generous souls at the outset of their enterprises, when they have unreservedly devoted themselves to the service of God and are being tried like gold in the furnace: nobody thought it worth while to help a little band of young women, whose project sounded very well in theory, but was generally deemed impracticable. They were looked upon as crazy enthusiasts. Indeed, as M. Desgenettes, the venerable Curé of Notre Dame des Victoires, remarked, they were in reality possessed of the holy folly of the Cross.

Meanwhile they had to work hard for their bread. Needlework was with difficulty obtained. At one moment it failed altogether. What

was to be done? Want stared them in the
face. Just then a little girl knocked at the
door, and asked if they had finished threading
the beads she had been told to call for. The
child had mistaken the house, but she went on
to tell them what that work was. The shop she
came from sold bracelets made of little white
seeds resembling pearls, and employed persons
to thread them. 'If you like, I can get you
some of that work,' she added; and for several
weeks the Helpers of the Holy Souls threaded
beads and lived on the scanty payment this
occupation brought them. By working hard
those who were clever at it earned about a shil-
ling a day. Holy poverty was, indeed, strictly
observed amongst them. Water has to be
bought at Paris, as well as other things: these
ladies had to limit themselves to a pennyworth
a day of that necessary of life. Their shawls
were turned at night into blankets, and, as some
of them were not provided with that article of
dress, they went to Mass one after another, making two or three do duty for six or seven persons. One chair was all the whole set of rooms
had to boast of: the need of seats was supplied
by the purchase of two narrow wooden benches:
the chair was allotted to the one of the party
who was most in want of rest. The beds were
folded up during the day; but, as they occupied
all the room at night, the chair and the benches

had to be piled up on the solitary table which
served both for meals and for working hours.
It must have been a strong vocation which
brought to Eugénie's feet, in that miserable
abode, a postulant, who exclaimed as she knelt
down before her, ' Mother, behold your daughter,
for whom you will have no answer.'

Eugénie had never felt so strongly as at that
moment the weight of the sacred burden laid
upon her—the awful consciousness of that spiritual maternity through which one soul becomes,
as it were, responsible for the souls committed
to her charge. She shrank from it with dread ;
but confidence in God, and an absolute submission to His will, gave a sweetness even to the
presentiment of sufferings to come. It enabled
her also to endure the various trials of those
first days of community life. They were hard
in every way to a person who had been used to
every comfort, and whose health was very deli-
cate. But, great as were the straits she was
reduced to, help always came in answer to her
childlike appeals. One day as the associates
were in positive want they prayed earnestly
to St. Joseph, and, even venturing to specify
the sum, petitioned for 200 francs ! It was at
Mass they had made this request, and the
day passed without any sign that it had been
heard. Towards evening Eugénie went to pay
a visit to their first benefactress, Madame ——,

and conversed with her some time. Just as she was rising to go away, that lady went and knelt down before an image of St. Joseph which stood in a corner of her room, and prayed for an instant; then, coming back to her visitor, she said, 'My child, St. Joseph wishes me to give you 200 francs.' 'O madame!' Eugénie exclaimed, 'that is exactly the sum we asked him for this morning.' The devout friend of the Holy Souls and their Helpers knelt again at the feet of her dear St. Joseph, and thanked him for having chosen her as the instrument of his fatherly kindness to the poor little community.

On another occasion, when the actual pressure of temporal difficulties had drawn from Eugénie, who had gone to pray in a neighbouring church, the cry of the Apostles on the apparently foundering bark, 'Lord, save us, or we perish,' she felt as if God's voice was saying in her heart, 'O thou of little faith! wherefore dost thou doubt?' This roused her from her dejection, and she entered into a familiar converse with our Blessed Lady, expostulating with that Holy Mother, and ending her prayer with these words—'Do, my good Mother, inspire some charitable soul with the thought of sending us 100 francs.' When she went home the Sister who acted as cook met her on the stairs, and, with some agitation, said, 'Mother, I cannot go to market; there is only one penny left in our purse;' and she turned the little bag inside out to demonstrate the melancholy fact. 'Well,' Eugénie replied, with a bright smile, 'this is just the very moment to rely on Providence.' When Mdlle. de Lamouroux, the pious foundress of the Good Shepherd at Bordeaux, found herself in a similar position, she called together all her companions and said, 'Come, children—join hands and dance a *ronde* for joy that we have not a single penny left.' Our little London saint, good Elizabeth Twiddy, when the Infant Orphanage of Mary's Home was reduced to its last penny, resorted to a successful expedient. She sent one of the children into the street to bestow this fortunate coin on a beggar. Our Lord immediately repaid the loan with more than a hundredfold interest. Eugénie's smile and her words were fully justified by all the annals of holy poverty. It is one of the disadvantages of persons in what is called a comfortable position in life that they can never dance Mdlle. de Lamouroux's *ronde*, never invest the last penny in the house like Elizabeth Twiddy, never smile bravely like Eugénie in the face of actual want. Miracles are not worked in their behalf; they do not know the superhuman joy of receiving assistance straight from God—of seeing, as it were, His hand stretched out to them as our Lord's to the sinking friend who had walked on the waves at His bidding.

Eugénie had scarcely uttered those words, full of confidence in Divine Providence, when the porter of the house came up and gave her a letter directed in an unknown hand. She opened it, and in an inner envelope, unaccompanied by a single word of explanation, found a note for 100 francs. It was never known who had sent this offering. There was no one to thank but the Blessed Virgin. Another time the sum of 500 francs was required for some pressing necessity. This time Eugénie had recourse to Our Lady of Victories. Having placed the matter in her hands, she went to call on a person who she thought would perhaps lend her the money. She met, however, with a decided negative, and did not know any one else in Paris to whom she could apply; but on leaving the house she met a gentleman, with whom she had no previous acquaintance, who came up to her and said, ' I think you are Mdlle. Smet, and that you have a special devotion to the Souls in Purgatory. Will you allow me to place these 500 francs at your disposal, and to recommend my intentions to your prayers?'

Illness was beginning to complicate the position of the Helpers of the Holy Souls. Eugénie's strength broke down, and her severe neuralgic pains returned with violence. The Abbé Toccanier wrote at that moment a discouraging reply to a petition addressed to the Curé d'Ars for prayers in behalf of the health of the poor foundress. 'Do not ask for miraculous cures. M. le Curé complains that St. Philomena sends us too many people.'

And again, shortly afterwards, 'The good Cure prays hard for you; but why do you want him to get you cured at once? You have offered yourself in sacrifice, and, now that God takes you at your word, you begin immediately to cry for mercy. The only reason I can find for asking him to pray for the improvement of your health is the interest of your infant community, to which you are, in truth, very necessary.'

A still greater trial was at hand for poor Eugénie: the friend and the benefactress who had been hitherto the mainstay of her institute, and the Père Aussant, who had been her spiritual director during its arduous beginnings, left Paris about the same time, leaving her destitute of the constant sympathy and consolation they had afforded her, and impressing on her mind and on her heart a fresh sense of her—in one respect —solitary position. The wounds inflicted by her total separation from her family reopened, as it were, under the influence of this new bereavement, and she wrote, in the fulness of her heart, to the Curé d'Ars a letter which the Abbé Toccanier, in M. Vianney's name, answered as follows:

'M. le Curé smiles when I tell him all you have to go

through, and he bids me to repeat to you what he desired me to
say to a good widow devoted to all sorts of holy works, and
who suffers cruel persecution —" Assure her that those crosses
are flowers which will soon bear fruit."

You have thought, prayed, taken advice, and thoroughly
weighed the sacrifices you are called upon to make; you have
every reason to believe that in undertaking this work you are
doing God's will; the energy which He alone can give will
enable you to accomplish what you have begun. M. le Curé
has said to me over and over again, in a tone of the deepest
conviction, " Their enterprise is certain to succeed; but the
foundress will have to learn that such a work can only be con
solidated by labour, anxiety, efforts, and sufferings." But he
always adds, " If God be with them, who shall be against
them ? "

Another time the Abbé writes to a third
person :

' I feel deeply concerned at the thought of the many and
severe trials which beset your friend. Tell her that the holy
Curé forbids her to look back, and exhorts her to obey the
blessed call she has received. The Souls in Purgatory must be
enabled to feel that their advocates on earth sympathise with
them from an experimental knowledge of suffering : and mind
you continue praying to St. Philomena, and begging of her to
obtain the necessary means for the accomplishment of this holy
project.'

These and many other assurances from the
Saint of Ars gave Eugénie courage to persevere
and even rejoice in the midst of continual
crosses. One of the most painful circumstances
attending this period of her work was the ever-
increasing conviction that her coadjutor, the
Vicaire of the Church of St. Merry, who had
given the first impulse to it in Paris, and herself,
into whose hands he had committed it, differed

so much on various points that it was becoming impossible to carry it on conjointly. She spoke to him frankly on the subject, and he fully agreed with her that a divided direction could only injure its progress. In consequence of this explanation he withdrew more or less, and in the end retired altogether from the undertaking. Eugénie then asked the Abbé Gabriel, the zealous Curé of St. Merry, to accept the functions of Superior of her community. He agreed to her proposal, and the first act of authority he performed in that capacity was to give to each of the Sisters a name in religion. From that time forward Eugénie was called 'Mère Marie de la Providence,' and it is under that name that we shall now speak of her.

The Associates, now regarded as Religious, went on praying, working, and suffering with patience and cheerfulness. At last they received some unexpected assistance. New members proposed to join them. It then became absolutely necessary to find a house. The Superioress searched for one in every direction, but without success. It seems as if the words, 'There was no room for them,' were destined to prove for a while applicable to all the religious families which tread in the footsteps of the Mother and Child who heard them uttered in the streets of Bethlehem on the night of the Nativity. One day the foundress received a letter from her

absent director, the Rev. Père Aussant, in which
he said :

> ' As you have so great a trust in Providence, ask Providence
> to lead you where God means you to be ; then walk up and
> down the Rue de Sèvres, the Rue de Vaugirard, and the Rue
> Cherche Midi, but you need not look at all the boards you may
> happen to see, for *your house* is in one of the by-streets. Go
> doggedly backwards and forwards, and when you shall feel
> an impulse to turn in a particular direction follow it.'

Full of faith in the virtue of obedience, Mère
Marie de la Providence went off with one of her
companions to the part of the town mentioned
by the good Father. As they walked down the
Rue Cherche Midi, she felt no particular inspira
tion till, just at the corner of the Rue de la
Barouillère, she was impressed with the idea that
it was down that street she was to go. And it
did so happen that before they had walked
half-way along it she observed a board on an
entrance-gate, with the words ' To be sold,' star-
ing her in the face. Her heart began to beat
quite fast, and she said afterwards that it seemed
as if some one was saying to her, ' You shall be
here or nowhere.' She looked at the house, and
it seemed to be just what she wanted ; but then
the landlord, she was told, had made up his
mind to sell it, and would on no account think
of letting it. She felt nowise disheartened.
With God all things are possible, and M. d'Assonvillier's resolutions would not stand against
the will of Providence.

A number of complications had made it quite impossible to remain any longer in the Rue St. Martin ; she concluded it must follow that another house would be provided for them. Twice, at different intervals, she sent to ask whether there was any hope of their obtaining a lease of the one in the Rue de la Barouillère ; but M. d'Assonvillier's man of business each time replied that he was determined to sell, and not to let.

The whole community betook themselves to prayer, and entreated St. Joseph to evince his power by bringing about on the following 19th of June a change in that gentleman's intentions. It was on the 19th of April that these prayers began.   For two months they did not let St. Joseph rest.   Each day their supplications became more fervent ; but, whenever their kind *chargé d'affaires*, who transacted their business, made any inquiry as to the house which Mère Marie de la Providence had made up her mind to have, the answer was always the same, and this went on up to the very time named in their prayer.   On the morning of the 19th, however, she received a letter from her said *chargé d'affaires* informing her that M. d'Assonvillier's lawyer had just sent him word that his client had, contrary to all his intentions and protestations, suddenly made up his mind to let his house, and particularly wished to let it to Mdlle. Smet : so eager had he become to conclude the business that, if convenient to the lady, he would meet her on the same day at his (the said lawyer's) residence, in order to draw up and to sign the agreement.

The joy of the little community can hardly be described. It was like the light of a new day, full of hope and blessings : they were now really about to begin that double apostolate they had so long contemplated, and by works of mercy towards Christ's suffering children on earth bring relief to His loved ones in Purgatory. They all knelt down round their foundress, and poured out their hearts in grateful thanksgivings ; then she sallied forth with one companion to face M. d'Assonvilliers and his lawyer. Her own *chargé d'affaires* was to meet her.

It was the first time in her life that she had transacted this sort of business, and she was quite in the dark as to the terms of the lease or the particulars of the agreement she had to sign. She kept repeating to herself that it was in the name of Providence she was engaging in this responsibility, and that Providence would see to it. Humanly speaking she looked for the payment of the rent to certain subscriptions which her parents and some other persons had promised ; otherwise she had nothing to reckon on, and no income whatever. The lawyer read the long series of conditions included in the agreement ; M. d'Assonvilliers keenly watching every detail; the foundress's friend, who knew the state of her finances, listening somewhat anxiously to all she was binding herself to pay, without having a penny in hand towards it; and Mère Marie herself perfectly serene and contented, and without the slightest misgiving as to the future. She had a right to feel that confidence after the miraculous answer to prayer she had received that day. It was her intense faith, and not a foolish rashness, that inspired her with this unshaken trust. Just as M. d'Assonvilliers was taking up a pen to sign the agreement and adjusting his spectacles on his nose, he looked straight at Mère Marie, and said, 'How glad I am, mademoiselle, that I have arranged this affair with you! They wanted me to let my house to some persons who are going to be nuns.' 'O, indeed!' Mère Marie ejaculated, not knowing quite what to say. 'Yes, and I can tell you I did not at all like the idea.'

The poor foundress felt a little uncomfortable at this remark; she said nothing at the time, but a day or two afterwards she had a misgiving on the subject. Straightforwardness was one of the strongest features of her character, and her joy was a little disturbed by this incident. She made up her mind to go and see M. d'Assonvilliers, and to tell him exactly the state of the case. This was a really heroic step to take in a matter where there was no positive obligation to speak, and where his withdrawal from his bargain—or, at any rate, the difficulties he might have raised on the subject—might have caused her such serious annoyance. But, as so often happens, honesty proved the best policy ; and Providence, again invoked with unhesitating confidence, smoothed away the apprehended obstacles. Her words, her frankness, her manner, won over completely the testy landlord to her side. His prejudices were dissipated, and he expressed himself perfectly satisfied that a religious community should inhabit his house.

CHAPTER IX.

HEROIC CHARITY.

BEFORE we proceed with our narrative, it will be well to describe the house obtained by so many prayers, and taken possession of with much grateful joy on the Eve of the Feast of the Visitation, 1856, and which still remains the mother-house of the Helpers of the Holy Souls. No. 16 Rue de la Barouillère was a small and not very convenient habitation at the time of their installation; it has since been remodelled according to the needs of an increasing congregation, and an adjoining one has been added to it. This con-

vent soon became dear to those who long to help
the many beloved ones removed from their sight,
but who feel the impotency of their own efforts,
their want of holiness, of courage, and of perseverance in the blessed work. The aspect of this
religious house is very touching. The inscriptions on the walls, which are taken from the
Holy Scriptures and the writings of the Saints,
all bear reference to the state of departed souls
and our duty towards them. In the quiet
chapel, where the Office for the Dead is daily
said, a number of Masses are also offered up.
The memorials of the holy Curé d'Ars, whose
spirit seems to hover over the place, bear witness
to his connection with this great work of spiritual
mercy. The Helpers of the Holy Souls do not
wear a religious dress ; they are simply clothed
in black, like persons in deep mourning. They
have to a remarkable degree the look of happiness which is peculiar to nuns. There is something singularly joyous in their countenances.
Their vocation, beyond all others perhaps, causes
them to rejoice in sufferings. Sufferings form
the treasure of their community, its spirit and
its strength. Joy in suffering—this thought
seems impressed on all they say and do, and
unites them to the Holy Souls, to whose service
they are devoted.

Like all the convents in Paris, this one has a
large garden. The professed Sisters have not

much leisure to avail themselves of its green
lawn and shady alleys, but the poor women who
meet every Sunday at the convent for religious
instruction and recreation enjoy there in the summer the sight and smell of the flowers, whilst
their little children play on the grass, and gather
the daisies which grow in abundance.

A day or two after the new community had
taken possession of the house in the Rue de la
Barouillère, a lady called to ask if one of the
nuns would visit a poor woman who was dying
a few doors off. 'It must be St. Joseph sends
you,' the Superioress said ; and immediately a
Sister went to the house in question. Her
patient was one of those old Frenchwomen who
hate the sight and even the name of a priest.
When the Sister said something about God she
answered that she was a Christian, but that she
never meant to go to confession, because she
hated priests. The Sister felt glad at that moment that nothing in her garb revealed her religious character ; she contrived by degrees to win
the poor woman's confidence, and finally succeeded in overcoming her prejudices. 'O, how
glad I am that you were not dressed as a nun !'
said her patient, some time afterwards, when she
had fulfilled her religious duties and received
Holy Communion. 'If I had had the least idea
of your being a nun I should not have suffered
you to approach me, nor listened to a word you

said.' This incident decided the new Sisterhood
to forego the satisfaction of wearing a religious
habit. This was no doubt a sacrifice; but in a
country like France, where there are many
merely nominal Catholics, and deep-rooted prejudices exist amongst a portion of the population against priests and nuns, their secular dress
often enabled them to approach and to win over
persons who had long kept aloof from all religious practices, but in whose hearts faith was
not absolutely dead.

Another poor woman whom they assisted
declared at the outset of her illness that she
would not allow a Sister to enter her room, as
she had made up her mind not to go to confession; but when they told her that a lady in
mourning had called she made no difficulty in
admitting her. Satisfied with the attentions of
her visitor, and especially because not a word
had been said about confession, she condescended
to express a wish to see her again, provided it
was not to talk about Almighty God. 'If, however,' she added, 'you would be so obliging as to
read me novels, I should not mind, once in ten
times that you called, letting you say a word or
two about religion.' The bargain was accepted.
The lady in mourning read aloud *Fabiola*, and
soon obtained permission to speak of religion
every other day. Before long the poor woman
begged herself that it might be every day. Soon

she went to her duties, and died peacefully a short time afterwards.

From the moment that the little community entered on their work of mercy their time was no longer their own ; they were sent for in every direction, and found themselves compelled to give up the employment which had hitherto provided for their support. They now trusted to Providence for their daily bread, and it never failed them, though they experienced, indeed, in those early days especially, many of the real sufferings of poverty. But though they often suffered, they did not starve. Their first refectory was a stable, and they wrote on its walls the words of our Lord, ' Behold the birds of the air : they sow not, neither do they reap nor gather into barns, and yet your Heavenly Father feedeth them.' So it has been with these children of Providence, whose trust has been rewarded by numberless graces and blessings.

On the 18th August, 1856, Monseigneur Sibour, the Archbishop of Paris, came to visit and bless the new convent. ' It is a grain of mustard-seed,' he said, ' which will become a great tree and spread its branches far and wide.' He approved of all that had been done since the house had been opened, and allowed Mass to be said in the chapel, and the Blessed Sacrament to remain in it. This took place on the ensuing 5th of November. On the 8th of the same

month the house was consecrated to the Blessed
Virgin in a most especial manner. The Mère
de la Providence had been kneeling before that
little image of the Immaculate Mother which
she had looked upon for years as her greatest
treasure. Once in her youth it had seemed to
her that from its lips she heard these words,
' One day I shall be in a chapel,' and she had
looked upon this intimation as a prophecy,
which was now realised. The beloved statue
was placed at the right-hand side of the altar in
the humble sanctuary of the Rue de la Barouillère, and as she prayed before it the thought
arose in her mind of delivering up into the hands
of her heavenly Mother all the cares and responsibility involved in her position as foundress and
Superioress. She told her daughters that such
was her desire ; they warmly sympathised with
her devout intention, and on the appointed day
the altar of the Divine Mother was adorned to
the best of their power in honour of her installation as the Superioress of the little congregation
devoted to the most forlorn of her children.
After Mass Mère Marie knelt down before the
dear image which had witnessed the earliest
aspirations of her ardent soul, and, with a voice
trembling with emotion, pronounced words
which revealed the faith and the love burning in
her heart. According to her usual practice, she
asked for a token that her prayer had been heard,

and that her Mother in heaven had accepted the office of Superioress of the Helpers of the Holy Souls. The details of the proofs which she petitioned for, and of the astonishing way in which they were vouchsafed, have not reached us, but they were such as fully to satisfy her clients that Mary Immaculate, at whose feet the keys of the house were laid, had indeed become their special Protectress.

A few days afterwards a Monstrance was presented to the congregation, and Mère Marie exclaimed, ' I see, then, that our Lord wants to give us His blessing ; ' and off she went to the Archbishop to obtain leave for the Exposition of the Blessed Sacrament and Benediction on several days of the year. When Monseigneur glanced at the list she had drawn up, he said, ' Why, you are asking, my child, for privileges which long-established congregations would not think of soliciting ! ' With that readiness of reply possessed by the French more than any other people, the Irish perhaps excepted, Mère Marie exclaimed, ' O monseigneur, don't you know that the youngest children in a family are always the boldest and most indulged ? ' The kind Archbishop smiled, and seemed about to sign the paper ; but, as he was taking up his pen, he stopped and said, ' No : really I cannot give so extensive a permission.' Mère Marie was not to be daunted. ' Monseigneur,' she urged, with

a voice full of emotion, 'do give it. The Souls
in Purgatory are holding your pen.' 'Do you
think so, my child?' his Grace said, as if impressed by the thought, and forthwith signed
the paper without further remark. A few days
afterwards this pious prelate was numbered with
the dead. He had fallen by the hand of an
assassin, and closed a life devoted to acts of
charity by a tragical death. But, between the
day of her last interview with Monseigneur Sibour and that on which they shed bitter tears
at his loss, the Helpers of the Holy Souls had
accomplished the important act which united
them for ever to our Blessed Lord as His
spouses. On the Feast of St. John the Evan-
gelist they made their first vows—temporary
indeed in form, but in the secret of their hearts
as indissoluble as the inward and entire consecration of their whole beings to Him could make
them. It was a solemn moment for Mère Marie—
even more solemn than to most of those who
made a similar offering. It had been so long
desired, so sighed for, and attained at last at the
price of so many sufferings. A strong sense
came over her in that hour, even whilst joy was
flooding her soul and the words of the *Magnificat* rising to her lips, that she was committing
herself to more than ordinary and ever-increasing sufferings—that God would have mercy upon
her according to His great mercy in the sense

which many holy persons have attached to those words—believing that the greatest of His mercies is to be given to drink of His chalice and to be baptised with His baptism: and, indeed, no sooner had the alliance been formed between the souls of these servants of the Holy Souls and their crucified King than the weight of His Cross was sharply pressing on their hearts. The news of the assassination of their best friend and protector, Monseigneur Sibour, which happened on the 3rd of January, 1857, came upon them like a thunderbolt, and it needed the words of a Saint to raise their courage under the terrible blow. On the 29th of January the Abbé Toccanier wrote to them this letter in the name of the Curé d'Ars:

'I own that I feel more inclined to weep with you than to write words of comfort. The death of your holy Bishop has indeed deprived you of a powerful protector, but he will watch over you from heaven. You are the children of Providence, and it must be made evident that it is on God alone you depend. The suffering Church must have its martyrs on earth. Our good Curé prays for you, and sends you his most heartfelt blessing. A house founded on the Cross has nothing to fear. It is marked with the Divine seal.'

On the 11th of April he advises them as follows:

'The good Curé recommends you not to trouble your head about certain pretended predictions respecting the duration of good works. The Church is now, as it has always been, militant; and the good it does is ever accomplished in the midst of labours, trials, and persecutions. Our risen Lord says to you, as He did to His Apostles, " It is I. Do not fear : I shall be with you. Is it not from His hand that you receive the daily Bread of your souls and of your bodies ? At the same time he exhorts you to confidence, the holy Curé says that you must also exercise prudence. He does not venture yet to advise you to buy the house. You must think more of the excellence than of the number of subjects you receive, most especially in these early days. The seed must be of the best quality.'

M. Vianney was often sending these messages to the little community, which looked upon him as their founder and their father. On the 30th of June of the same year, for instance, this note was written by his faithful secretary :

' Can you for a moment doubt that you are doing God's work when He vouchsafes to give you so many tokens of His love ? Your sufferings your trials your struggles are all means of advancing in virtue and paying the debts of others.'

And on the 14th of July he says :

' Our good Curé thinks that you have received so many visible proofs of the Divine goodness towards your community that it is impossible to doubt that your labours are pleasing to God, and that the fervent prayers of your Sisters, and the sacrifices they make, have greatly assisted the Holy Souls in Purgatory. As to what number you may have contributed to release, that is a question which, not being a prophet, he cannot answer ; and he says we must not be over-anxious to pierce the veil with which the Divine will hides from us those mysteries of suffering and expiation. He perceives that the devil does all he can to discourage you, and uses every kind of artifice for that purpose. Do not be disturbed by it. Such is the substance of the answer I received from him when I showed him your letter. I should like to have more abundant consolations and still greater lights to transmit to you.'

Amidst many privations and a very practical kind of poverty, the Helpers of the Holy Souls carried on their mission. They accepted every opportunity which occurred of practising abnegation, patience, and mortification in the dwellings of the poor, when sickness, old age, or infirmities called for their assistance. With the fervour which specially marks the early days of a religious Order, they gave themselves without intermission to this work of charity, and often the lay Sister who acted as cook to the community was despatched on errands of mercy, leaving the dinner of the Sisters to shift for itself. To illustrate the spirit of their apostolate amongst the poor, we will give the following specimen of the cases with which they dealt, and of the success which attended their ministrations.

In an attic on the seventh story of a house in their neighbourhood lived an old lady, who for twenty years had suffered from an ulcer, which by degrees so destroyed her legs that at last they were reduced to nothing but blackened and diseased bones. For years she had been unable to walk, and at last to stand. When first obliged to take to her bed, the members of a confraternity to which she belonged paid her frequent visits and afforded her assistance; but gradually almost every one ceased to climb up to the poor attic, and she was left in the most helpless solitude. The fact was that the stench caused by her disease had become so overpowering that persons had been known to faint in her room. A lady advised her to invite the attendance of one of the Helpers of the Holy Souls, and from that day for five months they exercised towards this poor sufferer the most heroic charity. Though a pious and good crea-ture in her way, Mdlle. Gramillet would have often tried the patience of her religious nurses beyond endurance if they had not looked upon her as the source of countless graces for their own souls and for the sufferers in Purgatory. She had a mania for the arrangement and re-arrangement of the scanty furniture in her room, of her bedclothes, and of everything about her, which took up hours of their time, and was a never-ending labour. The slightest speck of dust on the walls, the least fold in the curtains, she remarked: and with many apologies, indeed, but in the most stringent manner, insisted on their being removed. Nothing could remain in the same place for five minutes together. The activity of nature, forcibly repressed by her own helplessness, found vent in these continual exac-tions on the time and attention of those who attended upon her. But this was nothing in comparison with what was to follow. At the beginning of October, 1857, Mdlle. Gramillet was taken dangerously ill, and received the last Sac-raments. Naturally enough for a person who was pious, and whose life had been a continual course of pain and privation, she was glad of the news of her approaching departure ; but she was apparently destined to go through her Purgatory on earth, and those who attended upon her to share it. For more than three weeks she lingered, her body in a state of frightful decomposition, exhaling so horrid an effluvium that it required the spirit of martyrdom to endure it. An appalling number of worms issued from that living corpse, and the soul which lingered in it rebelled against its sufferings, and was angry because death did not come. But the work was at last consummated which God was intending to effect by this prolonged agony. Resignation and peace at last took the place of irritation and murmurs. The dying woman gently thanked her patient nurses, and sent a message of reconciliation to a relative whom for ten years she had refused to see. Then death came : it seemed as if the word of release was spoken when the word of pardon had passed her lips. She lingered some hours, waiting as it were for the presence of one of the religious who had been her ministering angel, and breathed out her soul in her arms. We scarcely venture to speak of the task they had to perform towards the earthly remains of this poor creature, but they did not abandon them until they were consigned to the grave.

A man who lived in a street adjoining the Rue de la Barouillère was a Freemason, and noted as a most desperate character. He always worked, bought, and sold on Sundays, had a violent aversion to priests and Religious, and scarcely opened his mouth without swearing and blaspheming. A woman who had lodged in the same house had been brought back to her duties by the efforts of the Sisters. She mentioned one day to her neighbour how carefully she had been nursed by one of the ladies in black. 'Well, I wish I had the same luck,' he exclaimed, 'for I am always alone now. My wife is out at work till midnight.' Upon this hint, which was conveyed to the nuns, one of them offered her services. She came in for the first time at a moment when the sick man was suffering great pain, and happened to be able to give him relief. He begged her to visit him every day, and she had often to sit for hours with him, listening to the most absurd speeches about religion, and especially against priests—the world went on so badly because people listened to them. This was the continual theme of the unfortunate man's declamations. But the nun found means now and then to put in a word, and to show him by degrees the senseless nature of his prejudices. One day she was agreeably surprised by his giving her a lilac which somebody had made him a present of, and saying, 'There now ; take that to your Mother, as you call her, and tell her she can put it before the statue of St. Joseph, my patron Saint. He will, perhaps, help you to convert me; and I hope you will be rewarded for all your goodness to me.'

The poor man grew rapidly worse. He still refused to see a priest, but said, 'Pray for me, and, if I get well, next Easter I'll go to church.' Each day his strength diminished. Then, of his own accord, he asked the Sister to make a novena to Our Lady of Liesse—the holy Virgin of his native place, he said. He also consented to wear a medal, and to learn the 'Hail Mary.' He said nine Hail Marys every day during the novena. At the end of that time he was not better in health, but his disposition was completely changed. He was like another man : he left off swearing, and expressed a wish to see a priest whom he had very ill received a few days before. When he saw him he said, 'Forgive me, sir ; I did not like priests, but you will be satisfied with me now.' He went to confession. Before the Blessed Sacrament was brought to him he insisted on being shaved, and begged his poor room might be nicely arranged. After he had been to Communion and received Extreme Unction, he threw his arms around the neck of the priest and exclaimed, 'O my dear sir, I have never been so happy ! I hate no one now. You were very right when you told me God was very good.' After this day his sufferings became acute, but he bore them with perfect patience the words, ' May God have mercy on me!' were continually on his lips. He kept asking his wife to forgive all his wicked conduct, and gave her good advice. Turning to the Sister, shortly before his death, he said, ' You have shown me the way to heaven. You may be sure, if I get there, you will come there also.'

Joseph's edifying end made a great impression on several persons. A woman of seventy-two years of age, in the same house, who had not been married in the church, and had never since approached the Sacraments, watched for the Sister on the stairs, and said, ' Take me to confession.' ' Are you in earnest?' asked the nun. ' O, yes! since I have seen M. Joseph so happy, and Madame D —— so good, I have made up my mind to do as they have done.' She confessed, went to Communion, and died suddenly, ten days afterwards, of a heart complaint. A little later on, still in the same house, the Sister's attention was directed to an aged couple who had lived together for years, but had never been married. The man had a severe illness. which prevented him from working. The woman had long toiled to support him, but now a whitlow had deprived her of the use of her right hand. When the nun came in, Helen —that was her name—was weeping bitterly; Henri was sitting on the bed reading a news-paper. He received the visitor with these words,

'Poor people have no friends,' and followed them up by a volley of oaths. Then he went on reading. The Sister, nowise discouraged, began to look about her, and tried to set things a little to rights; but there was no fuel, no bread, no clothes. She went out, promising to come back, and whispered to the woman to pray. Soon she returned with a little money and some provisions. Helen cried for joy; Henri muttered, 'Thank you.' Then she set to cleaning the room and attending to the poor woman, who, her left hand being paralysed, and her right at that moment helpless, was in a most disgusting state of neglect, and quite covered with vermin. The man raised his eyes from his newspaper, and watched her steadily for some time. After a while he exclaimed. 'This is too much! How can you bring yourself to do that, Sister?' The following morning Helen was suddenly attacked with apoplexy. When the nun arrived she was senseless.

'Pray, Henri, pray!' said the nun, struck with the sad spectacle of the woman's dangerous state and the man's despair. A look of scorn and anger passed over his face. Still, after an instant's hesitation, he uncovered his head and joined his hands. In the evening Helen recovered her consciousness. A priest had been sent for. He went straight up to Henri, and said,

'I hear your wife is ill, my friend. Keep up your spirits. She will soon get better, I hope. What part of France do you come from?'

'From Burgundy.'

'What! from Burgundy? We are country folks, then. Long live Burgundy, and all the good people in it! Come, let us shake hands.'

Whilst Père —— was talking to the sick woman, with whom he begged to be left alone, Henri kept wondering over the kindness of his manner.

'How good he is!' he said to a neighbour in the next room; 'not a bit of pride about him. To be sure, he comes from my own country.' Then, turning to the nun, with tears in his eyes, he exclaimed, 'Sister, I am a wretch to have said so much against priests. I did not know them.'

When Père —— came out he again spoke to Henri. 'That is a good little woman in there,' he said.

'We must not deceive you, M. le Curé; we are not married.'

'But you are going to be married. Come to me on Saturday; we will talk about Burgundy and arrange that matter.'

'And I will go and see you too, M. le Curé!' cried the neighbour in whose room they were. 'It is a terrible long time since I have brushed up my conscience.'

'Come by all means, then,' said the priest, with a smile. 'Too happy to see you; and as many more as like to come.'

On the following Saturday Henri kept his appointment, went to confession, and came home to Helen (who was getting much better) happier, he told her, than a prince. By means of the Society of St. Francis Regis the old couple soon got married, and went to Communion together the following day. They led a most edifying life during their remaining years, and died not long ago, blessing God and thanking the nuns, who had, as they said, put them on the way to heaven.

Altogether, thirteen persons were converted in that one house in consequence of the attendance of one of the Sisters on the dying Freemason. The gratitude of the poor—and, O, what a slander it is to say the poor are not grateful!—is often shown in a very touching manner to their nurses. Amongst other less remarkable instances we notice the following fact. One of the nuns was dying. Several poor women used to come and inquire after her. One of them seemed very much disappointed at hearing that she was not better. With great simplicity she said to the Superioress, 'She will be better soon, for I have begged Almighty God to take my life instead of hers.' It so happened that the nun did recover, and the grateful soul who had made the offering of her life died a few days afterwards.

The secular dress of the nuns, and their intercourse with persons in various ranks and positions in the world, often enabled them to render great services to those sufferers who, having known better days, shrink from notice, starve in silence, and hide the extremes of poverty under a decent appearance.

Their example has often awakened in the souls of others a generous desire to endure extraordinary sufferings for the Souls in Purgatory. The following story is an heroic instance of self-devotion, containing in itself the perfection of charity towards the living and the dead.

In the month of August, 1858, an Irish lady, Ann ——, called on the Superioress of the Sisters, and told her that she was a daily governess, but was obliged to give up her lessons on account of a severe operation she was compelled to undergo.

'Do not pity me,' she added, seeing in the nun's face the compassion she felt. 'I have often asked our Lord to suffer for Him, and to be as poor as He was; but I should be very glad, Reverend Mother, if one of your Sisters would be with me at the time, and dress the wound for me afterwards.'

The Superioress readily agreed to the request, and on the appointed day two of the

Sisters went to Miss Ann ——'s lodgings. She had been to Communion that morning, and was awaiting the doctors with perfect calmness. They decided that the operation could not be performed at that time—the health of the patient required some previous treatment. One of the doctors, a Protestant, was so much touched at the courageous serenity of the patient and the devotion and charity of her nurses, whose house he visited, that he left a sum of 100 francs in their hands, begging them to use it secretly for Miss Ann ——'s benefit. During two months they supported her, and dressed her wounds daily. At the end of that time it became absolutely necessary to proceed to an operation, as the cancer was rapidly increasing. The doctor declared that the patient must submit to go to the hospital, and the Curé of the parish offered to pay for a private room for her. When she got there her first words to the Sister who had accompanied her were these:

'I have nothing to give you in return for your kindness but my sufferings. Tell your Reverend Mother that I offer them all up for the Souls in Purgatory, and ask her to let you come to me when I have to go through the operation.'

Thursday was to be the day, but Miss Ann —— had prayed that it might be on Friday, that she might more particularly unite her sufferings with those of her crucified Lord ; and the doctors did put it off, on account of some accidental circumstance. On the Friday morning she offered up the coming day for the Souls in Purgatory, and then, leaning on the arm of one of the Sisters, walked quietly to the hall where the operation was to be performed. An ordinary person would have shuddered at the sight of the preparations, but a supernatural joy filled her heart. She begged that the crucifix should be placed opposite to her. The chief surgeon (sixteen were in attendance) said she would not see it, as she was to be chloroformed. She entreated not to be thrown into a state of insensibility, but the doctors insisted upon it. The evil was found to be so deep-seated that a long and terrible operation ensued. In the midst of it life seemed to be departing from the stiff and motionless frame, and the surgeons found it necessary to restore animation even at the price of excessive suffering. After the operation it was requisite to keep the patient awake, and they laid on the Sisters that difficult task. There was but one subject that never failed to rouse her. The thought of God and of the Souls in Purgatory kept her alive. For nine days she lingered in sufferings and in exhaustion, but saying, with a smile on her face, ' It is all for the Holy Souls !' A complication ensued, and on the 20th of November, 1858, the brave Irish girl went to receive her reward in heaven. Brave indeed ! for after her death a secret was discovered which stamps her sufferings with a character of heroic charity. She had for some time been giving lessons gratuitously to the young widowed mother of three children. One day this poor woman confided to her that her heart was breaking. She was threatened with a cancer, and the thought of leaving her children destitute orphans drove her to despair. Miss Ann —— made a novena with her; and on the same day, after a fervent Communion, she implored God to let *her* suffer and die, and to spare the mother for the children's sake. The widow recovered, and the holy girl soon after had proof that her sacrifice was accepted.

The Sisters watched over her last moments, and accompanied her to the grave. Miss Ann ——'s brother, a priest in Ireland, made them the best return in his power by becoming an honorary member of their Society, and offering the Holy Sacrifice of the Mass every month for the Souls in Purgatory.

CHAPTER X.

PERPETUAL VOWS—FAITH AND WORKS.

In the midst of the poverty which reigned within her house and around it, Mère Marie de la Providence coveted for one purpose alone the

precious things of earth. She longed to adorn
the sanctuary of her little chapel with some of
the gold and precious stones so lavishly bestowed on the adornment of the persons and
the dwellings of the rich and the great. It
seemed to her so strange that Christians should
dedicate to the service of the world all the beautiful things God has made, and so seldom devote them to the earthly temples where His
Majesty resides. She mused on the subject
until one day, as she was praying before the
image of Our Lady of Providence, the wish came
into her mind to crown that dear Mother with
one of those brilliant diadems which are the sign
of her Divine royalty. 'I will become a beggar
for your dear sake,' she said, as the desire arose
and grew in her heart. 'I will ask every one
of the rich ladies who pay us visits to give you
one of their many trinkets. How could any one
of them refuse to make you that little offering?'
And then she addressed to Providence one of
those strange requests which were so often
granted to her simple faith —she asked Providence, in case her intention was accepted, to
give her a sign of it by sending to the house
that very day some rich lady to whom she might
mention her plan, without, however, making any
direct request, and who would of her own accord
offer one of her bracelets for the Blessed Virgin's
diadem. The ensuing day was, as usual, so full

of occupations that Mère Marie did not think any more of what she had asked until, in the evening, she was summoned to the parlour, and found there a lady, very smartly dressed, whose rich attire reminded her of the bargain she had made with Almighty God during her morning prayer.

In the course of her conversation with the stranger, the Mère de la Providence spoke of the poverty of their institute, and added that nevertheless she thought of promising the Blessed Virgin a crown of gold and precious stones. The lady remained silent a moment, and then, taking off one of her magnificent bracelets, she gave it to Mère Marie and said, 'Give me leave thus to contribute to your pious purpose.' Tears came into the eyes of the Mère de la Providence, and she explained to her generous visitor how she had unconsciously brought her the answer she had asked for in prayer.

The next day another lady, unknown to the pious foundress, called upon her, and said that she was curious to know what were the means of support of this little community, which she had only just heard of. When she was told the details of their mode of life, and the supernatural object of their labours and devotion, she exclaimed, 'But how do you exist if you give yourselves up to unremunerative works of charity?' The foundress smiled and answered, 'Has not our Lord said, Seek ye first the kingdom of God and His righteousness, and all these things shall be added unto you?' The stranger smiled in return, but hers was an incredulous smile. Mère Marie had recourse to facts in order to convince her that Providence acts in a supernatural manner with regard to those who abandon themselves to Its guidance. She had many proofs of it to allege. Among other instances of this Divine co-operation, she related the answer her prayer had received on the preceding day. The lady to whom this was told was so struck with the fact that she at once gave to the good Mother one of her richest necklaces. From that day so many tributes poured in upon her for the Blessed Virgin's crown that she was enabled to make her an offering of two diadems, one of which was of gold and diamonds.

During the first year of their religious life in the Rue de la Barouillère, and the presence of the Blessed Sacrament in their chapel, the Helpers of the Holy Souls were greatly embarrassed as to the means of securing Mass. They were not rich enough to pay a chaplain, and only through the charity of various priests they obtained that the Holy Sacrifice should be offered up in their little sanctuary. The steps they had to take for this purpose involved a considerable loss of time, and kept them in constant anxiety.

The Superioress, who saw the bad effect of this uncertainty on community life, began, in November, 1857, a novena to St. Gertrude, to obtain an improvement in their position in this respect. On the eve of the Saint's Feast the Sister sacristan, who had made several unsuccessful applications that day, called at the house of the Jesuit Fathers, Rue de Sèvres. The Father-Minister promised her a priest for the morrow, and added, ' Try to secure him.' Mère Marie, struck with this message, could hardly believe that these words really contained an intimation that her prayer would be granted. To use her own words, ' she for once struck the rock twice,' and sent again to know what the Rev. Father meant. ' Tell your Superioress that it is just as if I had sent her a chaplain.' was his answer.

The Jesuit father who said Mass that day on St. Gertrude's Feast, and who continued to say it, not for many consecutive days, but many years, became the friend, the guide, and the faithful protector of the Helpers of the Holy Souls : and they loved to ascribe this priceless blessing to the intercession of St. Gertrude, to whom their foundress had turned in that her great and urgent need.

In the first days of January, 1855, M. d'Assonvilliers informed the Mère de la Providence that he was obliged to sell his house, and inquired whether she wished to buy it. She was convinced that God intended this house, in which they had been so unexpectedly established, to be the centre of their future works ; and without hesitation she signed an agreement to pay, on a given day, a sum she saw at that time no means of raising. No doubt crossed her mind as to the result ; and Providence justified her confidence. After performing this act of perfect reliance on our Divine Lord, she knelt down before the Tabernacle, and exclaimed, with her impetuous and childlike piety, ' At last, my beloved Lord, You are no longer a lodger here, but in Your own house.'

The daily increasing fervour of her love made her ardently desire at that time to complete the entire union of her soul with her Divine Spouse by perpetual vows. Even the Abbé Gabriel thought it early days for this step, and doubted greatly whether the Archbishop would accede to her request. ' Make them in your heart,' he said, ' and later on we shall see what can be done.' ' Do you give me leave, father,' she said, ' myself to petition the Archbishop for this favour ? ' ' Certainly,' her Superior replied ; and she and one of her companions, who acted as Mistress of the Novices, and coveted the same permission, went together to the archiepiscopal palace. She gives, herself, the following account of that visit :

'My hopes of success were at once confirmed by the circumstance that Monseigneur, having declined to receive several persons that day, made an exception in my favour and admitted us. I began by telling him how sorry I was not to have been able to see him before concluding the purchase of our house, and how successful had been the issue of our negotiations. He wished me joy in the most kind and fatherly manner, and then I said, "Our work is now securely established as regards temporal matters, but I still feel anxious as to the spiritual side of the question. And, though our Superior, l'Abbé Gabriel, thinks my request is rather too bold a one, I venture to entreat your Eminence to allow one of my daughters and myself to make perpetual vows." "Yes, I grant you leave to do so," he replied. "Eminence," I exclaimed, though my emotion was so great that I found it difficult to speak, "our happiness would be complete if it were through your hands that the gift of ourselves to God was made. I am afraid I am very indiscreet in asking this, but God will bless your charity, and your kindness encourages me to ask if the ceremony could take place on the 25th of this month, a memorable date in my life and in the history of our little community!" "That is quite impossible," the Cardinal rejoined; "I am engaged for all the coming days." "I am sure that cannot be the case." I boldly replied; "for, as I could not obtain an audience from your Eminence sooner, I asked your guardian angel to keep that day for us." Monseigneur then looked at his agenda, and was very much surprised to find that he had indeed no engagement for that day, and he at once granted our request.'

The two happy spouses of our Lord spent three days in retreat before the one on which they were to pledge themselves irrevocably to the holy life they had embraced. After two years of incessant labour, the Mère de la Providence had leisure in solitude and recollection to cast a retrospective glance on the mercies which had attended her arduous course, and writes:

'O my God, how strange was that year of 1856! Fourteen

persons living together, supported, we may really say, by a perpetual miracle! And, in spiritual matters, what graces were granted to me! I felt that You sustained me, for I was alone in my weakness, in the midst of all the exterior and interior trials in which I was plunged. Everything has happened as You intimated to me during the years which preceded the foundation of the community. You gave me to understand that I should one day be a religious, but not in the ordinary way —that You would remove from my path many obstacles, but that I should not actually be a nun till I was thirty-three years of age. Yes, I feel it, O my God—and I wish I could declare it to the whole world—rest is to be found in obedience and self-surrender. One of the greatest graces I have to be thankful for is the wish to obey which You have always given me. In all the circumstances of my life I can say, "I have obeyed." All I want to write down here are the marks of Your paternal care for Your poor child in spiritual ways, in order that by reading over this record I may always reanimate my faith and courage when I seem to have no help from earth or Heaven, caring for nothing on earth, and receiving no consolation from Heaven. During all the year 1857 you have, as it were, held me in Your arms, my Blessed Lord.'

In the ensuing passage we learn something of the work of grace in that chosen soul:

'What graces have been showered upon me, O my God! I feel encompassed with mercies. These three days will bring about a change in my life; they will do away with the past and be the beginning of a new existence. What You ask of me, my Lord, is to die to self in a spiritual sense, to give up all self-seeking relative to the state of my soul, and self-conscious-ness with regard to sanctity, so as to endure cheerfully that state of spiritual darkness when nothing is felt sensibly except temp-tation. . . . This is what You say to me by the voice which speaks in Your name —"God will take your work in hand, and He will make it His own." And, indeed, if I had to rely on myself, I should give it all up, for I feel quite incapable of any-thing; but I can do all things in Him who strengthens me, and I feel that, through Your grace, and if I will it correctly, the way and the only way in which I can advance in perfection will be by self-renouncement and abnegation. . . . I desire to live,

O my good Jesus, solely for the Souls in Purgatory, without any care for my own debts, numerous as they are—without even thinking of them—leaving it to You to do what You like with me, and wishing for nothing else but to be Your Providence for Your beloved spouses in Purgatory.'

On the last day of the exercises, when she was full of the happiness of having spent a time of more intimate intercourse with God, the following words summed up, if we may so speak, the feelings which filled her heart: 'Give me, O Lord, that rest which absorbs my soul in Thee, so that it may do nothing, when in prayer, but listen to Thy voice, and at other times fulfil Thy will in the present moment without disquietude about the past or the future.'

The emotions and the happiness of the day of her sacred espousals were too deep for words to describe. One brief sentence indicates their measure and their intensity. 'O, too short day!' she exclaims; 'only in heaven shall I find your like.'

Cardinal Morlot officiated, as he had promised, and on this occasion rejoiced the heart of the Mère de la Providence, and all her spiritual family, by a grant of Indulgences applicable to their beloved Holy Souls.

As soon as Mère Marie's community was established on a secure basis, temporally and spiritually speaking, she began to turn her thoughts to the extension of its works, and the spread of the devotion which was its life and the origin of its existence. It had never been her plan to limit its action within the walls of a religious house. Each convent of the Helpers of the Holy Souls was to be, according to her view, a centre of works of mercy, combining together the relief of sufferers on earth and of sufferers beyond the grave. With this idea and full of confidence that, if God called her daughters to devote themselves to a life of charity, He would provide them with the necessaries of life, she instituted, with the sanction of the Archbishop of Paris, an association of honorary members, who, in their measure, would contribute to carry out this holy apostolate, the motto of which is to pray, to suffer, and to work for the Holy Souls. The conditions of membership are such that the highest personages in the land, those most absorbed in business, or the poorest and most hardworking people, can fulfil them, and bear their part in this scheme of mercy. They consist simply in an annual alms, and in the daily recital of the Acts of Faith, Hope, and Charity, and the ejaculation, ' My Jesus, have mercy.' Numbers of persons sought at once admission into this confraternity. It seemed, in many instances, as if departed friends were appealing to those whose fruitless tears had been the only tribute paid to their memory, and bringing back souls on earth, by its means, to thoughts of prayer well-nigh forgotten.

The list of honorary members has gone on constantly increasing. The Holy Father vouch-safed to bless the association, and in 1860 attached special Indulgences to the prayers said by its members.

But there were those who sighed for a closer affinity with the Order devoted to the departed —who longed to consecrate themselves to the same thoughts, and, in a measure, to the same occupations, but who, on account of age, or health, or circumstances, or duties in the world, could not embrace the religious life. For such persons as these was founded a Confraternity of Associates, bound in a far more intimate manner to the congregation. In addition to the prayers said by honorary members, they recite every day the Vespers for the Dead. Once a month they assist at the Mass said in the chapel for deceased relatives, and accompany the Religious, or visit, under their direction, the sufferers whom it is their special object to relieve; and on Monday afternoons they meet at the convent to work for the poor. This charitable occupation is carried on in silence, or else spiritual reading beguiles the time allotted to it.

On the 21st of March, 1859, twenty-eight ladies entered into this pious league in behalf of the Holy Souls. They had learnt the spirit of this consecration, and how well it could adapt itself to the duties of their state in life, from Mère Marie de la Providence, who had, in her own former position, so perfectly united home duties with devotion and active charity.

In the archives of the society the proceedings of that day are thus related:

‘Our Reverend Mother began by addressing a few words to the twenty-eight ladies assembled in our house; then we all went into the chapel, and the nuns knelt on the steps of the sanctuary. At half-past eight his Eminence Cardinal Morlot stood in the midst of us, and spoke to those present of what the Triumphant Church in Heaven, the suffering Church in Purgatory, and the Militant Church on earth expected at their hands, and of the good which their generous self-devotion would effect. Then he blessed the silver crosses, on which the words “Pray, act, and suffer” were inscribed. Those who were about to receive them knelt at the altar-rail and received them from the Reverend Mother. During the Mass which followed this ceremony, the associates made their Act of Consecration, and sealed their pious engagements by the reception of Holy Communion.

Afterwards his Eminence again spoke from the altar, and attached to the crosses of the association the Indulgences of the *Bona Mors* and *Via Crucis*, and ended by reciting a *De Profundis* for the souls of the departed relatives of all those present in the chapel. Then diplomas of aggregation were delivered to each of the ladies by the Reverend Mother as the Superior-General of the Order, and his Eminence took leave of them with the warmest expressions of sympathy and approval of their self-devotion.’

On the day of their consecration the associates receive a little manual of prayers, headed by passages from Scripture—precepts for this life and promises for the next:

OLD TESTAMENT.	NEW TESTAMENT.

'Purify thyself by the work of thy hands.'

'Stretch out thy hands to the poor, that thy expiation and blessing may be perfected.'

'A gift hath grace in the sight of all the living, and restrain not grace from the dead.'

'Be not wanting in comforting them that weep, and walk with them that mourn.'

'Be not slow to visit the sick, for by these things shalt thou be confirmed in love.'

'In all thy works remember thy last end, and thou shalt never sin.'

'And when the Son of Man shall come in His majesty, and all the angels with Him, then shall He sit upon the seat of His majesty. And all nations shall be gathered together before Him; and He shall separate them from one another, as the shepherd separateth the sheep from the goats. And He shall set the sheep on His right hand, but the goats on the left. Then shall the King say to them that shall be on His right hand, Come, ye blessed of My Father, possess the kingdom prepared for you from the foundation of the world. For I was hungry, and you gave Me to eat; I was thirsty, and you gave Me to drink; I was a stranger, and you took Me in; naked, and you clothed Me; sick, and you visited Me; I was in prison, and you came to Me.

Then shall the just answer Him, saying, Lord, when did we see Thee hungry, and fed Thee; thirsty, and gave Thee drink? And when did we see Thee a stranger, and took Thee in; or naked, and clothed Thee? Or when did we see Thee sick or in prison, and came to Thee?

And the King, answering, shall say to them, Amen, I say to you, as long as you did it to one of these My least brethren you did it to Me.'—*Matt.* xxv. 31-40.

It was these teachings of Divine Writ that

had made Bourdaloue utter those words so thoroughly understood by Mère Marie de la Providence, 'It is not enough to pray for the dead: we must, above all things, sanctify ourselves for their sakes.'

CHAPTER XI.

TO PRAY, SUFFER, AND LABOUR.

ONE work of mercy leads to another. The Helpers of the Holy Souls instituted their Sunday conferences for women of the lower classes in order to confirm and strengthen the good results produced by their attendance on the sickbeds of the poor. These meetings were held at the convent. They commenced with short prayers for the dead, for never is the thought of the departed separated from any of their works for the living. Then the Epistle and Gospel for the day are read, with a short comment, some practical instructions are given, and hymns sung in unison. During this time one or two of the younger nuns take charge of the babies which the women bring with them, and amuse them with cheap toys. In summer they afterwards walk and sit in the garden, conversing with the Sisters, who have nursed most of them in sickness, and receive from them advice and encouragement to persevere in their good resolutions.

The work rapidly increased, and was placed under the patronage of the Blessed Peter Claver. Some of those who attend the meetings become apostles in their turn. They lend good books to their neighbours and their friends, and bring them to the Sunday conferences. If women in that rank of life can once be roused to work for God, and to try to save sinners, they often effect astonishing conversions. The Helpers of the Holy Souls found many a co-operator in the ranks of their humble associates.

Their own success, which was often a cause of astonishment to themselves, was no doubt owing to that law of grace by which great sacrifices purchase great results. To nurse poor creatures who frequently combine the most repulsive form of disease with those of long neglect, and whose souls are often as diseased as their bodies, is an extraordinary act of charity in women, many of whom have been reared in wealthy and comfortable homes, and in proportion to the self-devotion of their holy lives has been the fruit they have reaped.

There are in France a number of persons of the lower class who unite to an utter ignorance of all religious truth a violent hatred of priests and nuns, that exceeds by far what we see in England even amongst the bitterest Protestants they seem almost unapproachable on the subject of religion. Yet even amid this class of unbelievers the Helpers of the Holy Souls effect numerous conversions. The lady in black, who visits some of these haters of Christianity, does not utter a word about God till she has passed many an hour in the stifling atmosphere of a room where the Sacred Name is never uttered save in blasphemy and cursing. She, who once had servants to wait upon her, has now to wait herself on patients whom advanced age and want of education often render capricious and trying to the utmost degree. To make up a bed without sheets, cook a dinner with hardly any provisions, and light a fire without tongs or shovel, are problems she has often to solve, and she may be required to perform still more difficult and irksome things. One old woman used to insist upon her nurse brushing the furniture and even the floor several times a day with a bunch of feathers. The nun, who was required to go through this performance, had been in a high position in the world, but was too happy to spend hours upon her knees on the dirty floor for the sake of the soul she was bent on winning to God.

Day after day the Auxiliatrice watches for the moment when it will be safe to say something about the good God or the Blessed Virgin, as the case may be: she invokes in her heart the merciful Queen of Purgatory, and then leaves on the table a holy picture, or asks permission to hang on the wall a crucifix. Then, if the memories of the past, of a departed parent or child, or sometimes of a first Communion, bring a tear into the sunken eye, or force a sigh from the softened heart, she improves the opportunity, and proposes a visit from some priest well known as the friend of the poor—one who, in his turn, will come and say kind words, and sit by the bedside of the sufferer, and only speaks of confession, when the soul, touched by grace, is prepared for the suggestion. The Helpers of the Holy Souls study the art of winning hearts to God, and they teach that blessed art to their poor associates. Even the poor women of Father Peter Claver's confraternity become proficients in this knowledge, and draw their husbands, brothers, and sons into the fold of that Church so often hated from mere ignorance, so beloved as soon as known.

Every year, on the feast of their Patron Saint, there is a special service for the associates, and his picture is given to those of the members who are not yet in possession of it: they have the greatest confidence in the Saint's intercession; and, if all secrets were revealed, marvellous proofs of its efficacy might be here related. In the month of March a lottery takes place, when a prize is drawn by every member of the association. Clothes, pious pictures, etc., are provided by the ladies interested in the work. There is a lending library at the convent, and a Sunday class for poor girls, but the care of the sick still remains the principal active work of the community.

The Sisters of Charity yield a ready assistance in Paris to the Helpers of the Holy Souls. They sometimes come and ask them to take charge of some of their sick, and it is from the pharmacy, and often from the kitchen, of the Sisters of St. Vincent de Paul that they procure the medicines and the assistance they need for their patients. The physician of the Bureau de Bienfaisance sometimes points out cases to them. Friends and relatives among the destitute poor come and fetch them. An anonymous letter occasionally gives them notice of a distressing case. In each instance an experienced and prudent person is, in the first place, sent to ascertain that Christian prudence allows the Sisters to undertake the care of the patient proposed to them. They do not go out at night. If they are appointed to watch a sick person through the night, they go to his abode early in the evening, and leave it in the morning. In the day they spend several hours by the bedside of the sick, but return to the convent at stated times for the community exercises, in order that the religious spirit may be continually maintained, and active work sanctified by prayer.

During the first years of their community

life the Helpers of the Holy Souls, under the direction of their holy foundress, had followed a rule which she had extracted from those of various other religious Orders, selecting whatever appeared to her in each of them best adapted to the needs and the object of her own society. But the time had now arrived when the formation of a more definite form of government was to be given to the infant congregation. Father B——, of the Society of Jesus, had been acting as its chaplain during several months. Mère Marie attributed to the intercession of St. Gertrude the spiritual advantages which his charity had afforded them, for it was at the close of a novena which she had made to that gentle Saint that his ministrations had begun amongst them, and great was the consolation which, from the first, they had afforded them. But no intimate communication between him and the Reverend Mother took place for some time. It happened, however, that one day he made a slight remark which led her to express how grateful she felt for advice, and, with her habitual frankness, to add, 'You see, reverend father, that the community is only beginning, and that I am also a beginner; so that it is a twofold charity to help me, and to teach me what I have to teach others without having learnt it myself.'

From that day forward the Mère de la Providence found out that St. Gertrude had obtained for her, not only a chaplain, but a father ; for this holy man was permitted by his Superiors to devote himself, with all the ardour of his apostolic zeal, to the promotion in the new community of the highest desire of perfection. Following in the footsteps of all saintly teachers, he strove to establish it amongst them on the foundation of the deepest self-contempt. In all the most frequented portions of their house he inscribed on the walls words which he most wished to impress on their minds, '*Abneget semetipsum*,' and cultivated in this new institute everything that St. Ignatius teaches on the subject of the love of humiliations ; and then he gave them, as the most precious of gifts, the Rule of his own Society. When the Curé d'Ars was told that they had adopted St. Ignatius's Rule for their own, as far as is possible for a community of women, he exclaimed, ' O the good children ! It is all right with them, then. They could not have done better.' From that moment the Helpers of the Holy Souls advanced rapidly in their holy career. That blessed Rule became to each of them a constant theme of meditation, and the source of continual efforts towards heroic perfection.

Soon afterwards the Rev. Père Félix, pleading the cause of the Souls in Purgatory in an eloquent sermon which has moved many a heart to devote itself to their perpetual service, concluded his impassioned appeal with these words: 'Would that I could borrow the tongues of angels, and in accents full of heavenly melody implore you to give alms to our brethren in Purgatory! Yes, I claim from you in their behalf a threefold charity. Take as your own the motto of the religious Helpers of the Holy Souls, and act upon it—" Pray, suffer, work." Unite yourselves with them, and, by the might of almsgiving and the strength of heroic sacrifice, deliver the sufferers whom their example calls upon you to relieve.' This sermon was published under the title of 'The Dead, Suffering, and Neglected,' and produced a great effect. It revealed to many the existence of the new Order, and even determined some vocations to it. One Sister, now in the house in Paris, was living in a distant town in France when this sermon accidentally fell in her hands. As soon as she learned that a community existed devoted to the relief of the Holy Souls, nothing could induce her to give up the thought of joining it. She went to Paris and sought admission amongst the Auxiliatrices.

Père de Ponlevoy, whose name is ever connected with that of the saintly Père de Ravignan, took also the kindest interest in the little institute which was growing up under the shadow of St. Ignatius, and used often to preach in their chapel. Twice he gave retreats to these beginners in the religious life, and strengthened them in the spirit of their vocation. To one who was asking him for information as to the spirit of the infant community he wrote: 'I am passing through Paris on my way to the south of France, but I have just time to give you an excellent account of this new religious family. I know them very well; we give them frequent instructions. Their rules are formed on our own. The spirit of the community is good, and their works numerous and useful.'

The following letter from the Very Rev. Father-General of the Society of Jesus seemed to the Mère de la Providence a crowning instance of St. Ignatius's protection, and a pledge of his interest in her spiritual children. She had written to solicit from him a boon for the Holy Souls. He replied:

'Devotion to the souls in Purgatory has always been dear to our society; and one of our predecessors, Father Laynez, St. Ignatius's successor, looking upon it as the necessary result of the end of our institute, especially recommended it; consequently I felt inclined at once to agree to the request contained in your letter, and to apply, out of the number of Masses I have at my disposal, 500 for the relief of the Holy Souls. . . . I beg our Divine Lord to continue to shed His blessings abundantly on you, Reverend Mother, and on the fervent souls who have joined you in the holy work you have undertaken.

In the Sacred Hearts of Jesus and Mary, I remain
Your very humble servant in Christ.

PETER BECKX,
General of the Society of Jesus.'

Whilst Mère Marie de la Providence was favoured with so many graces and visible mani-

festations of the Divine protection, our Lord did
not withhold from her the trials with which He
usually purifies His chosen souls. As the immense
exterior difficulties which had surrounded her
undertaking were vanishing, or at any rate diminishing, her soul was undergoing strange sufferings. The pressure of this inward cross drew
from her at times, entirely devoted to God as
she was, exclamations which revealed how violent
was her anguish. 'Good Jesus, I am overwhelmed
by a nameless indescribable cross. Give me the
will to be crucified. The pains of Calvary have
taken possession of my soul. I am crushed, I
cannot lift up my head! My God, give me, I
beseech You, a love of suffering and sacrifice.
Take me, O Lord, and nail me to the Cross. I
am Your victim, but give me courage to endure
the sharpness of Your loving strokes. I have
before my eyes a cross, the pledge of Your love,
and at any cost I am resolved to take it up and
to carry it. The Five Wounds must be my continual devotion. O Jesus, give me courage, I
implore You!' Constant physical sufferings, which
seemed always on the point of overcoming her
moral energy, but which never did impede its
action, sometimes gave her a momentary feeling
of discouragement, which afflicted her all the
more painfully on account of its inconsistency
with the peculiar bias both of her natural character and her spiritual life. The burden of her

responsibility regarding the souls under her care
—the anxieties connected with the government
of a large religious family—sometimes weighed
heavily on her soul, and produced a sort of
anguish which one day found vent in a letter to
the Curé d'Ars.   In his name the Abbé Toccanier wrote her the following answer:

'The Curé says, " How can she wonder at the sufferings she
endures after having offered herself as a victim for the Souls in
Purgatory ? "   I pressed him to tell me what he thought of the
peculiar trial you were undergoing.   He answered, " It is Almighty God's will that she should go through this martyrdom,
in order that by means of it she may draw down blessings on
herself and on her house."   You know that I never do anything but repeat to you exactly his own words, not taking upon
myself to say whether they are inspired, or only the result of
his long experience in the ways of Divine Grace.   In either case
it must be a great consolation to you to receive such an answer
from him.   Our good Curé thinks that you have received so
many visible proofs of the Divine goodness towards your community that it is impossible to doubt that your labours are
pleasing to God, and that the fervent prayers of your Sisters, and
the sacrifices they make, have greatly assisted the Holy Souls.
As to the number you may have contributed to release, that is a
question that, not being a prophet, he cannot answer; and he
says that we must not be over-anxious to pierce the veil with
which the Divine will hides from us these mysteries of suffering
and expiation.   He perceives that the devil does all he can to
discourage you, and uses every kind of artifice for that purpose.
Do not let this distress you.   Such is the substance of the
answer I received from him when I showed him your letter.   I
wish I had still greater lights and consolations to transmit to
you.'

Though absent in body, M. Vianney had ever
directed in spirit the congregation, which looked
upon him as its founder and its father.   He
watched over every detail connected with its

establishment, and never allowed any deviation from its original intent. The Superioress had at one time been much urged to admit teaching among its works. Her own feeling was entirely against it, but for greater security she referred the question to the Curé d'Ars. As usual, M. Toccanier transmitted to her his reply:

'I told the Curé what you had written. His answer was one of the most prompt and decisive I have ever known him to give. I asked if he would think and pray on the subject, and then acquaint you with his decision; but he said, "Believe me, there is no doubt about it. She must go on as she is doing. Her ideas are right." Then he spoke of his own orphanage here. "God," he added, "has different views for each one of us. Each has his appointed work—his mission; and this applies more particularly still to those who establish an Order. There are plenty of schools for the rich, and trusting as the Sisters do in Providence, the bread of each day will not fail them." This seems to be enough to satisfy your mind on the subject, and to strengthen you in the resolution of labouring only for the Souls in Purgatory, and that by means of mercy towards the poor. You act in this way according to the spirit of our Lord, and you relieve at the same time His afflicted children in this world and in Purgatory.'

In 1859 the faithful friend and co-labourer of the holy Curé came to Paris, and visited the community. On his return to Ars he wrote the following letter to the foundress of the Auxiliatrices:

'I have on my table innumerable letters which seem clamouring for answers, but I must leave them to clamour for a while, in order to reply to one I have just received from you. Yes, indeed, I have talked to our good father at Ars of his spiritual family in Paris. I have given him ample details, and all the interesting particulars you related to me regarding the foundation of your congregation. We did not know the history of all the trials and the mercies that attended its beginnings. Tears of joy fell from his eyes when I told him about the Blessed Virgin's crown, the blessing of the Holy Father, and most of all when he heard of the heroic patience of your dear little Sisters in the Rue St. Martin in trying successively as many as ten different employments, and of all those marvellous interpositions of Providence by which your daily wants were at that time supplied. I ended my story by saying, " M. le Curé, all these daughters of yours are happy to unite themselves with you in suffering for the dear Souls in Purgatory. Whilst they nurse the sick and bury the dead, they strive as you do for the conversion of sinners. They would be so glad to see you. Pray for them very much." " Ah, that I will ! " he answered. " Poor dear children ! they well deserve it. Their work is truly a work of the good God." " It is possible," I added, " that the mother of that family may pay you a visit." " O, so much the better ! I shall be more glad of her visit than of that of a queen." '

On the 4th of August of that year the Curé d'Ars died ; but he lives in the hearts and the memories of the community which owes so much to his prayers and his guidance. His name is frequently on their lips ; often has his intercession obtained for them miraculous cures. Every memorial of him is carefully preserved and venerated. The simple pictures which recall his life of austere poverty, and represent the scenes of his prayers and labours, hang on the walls of their parlour in Paris, and speak to their visitors of the departed Saint of modern France.

In the preceding month of June the Abbé Toccanier had written to the foundress :

' My dear saintly Curé has heard with joy what abundant blessings have been showered upon you. Not knowing what else to send, I enclose a little picture, beneath which he has written his name, and a tiny lock of his hair.'

Previously to that she had received from M. Vianney a medallion painted on an agate stone, bearing an image of the Blessed Virgin and the Divine Infant. After the death of their mutual friend and father, M. Toccanier sent her a handkerchief steeped in his blood, and several things which had belonged to him; among others his rosary, so long and constantly used by his venerable hands. It passed into hands not unworthy of that precious bequest; and to the day of her death Mère Marie de la Providence carried it about with her as her most precious treasure.

The loss of her saintly guide was the greatest earthly trial that could have befallen that loving and devoted heart, which owed to him so much. She felt that, humanly speaking, that loss was irreparable; but she called to mind the words which he had himself uttered when death had deprived her, some years before, of that good Archbishop, Monseigneur Sibour, who had blessed and fostered the first steps of her community in its arduous career, and she took comfort in applying them to this yet greater trial. At that time M. Toccanier had written from Ars:

'I own that I feel more inclined to weep with you than to write words of comfort. The death of your holy Bishop has indeed deprived you of a powerful protector, but he will watch over you from heaven. You are the children of Providence, and it must be made evident that on God alone you depend. The suffering Church must have her martyrs on earth. Our good

Curé prays for you, and sends you his most heartfelt blessing.
A house founded on the Cross has nothing to apprehend. It
is marked with the Divine seal.'

That seal was not wanting to the spiritual
building this valiant woman had founded. It
was impressed on every step of her progress
towards its completion, but each cross brought
with it an increase of grace and strength.

CHAPTER XII.

NANTES AND CHINA.

THE number of Religious in the Rue de la
Barouillère went on rapidly increasing, and the
house could no longer hold them. Moreover, it
was impossible to carry on the novitiate in the
way prescribed by the Rule of St. Ignatius without a separate building devoted to that purpose.
The moment that Mother Marie recognised that
something was necessary to the welfare of her
institute, she never doubted that God would give
her the means of obtaining it ; and so she went
one day to inquire if her next-door neighbour
would like to sell his house. The answer was
that he had not the slightest thought of doing so.
His wife declared that nothing would ever induce

him to part with it. Not in the least discouraged, the good Reverend Mother began at once, with all her nuns, a novena to St. Joseph, and promised to say every day of her life the Little Office of her heavenly protector. The difficulties instantly vanished, and a few days afterwards the agreement was signed. The house was named St. Joseph, and, on the morrow of the day when the bargain was concluded, a celebrated artist, who knew nothing of their novena or their purchase, sent them a beautiful statue of the Patron Saint of the new novitiate.

This happened on the 29th of September, 1861. In the fulness of her gratitude, Mère Marie used often to exclaim, ‘O, if I could but make people understand how, in the midst of all God does for me, I feel my own nothingness, and what a wretched instrument He vouchsafes to make use of!’

It was, no doubt, a joy to see the number of her spiritual children increase and the borders of their tent enlarged: but this rapid growth necessarily involved painful consequences. Those who had hitherto worked together and been united in one family, under the wing of the same beloved Mother, were soon to part, and begin those emigrations which are at once a blessing and a trial to each new religious Order. Nantes was the first place where a little colony of Helpers of the Holy Souls swarmed from the mother-house.   We extract from the Mère Marie's journal her account of that foundation :

'On Wednesday, October 7. 1861, a young girl from Nantes called upon me. and spoke with much interest of our little society.   I begged her to pray for it, and to accept a small image of St. Joseph, which I advised her to carry about with her.   This young lady, whose name was Josephine —— , wrote several times from her home to ask me different questions. Contrary to my usual habit, I put off for a long while answering her, and fancied this had cooled her interest about us.   But she wrote again and again, and in the month of March told me that she was praying constantly to St. Joseph, and seeking his help for the project she had formed of having a house of our Order in her native town.   I said in my reply that this would require a very special assistance from Providence, and that I did not see at all my way to it.

On the 30th of March, 1864, I was told that a M. A ——— wished to see me.   He announced himself as Mdlle. Josephine's uncle, and said at once that his object was to know what would be required for the foundation of a house of ours in Nantes. "God's will in the matter is the first thing to be considered," I answered ; " and it would be a token of His will if Monseigneur the Bishop wished us to come.   At present, your niece's wish is all I have heard of.   Then we must have a house, and means of support for a few Sisters."

M. A — did not commit himself to anything, but it was agreed that the next time he saw the Bishop he would sound him on the subject.   I own that I was impressed with the fact of this proposal having been made during the month of St. Joseph.   "Is it," I thought, "a blessing vouchsafed to us through the intercession of our heavenly protector ? "

The spiritual guide God has given me opined that the plan was worth thinking of, and I felt then that something might really come of it.   This made me very nervous, and every time I thought of Nantes a sort of shiver came over me.   What was God's will ?   I was waiting and watching for some light on that point when, on the 19th of April, M. l'Abbé R—— , Vicar-General of the Bishop of Nantes, came to speak to me, by his lordship's desire, of the new foundation.   I repeated to him what I had said to M. A——, and he assured me of the Bishop's perfect approval of the establishment of a house of our Order in his diocese, adding that God would show us what was His will, and that I was right to have no wishes of my own on the subject. After meditating some time on this visit, I said to myself, "It is evident that this foundation will take place. But in what way? That is God's secret." Still I must confess it—I rather avoided any serious consideration of the question, and drove it from my mind as much as I could, until the 24th of April, the Octave of the Patronage of St. Joseph. I felt suddenly during Mass as if our Lord was urging it upon me, and gently reproaching me for my want of courage in not availing myself of this opportunity of extending our work; and, indeed, if I had waited to found the society till somebody came and said he would give me a house and means of support for those who were to live in it, we should be at this moment in the little rooms, Rue St. Martin. The only thing necessary after all was to secure the kind interest of a few families. I asked of God that help might be given to pay our rent for the first year: and as to the rest, Providence would provide, and we should act up to the principle of our little society "the spirit of faith." No sooner had this light flashed on my mind than I felt courage to act upon it, and to accept this foundation under whatever conditions Providence might ordain, and to look to It alone for the daily bread of this new family about to settle at a distance from us. After a few moments of recollection, I asked our Lord to give me in His goodness a token that my present dispositions were the result of His inspirations, and not of my own excited fancy, and that this token should be the receipt of a letter from Nantes. I had not heard from M. A—— since the 30th of March, and I did not know that he had seen the Vicar-General. During the whole of that day I felt strongly impressed by the idea that the Sacred Heart of our Lord would provide for that foundation.

On the following morning I had no sooner glanced at my letters than I saw that there were two from Nantes—one from M. A——, and another from his niece. Before I opened them a silent thanksgiving rose from my heart to our dear Lord, who had thus speedily answered my prayer. The renewal of my correspondence with M. A—— gave me an opportunity of informing him that I had altered my views with regard to the foundation. We made three consecutive Communions for the Souls in Purgatory, which have been most devout to the Holy Ghost, in order to find the house we were to have. We asked for prayers at Notre Dame des Victoires, and I did nothing but ejaculate. "My God, let this come to pass if it is Thy will."

Some one told me of a house in a good situation. I begged

our Lord to keep it for us. On the 24th of May, Feast of Our Lady Help of Christians, I asked our Blessed Lady, the Superioress of our little society, to let me have that day a good letter from Nantes. That very morning I received one from the Vicar-General, full of assurances of the Bishop's (Monseigneur Jacquemet) interest in our society, and of his desire to see us established in his diocese. I wrote to thank the Bishop and the Abbé R—— —, and on Thursday, the 2nd of June, I felt inspired to place myself in a more special manner than ever under the protection of the Sacred Heart of Jesus. I asked the Blessed Margaret Mary to give me her heart, and besought our Divine Lord to take into His own hands the foundation of Nantes, reminding Him that He never denies us what we ask on the Feast of the Sacred Heart. I implored Him to send me on that day which was the morrow some good news concerning Nantes, and that He would vouchsafe to inspire M. A ——— with the thought of securing to us the rent of our house for a few years, which was what he had originally hinted at ; and that if this happened I should see that it was indeed His blessed will we should begin at once the work at Nantes. On the following day I received a letter informing me that the landlord of the house we had in view was disposed to accept much lower terms for it than he had named at first. It did not occur to me at the moment that this was an answer to my prayer ; but when I went into the chapel and saw our Blessed Lord exposed on the altar I remembered my petition, and felt that it was granted. Later in the day came a letter from M. A—— renewing his proposal just in the manner I had begged our Blessed Lord to inspire him to do. He had complied to the letter with my request, and on the very Feast of the Sacred Heart. I cannot describe what I felt : no doubt remained in my mind as to the will of God, and every day of the Octave I recited the Office of the Sacred Heart.

On the 14th of June the Bishop of Nantes wrote to me the following letter :

" Reverend Mother,—With all my heart I welcome you to my diocese and my episcopal city. Yours is an eminently Christian work, and one which the Church did not yet possess. Your arrival will be hailed with joy by our good and religious populations. Come, then, dear Reverend Mother, and all of you, my dear daughters in Christ. I bless you in anticipation. The state of my health will not allow me for the present to see much of you: but I hope to make up for this privation later."

Some days afterwards M. A—— urged me to come to Nantes in order to sign, on the 1st of July, the agreement for the lease of our future house. I thanked our Lord that this kind friend, without knowing our special devotion to the Sacred Heart, had fixed upon the first Friday in the month for so important a step towards the new foundation.'

The promises of the good Bishop were realised ; his pious flock understood and sympathised to the utmost with the work of the Helpers of the Holy Souls, and entered into the spirit of their active and incessant devotion to the dead. All classes in Nantes concurred in establishing the new convent on a satisfactory footing, and the generosity and co-operation of their first benefactors have gone on increasing ever since.

Monseigneur Jacquemet, as long as he lived, was a most kind father and friend to the daughters of Mère Marie de la Providence ; and his successor, Monseigneur Fournier, has never ceased to evince his interest in their Order and their work.

We have already said that one of the Jesuit Fathers in Paris, the Reverend Father B——, had devoted himself to the rising community with unexampled solicitude. He seemed to have it at heart to instil into the new Order the spirit of St. Ignatius, and the apostolic zeal which is its grand characteristic. He laboured incessantly for this end, and every day the Mother of that spiritual family kept rejoicing and thanking our Lord and St. Gertrude that so great a blessing had been vouchsafed to them.   It was, therefore, no ordinary trial, no common occasion of testifying a blind and faithful submission of heart to God's will, when, with the suddenness which attends such events amongst the Jesuits, she learned that her director, father, and friend—the novice-master, as it were, of her spiritual children —was going off to China—leaving Paris perhaps for ever.   She said *Fiat* with her usual courage, but no light as to the meaning of that trial softened it then.

Two years afterwards, in 1867, Monseigneur Languillat, Vicar-Apostolic of Kiang-nan, came to Rome in consequence of the invitation which the Holy Father had addressed to all the Catholic Bishops, to meet in the Eternal City for celebration of the Centenary of St. Peter, and on his way back visited Paris.   He knew the deep interest which the Rev. Father B——, missionary priest at Shanghai, took in the religious family whose first steps he had guided, and kindly wished to tell him on his return that he had seen the convent of which he had often spoken to him.   So, on the 4th of August of that year, the prelate from that far-distant land asked to say Mass in the little chapel of the Helpers of the Holy Souls.   Whilst he was offering up the Holy

Sacrifice the thought came into his mind that the Religious in whose house he was were possibly the very nuns he was seeking for to take charge of a little band of Chinese virgins in his diocese, and of his orphanages of native children. So strongly did this idea take possession of his mind that, after making his thanksgiving, he went straight up to the Reverend Mother, and said, ' I think I am come to seek helpers amidst the Helpers of the Holy Souls.'

' How so, my lord ? ' she answered, quite surprised.

' Why, do you mean to be Helpers only in this little corner of the world ? ' he replied, with a smile.

It so happened that that very morning it had occurred to Father de Ponlevoy, the Provincial of the Jesuits and Superior of the Chinese Missions of the Society, that the Helpers of the Holy Souls were destined by Providence to co-operate with the missionaries, and to take charge of the Chinese orphanages. He did not know that Monseigneur Languillat had been saying Mass at their convent ; but as soon as he saw him that day he mentioned the idea which had struck him, and this coincidence appeared to both a token of God's will.

As to Mère Marie, she had kept in mind the words of the pious Bishop, and said over and over again to herself, ' Are we to be Helpers only in this little corner of the world?' When she heard that Monseigneur Languillat had called and wished to speak to the Superioress, her heart began to beat very fast. The prelate and the Père de Ponlevoy had come together to submit to her the possibility of a foundation in China.

'Do you think it would be impossible?' the Father Provincial asked.

'Impossible, very reverend father!' she exclaimed. 'Is "impossible" a Christian word? I own that I have never thought of such a thing. Our little community has been so recently founded that it is barely established in France. How could I have dreamed of China?'

'But if it is God's will?' the father rejoined.

'O, if I saw by some clear tokens that it was so, of course I should have nothing to say but *Ecce ancilla Domini.*'

The Father Provincial then told her how the thought of that foundation had occurred simultaneously, and irrespectively of any previous communication on the subject, to Monseigneur Languillat and to himself, and added that his own opinion was that Providence had brought about this opening, and asked if she would let them see and speak to the assembled community.

When they were all present he said a few words to the assembled nuns about the Chinese Missions, and begged the Bishop to recite a

'Hail Mary' in the Chinese language. Then he asked if any of them had a desire to devote themselves to the foreign missions; and the Reverend Mother added, 'My children, let those amongst you who would wish to go to China stand up.' Most of them rose, and the Bishop and the reverend father withdrew, thanking God in their hearts for the bright spark of apostolic zeal which had been kindled in those souls that day.

The good Mother betook herself to praying most fervently for light on the subject. She was not alarmed at the boldness of the undertaking, or, on the other hand, dazzled by the offer of so glorious a mission. We find her writing at that time:

'I really feel quite in a state of indifference. I do not incline to the right or to the left. I can hardly account for, and am surprised at, having no will in a matter of such importance. This is not the case with my daughters, N. N., which shows that a vocation for the foreign missions is of long standing in our little society.'

Thus she kept seeking for light, and asking in every direction for prayers, whilst her nuns were pressing her to decide in favour of their apostolic desires. The Superioress of the house at Nantes wrote to her at that moment:

'Under the present circumstances, I cannot conceive a greater mortification than *not* to go to China.'

But Mère Marie would come to no decision without the sanction of her director. She was determined not to act except under obedience, and patiently waited until her spiritual father—that Père Olivaint whose last days rise before us in connection with his peculiar devotion to her Order—came out of retreat—one of those very retreats the secrets of which are revealed to us in the wonderful journal of his meditations. Let any one read the record of that particular one entitled *The End*—that of the year 1867—and no wonder will be felt that, when his holy penitent submitted to him the question whether or not her spiritual children should enlist in the ranks of Christ's apostolic servants, and perhaps in those of the white-robed army of martyrs, he should have said, ' I think it is God's will,' or that she should have accepted his words as the voice of God, manifesting to her His Divine pleasure. No sooner had this conference taken place than Mother Marie de la Providence wrote thus to Monseigneur Languillat :

' My Lord. —I have been in daily hopes of hearing that you had returned to Paris, but, as you are still absent, I must communicate to you without any further delay the Rev. Father Olivaint's decision with regard to the important step we have to take. It coincides entirely with that of the Father Provincial. They both tell me that it is God's will we should go to China. Acting therefore with their sanction and by their desire, I accept the proposal conveyed to me by the Father Provincial. It is through you, my lord, that the Divine Heart of Jesus granted to the Helpers of the Holy Souls the grace of the foreign missions —a grace which involves, indeed, a more complete immolation and greater sufferings, but also more abundant means of assisting and delivering the Souls in Purgatory, the sole object and end of our institute.

It only remains for us to consider, with your lordship, the time and the manner in which we are to carry out the resolution taken before the holy Tabernacle. It was on the 13th of August—the last day of a novena to the Holy Ghost that I accomplished seeing both the Reverend Fathers de Ponlevoy and Olivaint. Now that we have become your children, how earnestly we long to see your lordship amongst us! You have the right to say to the Helpers of the Holy Souls, " Thousands of virgins in China are expecting you. Come and teach them to pray." '

We give the Bishop's answer to this letter :

' Blessed be the day when Providence led me to visit your house, and for the first time to offer the Holy Sacrifice under its roof. I little thought when I entered your chapel that I was about to detach a sprig from that tree—so strong and fruitful a one from its earliest days—and, carrying it across the seas, plant it in realms afar, even in China. I feel convinced that the veneration for the dead, which in that country amounts to idolatry, will now be hallowed and Christianised. You will be welcomed, not only by the Christians, but by the pagans, who will see that we are not wanting in devotion for departed souls. When I call to mind all the providential circumstances of the eventful day when, having consulted men whom I fully believe to be influenced by the Spirit of God, and having carefully put into practice all the rules for the discernment of spirits, I saw difficulties vanish in a way I could not venture to expect, and even conduce to the success of our pious design, I cannot help exclaiming with the thoughtful and holy persons who take the same view of the subject, " The finger of God is there." Come, then, dear Helpers of the Holy Souls ; come to China, and found your third house in Kiang-nan. Come, not to Mount Thabor— you do not look for it on earth—but to Calvary, which you love ; and to a Calvary that will comprise everything contained in your motto. Come and pray and work and suffer in China—in the mission which the Church has entrusted to the care of the weakest of her children.

✝ ADRIEN LANGUILLAT, Bishop of Sergiopolis, Vicar-Apostolic of Nankin.

Paris, October 10th, 1867.
  Feast of St. Francis Borgia.'

So conscious was Monseigneur Languillat that no time should be lost in providing his flock with the Helpers he had secured, at once for the living and the dead, that he pressed the Reverend Mother to fix their departure for the ensuing 15th of October. She agreed to his request, and instantly prepared for this trying separation by seeking for her spiritual daughters, about to leave their native land for so arduous and distant a mission, the best viaticum for their long voyage—the greatest encouragement to face the toils and dangers of their new destination—viz., the special blessing of the Holy Father.

The answer to this petition reached the Rue de la Barouillère a few days before the departure of the six nuns chosen amongst all those who had offered themselves to lay the first stone of the Chinese mission. The Sovereign Pontiff had written as his answer the following words :

'May the Angel Raphael accompany you, and bless all your footsteps.'

That heavenly protector conducted them on their way, and on the first Friday of December—the day consecrated to the Sacred Heart of Jesus—they set foot on the shore of that Eastern land hallowed by the labours, prayers, and tears of St. Francis Xavier, the blood of martyrs and the holy perseverance of successive generations of valiant confessors of Christ.

The good father who for so many years had been their guide and director at home welcomed them to the scene of their future toils, and continued to be at Shanghai what he had been to them in Paris. As to their spiritual Mother—whose affections were as warm, we might almost say as impetuous, as those of a parent for beloved children—she suffered intensely from this all but lifelong parting from some of her first and most devoted companions. But in the midst of that suffering there was a depth of joy, an ardent thankfulness, which shone in her countenance whenever she spoke of those who had gone forth from amongst them—'*Ad majorem Dei gloriam*,' the motto impressed on their hearts, and acted upon in their lives.

CHAPTER XIII.

THE CHINESE FOUNDATION.

IN 1855, on the Feast of the Compassion of the Blessed Virgin, under the pretty title of 'Garden of Mary'—in Chinese, Sen-mou-ieu—at a place called Wan-dan, a little congregation of Chinese virgins had been formed for the service of the Mission. In order to veil their religious character from the eyes of the surrounding pagans, about twelve orphans were added to the inmates of this sort of convent; and, later on, a school for the education of those maidens and of the oldest of the children was likewise established in the same spot. The approach of the rebels, a few years afterwards, dispersed this little community. Some of its members, however, clung to the foundress, and went with her to Shanghai, where they spent four years under her direction.

At the end of that time the little community was transferred to Wan-ka-dan, where suitable buildings had been erected. The virgins who wished to consecrate themselves to the work of the Mission were located apart from the scholars. In February, 1868, the direction of this house was given to the Helpers of the Holy Souls, and in the following year it was again removed into more spacious quarters at Zi-ka-wei, and the Orphanage of the Holy Children incorporated with the 'Garden of Mary.' The house at Wan-ka-dan was afterwards occupied by the Carmelites. The Helpers of the Holy Souls enjoy the consolation of often visiting these holy recluses, and feel strengthened and supported by the consciousness that pure hands and hearts are continually lifted up to heaven in behalf of the people and the objects for which they work. One of the nuns at Zi-ka-wei thus describes their convent :

'Our front door, which is the only entrance to the house, opens on a road bordering the canal. Three Chinese letters are

carved on its portal. The meaning of this inscription is, " Temple
where the Sacrifice of Perfumes is offered," and this satisfies the
curiosity of the natives, whose boats are continually passing to
and fro along the canal. Nothing meets their eye but the front
of our pretty chapel. The inside of the enclosure is hidden by
tall hedges : it contains a large rectangular square, surrounded
by a variety of buildings appropriated to our works of charity.
The Sen-mou-ieu, or Garden of Mary, occupies the side opposite
to the site to the entrance, and comprises the school and the congregation of native Sisters. On the right-hand side is the building occupied by the Helpers of the Holy Souls, and, facing it
to the left, the Orphanage.'

It cannot be denied that the vocation to such
a Mission as that of China requires, in those who
devote themselves to it, a more than ordinary
zeal and apostolic fortitude. St. Francis Xavier
says, in one of his letters to the religious of his
society :

' Ah, I fear that, amongst those who come from Coimbra to
the Indies, there may be some who, when they find themselves
tossing on a stormy ocean, may wish themselves in the seminary
rather than on board the tempest-driven vessel. There are feverish fits of virtue which sea-sickness speedily cures, and perhaps
not even all who may land at Goa with unabated ardour will
prove equal to the trials to be met with amongst a barbarous
people, and in the midst of all the dangers that will surround
them. If virtue has not laid deep root in their souls, zeal and
ardour will cool by degrees, and end by disappearing, and he
who pined in Portugal to be sent to India will pine in India to
return to Portugal.'

The same warning might be addressed to
every nun who desires to offer herself for the
Chinese Mission. Continual abnegation must
be the watchword, the motto, and the daily
practice of Christ's helpers in that heathen
land.

It fares badly with her if she has fallen short of her high destiny—if aught human has mingled with the supernatural desire of suffering with and like her Lord, and for the sake of souls, for whom we never work in vain on earth. But, if she has realised the sublimity of her vocation, nothing daunts, nothing disheartens, nothing saddens her spirit— not even the stolid indifference of the heathen—not even the slowness of the growth of that seed which she sows in tears, and which will be reaped perhaps in joy by others, when she has laid down her life on a foreign soil. She prepares her soul in patience, and in patience labours to win those whom her Divine Lord has marked out for her portion. She unites to the outward apostleship of her life the secret apostleship of personal sanctification, in her case amounting to heroism.

The Helpers of the Holy Souls preserve the habits, the dress, and to a certain degree use the same food as in Europe, but privations are not wanting of that sort also. The nights are often intensely cold, the mornings and evenings damp, the heat of the sun at noon overpowering. They have no water but that of the canal, which has to be boiled and filtered before it can be used.

The flatness of the country, only relieved by the hillocks in which the Chinese bury their dead, gives a melancholy and monotonous character to the surrounding scenery ; but, if the aspect of nature is depressing, there is a well-spring of joy in the souls of the nuns, which, if the world did but know of it, might well excite its envy.

The Orphanage of the Holy Childhood is a most arduous, trying, and at the same time interesting work of charity. It shelters more than two hundred poor little girls, abandoned by their parents chiefly on account of their ugliness or their infirmities. These unhappy creatures are left on the roadside, or at the door of the convent, or sometimes thrown over the wall into the enclosure, scantily covered by a few rags, or wrapped up in straw, often half-devoured by vermin and a variety of diseases. Many of them die, but not before Baptism has opened for them the gates of heaven. Those who survive are employed, according to their age and strength, in the garden or in spinning and weaving; they are taught household work, and at stated hours learn their prayers, and are instructed in the Catechism. Those who grow up strong and healthy are easily married, if they desire it, in Christian families, who are most desirous to obtain for their sons well-educated young persons, able to make themselves useful in all manner of housework and needlework. Others are received into native Christian families rather as adopted children than as servants, and the nuns continue to watch over their welfare. The permanent inmates of the Orphanage are therefore the lame, the blind, the helplessly infirm, for whom a hospital has been provided in a separate building from the school. Great sufferings are constantly witnessed within its walls; deformity and disease, produced by neglect in infancy, sadden these innocent lives; but the patience of the little sufferers, their keen enjoyment of the pleasures which the nuns contrive for them, and their edifying death, throw a halo of brightness even over this abode of infirmity and pain. Christmas—with its *crèche*, and its trees, and its sports, such as the poor little things can join in—is hailed there as elsewhere, and their joy brings to the mind of their devoted mistresses many an echo, no doubt, of similar joys in their far-distant homes in the days of their own childhood. Strange power of grace, strange spirit of sacrifice, which turns even the sharpest pangs of memory into subjects of thanksgiving, and every pain that darts through the heart into a new offering to that Divine Heart of Jesus, which has known the tenderest emotions of human affection!

The poor little Chinese children die holy deaths, or grow up, generally speaking, in feelings of the deepest piety. One of them spent her recreations, during a considerable length of time, in carrying earth for building, in order to earn something to give as alms for the jubilee.

Another worked in the same way to buy a bit of trimming for the cap of the baby confided to her care.

A blind child had received as a prize a red handkerchief, which those who could see admired very much, and the nuns asked her if she would like to exchange it for something else ; but the poor sightless little girl refused to part with it. Having treasured it up for several months, on Christmas Eve she wrapped up in it a few pieces of money, and laid it at the feet of the Infant Jesus.

A pharmacy is attached to the Orphanage, and one of the native Christian Sisters visits the sick, and gives medicines to those who seek her advice, having been trained and instructed for that purpose. A day-school has also been established within the precincts of the convent. The school generally consists of about one hundred pupils, who come, many of them, from a great distance, and are often grown-up women. Sometimes a grey-haired scholar sits amongst the children, diligently studying the Catholic prayer-books and Catechisms, in order to become himself a teacher of religion in some distant district.

They are carefully instructed in Christian doctrine, Bible history, and the lives of the Saints, and likewise taught to read in the Mandarin language. The classical works of Chinese authors are also read and explained. Writing, needlework—including the making of vestments, of altar-linen, and of artificial flowers—are also comprised amongst their occupations. The younger children make shoes. In China, the women, even of the highest rank, are their own shoemakers. They consider it quite an unbecoming thing to allow any one to take the measure of their tiny and more or less deformed feet ; they therefore all embroider their shoes, and manufacture the soles with tissues of linen paper and dried leaves, which are supposed to be waterproof. But the material is so brittle that an incredible number of them is required in the course of a year.

We must now speak of that confraternity of Chinese virgins which, under the patronage of Our Lady's Presentation, had been formed into a semi-religious community some time before the arrival of the Helpers of the Holy Souls, and which has now become a sort of appendage, and a most important one, to their institute. These Chinese maidens or widows are trained in the spirit of the interior life, and in the practice of good works. They go through a kind of novitiate, which lasts two years, and then bind themselves, by a simple promise, to the mode of life they have adopted. They are of immense use in the missions, and are employed in various ways which are not compatible with the rule of the nuns ; for instance, in schools at a distance from the convent, or in houses called *Kon-sou*, which serve the purposes at the same time of a church, a school, and a place of instruction for catechumens. Two or more of these native teachers reside in these buildings, watch over the humble sanctuary, baptise and teach the children, nurse the sick, and thus carry on a humble apostleship in distant and scattered villages.

It was on the 8th day of September, 1869, that the novitiate of these Presentation Sisters was opened, and thirty persons were admitted into it. The novices go every day to the Orphanage to attend on the sick children, and spend the rest of their time in prayer, the study of religion, and needlework. They are most edifying in their zeal for penance and their spirit of abnegation. Se-mou-mou, first Directress of the 'Garden of Mary,' as it was called, though past sixty years of age, begged to be received as a novice, and give the highest example of fervour and obedience. It was touching to see this aged woman humbly asking permission for everything she wished to do, or for little exemptions which her infirmities required. 'I am good for nothing,' she said one day. 'I cannot do all that a novice ought to do. If the Reverend Mother permits it, I will weed the garden, and teach the little children to say their prayers, so that I may at least still do something for the Mission;' and yet it was this holy woman who had founded and governed the works of this confraternity from 1855 to the time of the arrival of the nuns. There have been already many vocations out of this community to the Order of the Helpers of the Holy Souls, which goes among them by the name of the 'Help-the-Dead Society.'

More than a hundred poor women assemble every Sunday, under a verandah which surrounds the central court, to learn the Catechism and converse with the Sisters. This is the Blessed Peter Claver's association. On two or three days of the week the young girls of the neighbourhood come to be instructed in religion, and are rewarded for their assiduity by medals fastened to French red ribbon. St. Philomena is the patroness of this little society. Again, another class of persons engages the constant solicitude of the nuns. A large number of Christian women live on board the boats that are constantly going backwards and forwards along the canals of Kiang-nan. They are invited to visit the 'Garden of Mary,' when they stop for a day or two at Zi-ka-wei, and to approach the Sacraments. The children of this fishing population are often kept for two or three months at the convent to be prepared for their first Communion, and on the following year return there for a month to commemorate that blessed epoch in their Christian life. They become sometimes by these means little missionaries in their families.

Every year the spiritual exercises of St. Ignatius are given to four or five hundred women, many of whom come from a great distance. Most of them are virgins consecrated to a pious life. They arrive in boats, bringing with them a parcel of provisions and a sort of rug, which serves the purpose of a bed. They sleep in the passages and the outhouses, as well as in the dormitories. Every corner of the building is crowded with these pious visitors. But nothing can exceed the silence, the fervour, the recollection of this multitude of women. The nuns are always astonished and edified by their conduct. Many of these Chinese women work during whole nights, in order to earn the means of attending the retreat, and of bringing the religious some trifling present, such as chickens, ducks, pigeons, preserves made with salt as well as sugar, which does not quite suit European taste, and cakes baked with oil, butter being unknown in that country.

The Helpers of the Holy Souls supply altar-linen to the missionaries, who go up the country carrying with them their sacristy in a box. In several European towns their associates have undertaken to be the angels of the Chinese Mission, and forward to the nuns all sorts of articles for the portable altars of the priests.

Many of the charitable works above described have been established at Shanghai, and also a boarding-school, where girls of every nation under the sun are educated together. Many of them are Protestants, who become attached to the Catholic religion, and often carry away with them impressions which, by God's mercy, may tell in after life. To this school has been added one for the middle classes, under the title of 'School of Providence.' More than a hundred young girls are brought up there, and the greatest number of them are gratuitously supported and educated. All ranks of people at Shanghai have shown from the very outset a great interest in this institution, on account of its strongly moral and civilising influence. The Sisters had been assisted in carrying it out by persons of all nations and all creeds, even by the Chinese pagans. The children of this school are principally Eurasians; experience has shown that, under careful tuition, they are capable of a high amount of religious and intellectual development. When once they have realised the doctrines and teachings of the Catholic Church, their hearts turn to God with extraordinary energy and simplicity. The power of self-conquest and sacrifice which these young creatures evince would astonish and put to shame many languid and tepid souls in Catholic countries.

If there is occasion for patience, and need to

fight against discouragement in China, as regards the bulk of the population and the difficulty of conversions, it must be owned that the native Christians give great consolation to the missionaries, and striking examples of zeal and devotedness. As to the particular vocation of the Helpers of the Holy Souls, it is wonderful how it seems to respond to the feelings of the Chinese, and to stimulate the efforts of their associates. Nothing seems to them too irksome, and no sacrifice too great, when they are reminded that the Holy Souls will be benefited by their works. They put by their hardly-earned gains in order to give alms and to make offerings for Masses said in their behalf. One young girl, employed in the Orphanage, who had struggled long under much suffering and met with many disappointments, came one day in tears to the Reverend Mother. ' I can bear it no longer,' she said. ' O my child, how afraid the dear suffering souls must be that your courage may give way!' was the answer she received. A light shone in the face of that young Helper of the Holy Souls, and she said, ' That thought can make me bear everything. My heart is glad since you have said those words ;' and she resumed and persevered in a position of no ordinary difficulty.

' How happy you look!' one of the nuns said to a Chinese postulant, on the morning of All

Souls' Day. 'What are you thinking of, my child?' 'Mother,' was her answer, 'during Mass I offered up my body and soul to our Blessed Lord, and begged Him to let them suffer as much as He pleased for the dear Souls in Purgatory.' Another told her Superioress that she had made the heroic vow for the Holy Souls, and begged them as they entered heaven to obtain that at the same time a great number of pagans should enter the Church. A girl of twenty—in the novitiate—who belonged to a family of high position, received a letter from a rich aunt, who said she would make her heiress of all her wealth provided she came to live with her. To the question which was put to her as to her intentions, in consequence of this proposal, she replied, 'No, indeed ; I have chosen the Heart of Jesus for my abode, and I will not leave Him. I am doing penance to obtain my father's conversion.' Soon afterwards she told the Superioress that her aunt had declared that henceforward she would give her neither clothes, money, nor anything at all. 'Never mind, my child,' the Reverend Mother said ; 'we will take care of you.' 'O mother, I am not uneasy ! When I read my aunt's letter I thought of what our Lord said to the Apostles about not taking with them money, nor scrip, nor bag, and that they had not wanted for anything. I said to myself, " As I have given up both my soul and body to our Lord, He will certainly provide for me." ' Another of these pious children of the Garden of Mary always selects the most disgusting case amongst the children as her particular charge, and instructs the poorest woman in order the more to benefit the Holy Souls by that humble choice.

We have dwelt at some length on the work of Mère Marie's children in China, because it gives the measure of what zeal can effect, even by a handful of poor nuns, when God imparts strength to weak and courage to timid women. It may also suggest to souls burning with the desire to aid the living and the dead that a field for work and self-sacrifice and heroic labour is to be found in an Order which, both at home and abroad, carries on a supernatural apostolate in behalf of the dead.

We doubt, indeed, whether the Chinese Mission is more trying to the delicately-reared and sensitive daughters of European parents than the work in London, where our poor dwell in a state of wretchedness which astonishes even those who are used to visit the abodes of the destitute in Paris and other large towns. The late lamented Superior of the Sisters of Charity, the venerable Father Etienne, said some years ago to one of his daughters, who had offered herself for the Chinese Mission, ' My child, *your* China is in London.' He knew that her cross was as heavy in the great city where she was labouring as the one which her ardour for suffering was prompting her to take up. But God sometimes calls a chosen soul to add to her sacrifices the total surrender of familiar associations—the living death of an apostolate in regions as strange to her as those of another world; and when that call is given it must needs be obeyed. O strange diversity of the workings of grace! Wonderful dissimilarity in God's dealings with His children! Variety of paths leading to the same end! Beautiful harmony of lives, however dissimilar, which the Church sanctions and blesses! The more we study that word '*vocation*,' the more we find in it depths of mercy and of beauty which the world can never fathom.

CHAPTER XIV.

THE LONDON FOUNDATION AND THE LAUDA.

AT the close of the last chapter we alluded to the work of the Helpers of the Holy Souls in London. We will now relate what led to the first thought of their coming amongst us—a thought and a desire which arose in many a mind and heart long before its actual realisation. An English lady had visited their house in Paris in 1863, and a few months afterwards wrote as follows to the Mère Marie de la Providence:

'People are beginning to think and to hope that you will come to England. Several persons have spoken to me about it with much interest. I tell them that we must not be in too great a hurry about it, but wait and pray. Pray, then, and join your prayers to ours. Somebody was saying to me this morning that there is no country in the world which has more need than our own of your Order. How many foundations made in behalf of departed souls have been destroyed by heresy! How many converts there are whose parents and friends have died outside the pale of the visible Church—in invincible ignorance, they hope; but what a pressing call for prayers for those dear souls! Ask, I beseech you, that one of my dearest wishes may be fulfilled—that of seeing you one day established in London. I am told that the Bishop of Southwark feels the greatest interest in your community. Last month he spoke of it in his charge.'

Enclosed in this letter were a few words dictated to the Rev. Father Gordon by the Very Rev. Father Faber, and addressed to its writer, who had asked him for his prayers in behalf of an English foundation of Helpers of the Holy Souls. The date of this note is July 11th, 1863. It was one of the last utterances of him whose name is so justly revered and loved, not only by his friends and countrymen, but by Catholics all over the world:

'As for the Helpers of the Holy Souls, I have prayed for them, and now I will do so more than ever. I always felt greatly interested about them, first because of the Curé d'Ars, and then for their own sakes, seeing what immense glory their work gives to God. I will do all I can in the way of prayers whilst I am on earth. As to Heaven, that is rather their business than mine. They must begin by getting me out of Purgatory.'

In the spring of 1864 Thomas Grant, the late holy Bishop of Southwark, wrote thus to Mère Marie de la Providence:

'On this great Festival of our Immaculate Mother, a Catholic lady has begged the Bishop who now writes to you to ascertain if it is possible for your religious to give us hopes that a house of your pious institute could be founded in a district comprised within the immense diocese of Southwark. You know that this large capital is divided by the River Thames. The north side belongs to the Archdiocese of Westminster, whilst the southern side appertains to the Bishopric of Southwark, founded by the Holy Father. In that part of London there are various suburbs; one of these, called Battersea, is to be erected into a parish, or, as we call it here, *a mission*. The aforesaid lady thinks that, if your nuns could take up their abode near this mission, or rather near the chapel which will be in the centre of it, you would by your suffrages greatly forward our Heavenly Father's kingdom, and save many souls. O, remember that thousands of churches have been shut up in this country that our monasteries have been demolished that the Holy Souls in Purgatory have lost the numerous foundations for alms and prayers made in Catholic times. The Holy Souls require a perpetual reparation, which will radiate from your convent over the whole of England.

This lady wishes to help you to make such a foundation. I beg of you this favour, and I am happy to join in the request. Perhaps you have no Sisters who speak English. Do not let them be afraid. Charity can give the gift of tongues. For how soon would you promise them? If they have to suffer in this country, and amongst heretics, the Holy Souls will be grateful and happy. I bless in anticipation your meditations on this letter, and remain, Reverend Mother,

Your obliged and obedient servant,

✠ THOMAS GRANT.'

On the 7th of February the Mère Marie de la Providence replied to this letter in the following terms:

' My Lord,— I did not answer at once the letter that I have
had the consolation of receiving from your lordship, because I
felt the need of meditating upon it in silence for a few days
before attempting to express my gratitude for the proposal
which has been transmitted to me by your fatherly kindness. I
have always thought that our Lord would one day call us to
that land consecrated by the blood of so many martyrs, and I
fondly hope that our little society will establish itself in a country
which has discarded and attacked the consoling belief in the
doctrine of Purgatory. But, my lord, is the moment for it
arrived? I have asked myself that question on my knees before
the Tabernacle. You, of course, are aware that an establishment of this kind always entails considerable expense, and perhaps you do not know how great is our blessed poverty. Is your
lordship aware of the nature of our works? All the time that is
not taken up by our religious duties we devote to the care of the
sick poor in their homes. Thus we labour for our only end -the
relief of the Souls in Purgatory. Your lordship will understand
that, as our works are gratuitous, we must depend on Providence
alone for the necessaries of life. Our first foundation last year at
Nantes has exhausted our means and our subjects, for we never
shorten the two years' novitiate which precedes the first vows.
On these accounts we have been obliged to refuse many offers
made to us since the foundation of our house at Nantes.

The part of London where, according to your proposal, we
should establish ourselves seems to teem with wants, which will
have to be supplied if a parish is formed there, and this would
add still further to the difficulties of our foundation. Still, in
spite of all these obstacles, and others besides for instance, our
ignorance of the English language — we cherish the hope that
the Divine Heart of Jesus will grant us one day the favour of
praying, suffering, and working for the Souls in Purgatory in
your lordship's diocese.

We are very grateful, my lord, to the Catholic lady so gene-
rously inclined to help us, and we trust that the Souls in Purgatory will pay the debt of gratitude we owe her. Craving your
paternal blessing for our little society, and the assistance of your
pious prayers, I entreat your lordship to accept the expression
of the deepest respect, with which I remain.

My lord, your very humble servant in our Lord,

MARIE DE LA PROVIDENCE.'

The Bishop of Southwark did not rest contented with the reasons alleged against the immediate foundation of a house in England, and on the 10th of February wrote again to urge the point :

'" Pray, suffer, and work for the Holy Souls in Purgatory," Reverend Mother. It was a pious solicitude for the soul of her husband, a religious charitable man entirely devoted to the Church, which led the pious lady I spoke of in my first letter to think of your institute.

She begs me to thank you for your kind intentions, and, in uniting my own grateful acknowledgments to hers, I must tell you that, after praying as you have already done, you must think of acting : as to suffering, it is sure not to be wanting. We shall have difficulties, but it is the business of the Holy Souls to overcome them. I bless the *three* communities, Paris, Nantes (and Battersea).

Your obedient and obliged servant,

+ T. Grant,'

Circumstances, however, did not permit Mère Marie to comply, at that time, with the earnest request of the holy Bishop. She renewed in a subsequent letter her expressions of gratitude and regret at being obliged to decline his offer. Having prayed and suffered, she was obliged to wait till Providence gave her the means of acting. But she never lost sight of this favourite hope of her heart, or ceased to speak to her spiritual daughters of the English foundation as an event which sooner or later would come to pass. Some of them prepared themselves for that mission by studying the English language, and London was ever before their minds as the scene of future labours. But it was not till two years after her death that these mutual desires were realised. During the intervening period some English ladies interested themselves in the enrolling of honorary members, and remitted to Paris the alms of the associates. A tie was thus formed between the Helpers of the Holy Souls and devout persons in England, so that, when, in the early part of the year 1873, a proposal was made to raise funds for the establishment of a house in London, it met with a prompt response.

His Grace the Archbishop of Westminster gave his cordial assent to the scheme. Two or three zealous persons undertook the labour of collecting a sufficient sum to start the new convent, and the generosity of a devoted benefactress secured a home for several years to the London Helpers of the Holy Souls.

This house is now well known to most of the Catholic residents in London. No. 23 Queen Anne Street, Cavendish Square,* with its pretty chapel and its works of charity, is familiar to the associates and to the friends of the community.

When the Carmelite church was opened at Kensington, the Rev. Father Gallwey, S.J., preaching on that occasion, said that the new sanctuary would be to the inhabitants of London as it were the Lady chapel of their vast city.

* Now removed to Park House, Gloucester Gate, Regent's Park. N.W.

The chapel of the Helpers of the Holy Souls may also be looked upon as a mortuary chapel, where those whose hearts and thoughts are with the departed can pour forth, with a sense of peculiar affinity, their prayers for the loved ones ever present to their minds.

It is in a very expressive and real manner the Sanctuary of the Dead, and those who enrol themselves, not merely as honorary members, but as active associates, under the banner of the Servants of Purgatory—who accompany them to the bedsides of the sick and dying poor—or who work with their hands in religious silence under their roof to clothe the naked and comfort the destitute, can feel that they too belong to the army of Helpers which Mère Marie de la Providence raised up for the departed.

For more ample details regarding the institute, the associates, and the works of charity of the Helpers of the Holy Souls, we refer our readers to the most interesting and beautiful little work of the late Rev. Charles B. Garside, M.A., published in 1874, entitled *The Helpers of the Holy Souls*, and dedicated to his Eminence the Cardinal Archbishop of Westminster.

In relating the little history of the London foundation we have anticipated the course of time, and must revert to the incidents which marked the close of the life we have been depicting. One of the last consolations afforded to the foundress was the establishment of a house in Brussels, where her nuns were welcomed with the most hospitable kindness. Catholic Belgium had already given several zealous members to the infant community, and it promised to take speedy root in that congenial soil.

In the course of a few years a great work had been achieved. Mère Marie de la Providence could not but feel, in the midst of the most profound sense of her own nothingness, that God had done great things for her and through her. And at the same time a conviction rose in her mind that her end was not distant. Her bodily sufferings for years had been frequent and severe : so it was not that alone, though they did increase in intensity and left her no longer any intervals of ease, which made her foresee her approaching death. There was something beyond the state of failing health that convinced her the hour was at hand when she might utter the words, ' *Consummatum est.*' Even two years before her death, in 1869, she said to the nun who was helping her to write the history of the foundation of her Order, ' We must make haste. I feel as if the time I have yet to live was simply granted as a reprieve. Just a log put on the fire to keep it going a little while,' she added, with one of her bright smiles, and then told her that she often seemed to hear a voice in her soul warning her to prepare for death. She was convinced that God was only keeping her on earth to complete the work assigned to her, and that work could not be said to be completed until it had received the full sanction of the Church.

The Sovereign Pontiff had often expressed his kindly and fatherly interest in the community; but the '*Lauda*,' the first step in the solemn recognition of a Religious Order, had not yet been solicited. It seemed too recently established to hope that it could yet be granted. But, pressed by that inward voice which was impressing upon her that her life would not be much prolonged, the foundress made up her mind earnestly to sue for the approbation which was to constitute her community into a society approved by the Church and devoted to the Holy Souls. Forty Bishops wrote to her letters on this occasion, from which we extract the following passages:

Père de Ponlevoy says, in the name of Monseigneur Languillat:

'I attest, in the name of Monseigneur Languillat, Bishop of Sergiopolis, and Vicar-Apostolic of Nankin, that we are all acquainted with that congregation, and have watched its progress from the time it began. I know its history, its spirit, and its rules, which are nearly the same as our own, and all its works of zeal and charity in France and in China. I now wish and hope that the Church will set its seal on this work of God.'

The Bishop of Nantes says :

'These religious founded a house five years ago in my episcopal city. I have carefully studied their spirit, and examined their manner of life, in order to judge whether the new congregation was likely to bear fruits of edification. In 1867 I already mentioned them in the account of the state of my diocese which I sent to Rome, and spoke strongly in their favour. The Sisters are guided by the truest religious spirit, most faithful in the observance of their rule, and diligent in practising all the works of mercy and charity belonging to their institute ; and, as regards the principal end of their society—the relief of the Souls in Purgatory—they pursue it indefatigably, and, by their example and prayers, stimulate Christian persons to constant devotion in behalf of the faithful departed. When I consider the actual state of society, and the decrease of faith amongst people who give themselves up entirely to the pursuit of worldly riches and business, and seem entirely to forget the life to come, I cannot help earnestly thanking God that He has raised up this new religious family. I have already had occasion to know that these pious women, by the force of their example — a far more powerful argument than any words can bring forward have induced many souls to think of eternity. Men admire a charity which is inspired by a true faith, and are thus led to invoke as a Father that God who is to be one day their Judge. . . . I am inclined to think that our Lord, who governs His Church with so much goodness, and disposes and makes all things work together for the salvation of men, has raised up in our day the Helpers of the Holy Souls in order to remind those who forget to think of their salvation of the mercy and the justice of God towards departed souls.'

We may also quote what Monseigneur Guibert, then Archbishop of Tours, and now Archbishop of Paris, said on this occasion of the society founded by Mère Marie de la Providence :

' It will be very useful to the Church and to religion, and is already remarkable for its exact observance of rule, and the practice of all religious virtues.'

The Rules and Constitutions of the Helpers of the Holy Souls were accordingly examined at Rome; and on the 24th of August, 1869, thirteen years after the first foundation of her society, the foundress received the *Lauda*, or first Brief of approbation.

With renewed ardour she applied herself to the task of drawing up the annals of that work, the object of all her hopes and anxieties. 'This once finished,' she used to say, 'I can then die.' Every moment of reprieve from her ever-increasing sufferings was thus employed. We find her writing in her scribbling-book:

'The only thing I can do is to work a little at the annals of the society. O, what a change I see in myself! If it were not for the sake of obedience, I should leave out all those little details that have reference to that wretched self which I should like to get rid of altogether. But I have no option in the matter. I beg of our Lord to give me grace to accept from moment to moment what I have to bear.'

Her life had become a perfect martyrdom. We may judge of what her sufferings were during the last year of her life by the answer she made to one of her nuns who asked her if she was at any time free from pain. 'It would be a great repose,' she answered, 'if the pain were sometimes only a little mitigated. Looking at the crucifix is the only thing that enables me to endure it.' Day after day she used to sit before a little table gazing at the image of her crucified Lord.

That last year of her life was no ordinary epoch in the history of her country. God had reserved for the dying child of His providence, during the prolonged agony of these last twelve months, a strange and terrible chalice. We shall follow her in the next chapter through every step of that way of sorrow, and learn how those do and can suffer who offer themselves up, as she had done, to be a victim as well as a Helper for the Holy Souls.

CHAPTER XV.

CONSUMMATUM EST.

A DARK cloud bursting with terrific power, and causing a horrible devastation over a smiling landscape, is but a feeble image of the sudden and awful ruin which, a few months before her death, fell on the native land of Mère Marie de la Providence. The writer of these pages saw her in the spring of 1870, struggling with indomitable courage against physical suffering, and occupied in spreading the devotion to the Holy Angels, which had lately been revived by the establishment of a confraternity in its honour. She spoke of the excruciating sufferings she was enduring with the most beautiful submission, and acquiescence even in their increase, if such should be God's will. 'Give me as much suffering as I can bear,' she used to ask ; and she did not set in her own mind any limits to the powers of endurance grace would give her.

Additional sufferings came, and not only bodily pangs, but griefs so acute that those who have never seen their country invaded, lacerated, torn, and crushed by a horrible war can hardly conceive or realise them. The state in which the servant of God found herself in the autumn of that fatal year would have required repose and stillness for the body and peace for the mind to mitigate its sufferings ; and, instead of that, day after day, heart-breaking news arrived of deepening perils and approaching desolation. Defeat succeeded defeat. Paris became the scene of a revolution, the harbinger of social misery and religious persecution. Soon the enemy was besetting its gates, and laying siege to the most beautiful, the most brilliant, the most active, for evil and for good, of all the capitals of the Christian world.

The horrors of the bombardment of Strasbourg had spread such dismay throughout France that there was a general impulse to hurry out of the beleaguered city. The stations were crowded with passengers, and a ticket was sought for with feverish anxiety.

When it was proposed to the foundress of the

Helpers of the Holy Souls to quit Paris with her community, she calmly and steadily refused. Obedience ruled her decision. She had asked Père Olivaint what she should do. 'I think,' he had said, 'that we shall want Carmelites to pray for us, Sisters of Charity and Helpers of the Holy Souls to nurse the sick and wounded.' This had been enough; and no one would have dared to suggest to the all but dying Mother Marie to leave the house and city where her children were to live or die as God should ordain.

The organisation of an ambulance in the Rue de la Barouillère was her last act of active charity towards the living, but the one sole thought which soon took possession of her soul was that of Purgatory. She seemed immersed, as it were, in the sense of the awful number of souls which were hourly passing from this world into eternity. The roar of the cannon, the bursting of the shells, sounded in her ears like the signal-guns of suffering souls calling for aid from their Helpers on earth. 'My God, my Jesus, have mercy!' was the cry continually rising from her lips, parched with fever; and when any other subject was mentioned before her, she used to exclaim, 'I can think only of those who are passing into eternity—who are appearing before God. That is the real, the terrible truth. O, speak to me of Purgatory!'

She often said, 'When my pains seem to be

unbearable, tell me I am in the place of expiation : it will give me courage.'

On the 1st of November, a sad and memorable day, though her trembling hand could hardly hold a pen, she wrote in her diary :

' The Commune is proclaimed ! So they say. But I will not disquiet myself about anything. I rely on the Divine Heart of our Lord. He will take care of my poor daughters. I am suffering martyrdom. This is as it should be. This is the proper way of celebrating the seventeenth anniversary of my first thought regarding my dearly-loved Souls in Purgatory. Yes ! on this day just seventeen years ago our Lord inspired me with the thought of founding this community. How many favours I have since received ! And, if I had faith enough to feel it, what an immense mercy my sufferings are ! To-day I feel as if I were on fire ; my hands are burning. Jesus, I want nothing but that Your will should be done. I do not ask to be cured, only let Your will be done. O Jesus, my Master, let every pain be an act of love soliciting the deliverance of a Soul in Purgatory.'

In spite of her sufferings and weakness, she insisted on hearing that day the Mass said for the convalescent soldiers, and was present at their dinner and supper. ' For You, my God, for You,' she murmured all the time ; ' for I have no strength—no power left.'

On the 5th of November she wrote :

' Anniversary of the first Mass said in our chapel in 1856. I suffer intensely. Help me, Jesus, Mary, Joseph ! I advise our fourteen lay Sisters to make an offering of lilies to our Blessed Lady on the 8th, the fourteenth anniversary of the consecration of our society to that good Mother in heaven. They will do this by aiming at great purity of intention.'

The last time that this holy woman took up her pen was to write down an abstract of a conversation which had just taken place between her and the Père Olivaint. She was going through a slow martyrdom, and advancing surely and consciously towards its consummation. God had set His seal upon him also, and marked His faithful servant —though he knew it not then, except by a presentiment which finds expression in some of the passages of his meditations—for the honour of a death as closely resembling His own as any man perhaps has been favoured with since St. Peter and St. Andrew died on the cross. The narrative of the treatment of the martyrs of the Commune reads very like the history of the Passion of our Lord. Blows, scoffs, and brutal ill-usage in the streets of the city where he had gone about doing good —such was the fate, the glorious fate, in store for the priest who stood by the bed of the foundress of the Helpers of the Holy Souls; and these were the words that passed between the penitent and her spiritual father, both on the verge of that eternal world they were so soon to enter:

'I said to the reverend father, "'*Fiat*' is always on my lips." "Aim," he answered, "at the closest possible union with Jesus; that good Master is not by your side only -*He is within you.* Why do we communicate if it is not to possess Jesus? You suffer tortures, but He suffers with you—He bears them with you. God's will. Yes, all is comprised in that. Rely on our Lord. O, you would be without excuse if you, for whom our Lord has done so much, had not a great faith in Him." I then told the reverend father of the many graces I have received in my life, and of my daily prayer that through the Cross I may love Him more. " For twenty years," I said, " I have made that prayer, without, perhaps, fully realising what I asked for." He answered, " My child, our Lord gave you His Cross eighteen months ago, and during the last six months it has become sharper. O, let that Cross be to you a token of His love. Love even unto death ; suffer unto death ; take heart. Long live the folly of the Cross ! You say that you feel yourself to be God's property— a thing belonging to Him. That is right. Cling to that thought, and prize it.'"

Thus did the future martyr teach his penitent to smile on suffering; and he was wont to say, with a kind of heroic playfulness, ' I don't understand people dying fretfully.' Befitting words for one who, a few months afterwards, when he could have made his escape, chose to remain at his post, and brave a cruel death, in order to encourage by his presence the cause of justice and the principle of duty. And she whom he sustained by his ministrations in her last struggles with a mortal disease, used to exclaim, as she looked upon the blood flowing from the wound which was killing her, ' My God, how glad I am to shed my blood for You ! To accomplish Your blessed will, Jesus on the Cross suffered more than I do. O will of God, will of God, these words give strength to bear everything.'

Even when crushed by bodily sufferings, Mère Marie found strength, in her ardent charity, to direct, and even sometimes prepare food with her own hands for the poor, whom her nuns continued to visit amidst all the horrors of the siege. She used to send out every day soup to the sick, and watched over all the details connected with the relief of the wounded.

December was marked by increasing pains and an increasing fervour of love, which struck all those who approached the voluntary victim of her devotion to the Holy Souls. On the festivals she used to say, ' For me there are no feasts now but those of eternity : here I can do nothing but lose myself in the depths of God's will.'

At the close of that terrible year of 1870, and the beginning of 1871, which opened amidst such dire calamities, she said to her spiritual children assembled round her bed, ' Cling to the Cross, our only hope. Life is short, eternity endless. Let us think only of eternity.'

The doctor having pronounced that she might die at any moment, Père Olivaint proposed to her to receive Extreme Unction : she agreed to it with a joy which lighted up her dying face. The bombardment was then at its height, and the voice of the priest was sometimes drowned by the fearful voice of the explosions. Shells were continually bursting on every side of the house where that peaceful scene was going on. Death did not seem a strange thought to any of those who were taking part in it. Heaven was opening, as it were, its portals above that awful desolation, and the voice of God's servant sounded like the voice of an angel, leading the way to another and brighter world.

After receiving the last Sacraments, Mère Marie de la Providence accomplished the act which the rule enjoins on all religious persons on their death-bed. She placed herself in spirit at the feet of all her Sisters—of those who for so many years had given her the name of Mother —and distinctly and earnestly, though sometimes interrupted by the difficulty of breathing, she humbly begged forgiveness for all her failings, and the faults by which she had scandalised or grieved them.

Père Olivaint then said, 'It is time now to address your last recommendations to your daughters.' Upon which she made an effort to raise her voice, and uttered these words—'Let them continually increase in zeal for the Holy Souls in Purgatory, and in the spirit of their Order: let the houses of China, Nantes, Brussels and Paris be one in heart and soul.' 'And all the future foundations also,' Père Olivaint added, with a kind smile. 'Charity! that is what I recommended,' the dying foundress ejaculated ; and her director, who was well acquainted with her thoughts, added, 'And the interior spirit, without which there can be no religious, and, indeed, no Christian, life.'

From that day to the 6th of February, the eve of her death, Mère Marie de la Providence received the Blessed Sacrament every day. The 19th of January was the anniversary of the foundation of the community. On that day she said. ' Almighty God has showered blessings on our society: it is right I should suffer a great deal.... O, if you did but know what I feel— that it is entirely His work, and not mine! He has chosen the most wretched of instruments to effect His purpose. Blessed be God!'

On the Feast of the Conversion of St. Paul she was unable to pray audibly, but asked that the *Te Deum* should be said for her intentions, and in thanksgiving for the immense graces she had received. Longer by far than the physicians expected did the servant of God struggle with the mortal disease which was destroying her by degrees. There were dreadful moments of oppression and agony, during which every one thought she must breathe her last, and still the energy of her soul and the strength of her constitution triumphed over these attacks, and she rallied again.

To the end her mind remained perfectly clear, and pious ejaculations rose to her lips, especially the words, ' Jesus, eternal joy of the Saints!'

' It is strange,' she remarked, ' how continually present to me are those words.' The cry of

our Blessed Lord's agony was also ever bursting
from her heart. 'I can no longer pray or even
listen to prayer,' she often said, 'but I can still
say "*Fiat*;"' and with the rosary of the Curé
d'Ars in her hands, she repeated on every bead,
'Jesus, *fiat*.'

'O, poor us. poor us!' she would often mur-
mur, 'how can we care for anything but Jesus
and His Cross? It is in weakness and illness
that we learn to prize it.'

She frequently offered up her life, but did not
speak of her death as close at hand. We cannot
fathom God's dealings with souls, but in this case
we may believe that this ignorance of the near
approach of death was an answer to prayer.
With her bright smile she had often said,
'Amongst the things I was most afraid of—
that did not involve sin—there were five I particularly dreaded :

'To have to leave my family :

'To found a community :

'To have nothing to depend on for the
    support of my daughters ;

'To get into debt :

'And to have a cancer.

'Well, by God's goodness, every one of them
has happened to me !'

She had dreaded these trials, but she had
never asked to be delivered from them ; but
one petition she had frequently and earnestly

addressed to her Divine Spouse—this was to die well prepared, without any definite expectation of her decease, yet immediately after receiving absolution.

Strangely was that petition granted. More than a year before her death she had heard a voice warning her to prepare to depart this life; but, as the moment fixed by Providence drew near, she did not seem conscious of its close approach. We shall see that the last part of her request met also with a striking fulfilment.

On the morning of the 7th of February her oppression of breathing became so terrible that she was not allowed to communicate; she several times inquired if it was indeed impossible, and wished the Superior of the community to be consulted on the point. It was only out of obedience that she could accept that privation. The Church was commemorating that day the agony of our Lord: she united herself in spirit with a mystery which had always been one of her special devotions.

Each hour she became worse, and sometimes it seemed as if her agony had begun; still her mind remained as clear as ever. She said several times to the nuns who were with her, ' Père Olivaint will come at three o'clock.' They thought that he must have told her the day before that his visit would be earlier than usual, for he generally came late in the evening. At one o'clock she again said, 'The father will come at three.' 'Did he tell you so?' one of them asked. 'No,' she replied; and fell into a doze. As the clock struck three she roused herself, and said, 'Go down to the parlour; the father is coming.' The portress had not yet given the usual signal, but it was nevertheless the fact—Père Olivaint was opening the second entrance-door at that very moment. The nun who had come from Mère Marie's room to meet him said, 'I suppose you had told our Mother that you would be here at three o'clock?' 'O, no,' he answered, 'for I did not know it myself; I did not intend to come till five, after a visit I have to pay at the Batignolles, but something impelled me to stop first at the Rue de la Barouillère.' Had he not followed that inspiration, Mère Marie would have been dead before he arrived.

As it was, he conversed with her for half an hour, heard her confession, and gave her absolution. From that moment she did not utter another word, and fell into a gentle doze. The nuns who were in her room sat at a little distance from the armchair, keeping their eyes fixed upon her face, and now and then whispering to each other that their Mother was asleep.

One of the physicians who had attended her with unwearied devotion came in, and went up to the bedside. He turned round and said,

'Your Mother is on the point of death.' The whole community was hastily summoned, and hurried to the room where Mère Marie de la Providence was about to yield up her soul into the hands of her Divine Lord, whom she had loved so ardently and served so faithfully.

The prayers for the dying were said, and before the last invocations had been uttered the valiant woman expired, leaving behind her one more proof that nothing is impossible to those who forsake all for God's sake, and then follow day by day the guidings of His Providence.

Would that some one reading this simple record of a noble life might be inspired to tread in the footsteps of the foundress of the Helpers of the Holy Souls, and led to conceive and carry out some work akin to hers!

Every such biography should end with the words which our Lord uttered after relating the parable of the Good Samaritan, 'Go and do thou likewise.' All can do something. O, let no one be content to do nothing! If a stimulus be wanting, where can a greater one be found than in the thought of acting, praying, and suffering for those whom we have loved on earth, and who, according to the opinion of the greatest theologians, know what we do for them, and pray for us, even though they cannot pray for themselves? St. Catharine of Bologna used to say, 'When I wish to obtain some favour from the Eternal Father, I invoke the souls in the place of expiation, and charge them with the petition I have to make to Him, and I feel I am heard through their means.'

In conclusion, we cannot resist quoting the words of a writer * who has devoted his talent and his pen to the advocacy of the cause for which Mère Marie de la Providence lived and died. It contains thoughts which may bring consolation to many an aching heart, and stimulate the zeal of many a desponding mourner:

'Let us, then, if we feel inspired to do so, ask the prayers of the Souls in Purgatory; but, above all things, let us pray for them, and, like those religious, join to our prayers acts of self-denying charity to the poor. Let us always remember that to the Eternal Lord of all things everything is present, the future as well as the past. We call Him the King of Ages, because the order of events depends wholly on His will, and nothing in their course or succession can alter or change the effects of that will. He looks upon what is to come as if it were present or already past. In consideration of the prayers, the suffrages, and the good works of the Church —which He foresees—He grants proportionate graces, even as if those prayers and good works had been already offered up. In the same way,

* The Reverend Père Blot, author of *Les Auxiliatrices des Ames du Purgatoire*.

what we do for the dead, even though it be
subsequent to the judgment passed upon them,
may, through the Divine foresight, have availed
to obtain for them graces which have mitigated
the severity of that judgment.'

Amongst the Helpers of the Holy Souls
several have made great sacrifices to God in
order to obtain mercy for souls long ago called
away from this world. We can all imitate their
example. 'O, if it were not too late!' is the
cry of many a heart tortured by anxiety for the
fate of some loved one who has died apparently
out of the Church, or not in a state of grace.
We answer, 'It is never too late—pray, work,
suffer! The Lord foresaw your efforts. The
Lord knew what was to come, and may have
given to that soul, at its last hour, some extraordinary graces which snatched it from destruc-
tion, and placed it in safety, where your love
may still reach it, your prayers relieve, your
sacrifices avail.'

May our Blessed Lady, the Queen of Purgatory, bless this effort to make known the spirit,
life, and labours of the Helpers of the Holy
Souls—the exiled children of her maternal
Heart!

CHAPTER XVI.

SEQUEL TO THE LIFE OF MÈRE MARIE DE LA PROVIDENCE.

SINCE the *Life of Mère Marie de la Providence* was published in 1875, the congregation she founded has very much increased and extended, several new foundations having been added to those mentioned in the foregoing pages. At Cannes, at Orleans, Tourcoing, Montmartre, Jersey, Liége, Turin, and Rheims new communities have been established, which successfully propagate devotion to the Holy Souls, and carry on works of spiritual and corporal mercy in the spirit of their holy foundress.

At Cannes these servants of God were invited to counteract, as it were, by their prayers and their active charity, on the one side the dissipation and worldliness which prevail in resorts where people congregate as much to distract their minds by frivolity as to benefit their health, and where the sight of suffering invalids and persons more or less drawing near their end contrasts painfully with the levity of reckless idlers ; and, on the other hand, to assist in keeping alive the faith amongst the native population, assailed as it is by the blind zeal and powerful bribery of an unprincipled Protestant propaganda. In both these directions they have laboured assiduously and obtained blessed results. English Catholics and English people who respect the Catholic Church and the faith of others, even though they remain outside its pale, would be struck, if they visited this convent, with the patient persevering manner in which these few earnest women, undistinguished by any peculiarity of dress and with but few visible means of influence, stem the tide of infidelity and heresy which desolates that fair land.

An interest of another order attaches itself to the foundation at Montmartre—the hill of martyrs, the scene of St. Denys' martyrdom, the birthplace of the Society of Jesus. Ages ago a little chapel was erected on the spot where the first Bishop of Paris and his companions, St. Rusticus and St. Eleutherius, were put to death. Tradition ascribes to St. Geneviève, the shepherdess of Nanterre, who remains one of the Patron Saints of the proud and luxurious city of Paris, the erection of that modest sanctuary. For some hundred years it was the property of seculars, and its only endowment consisted in the offerings of pilgrims who came to pray there; but in 1096 the owners of the chapel made it over to the monks of St. Martin-in-the-Fields; and in 1133 Louis le Gros and his wife Adelaide de Savoie concluded a bargain with these religious, through which they became possessors of the Chapel of the Martyrs and the land surrounding it: thus it became a dependency of the ancient Abbey of Montmartre. The king rebuilt and ornamented the little sanctuary, which continued to be frequented by great numbers of pilgrims.

In the sixteenth century St. Ignatius of Loyola and his companions, Francis Xavier, Peter Favre, James Laynez, Alphonsus Salmeron, Nicholas Bobadilla, and Simon Rodriguez, met at the Chapel of the Martyrs, and there consecrated themselves to God by the vows of religion, thus laying the foundation of the Society of Jesus. At the time of the first French Revolution inscriptions and a picture commemorative of that event were to be seen on the walls.

Half a century afterwards, Henry IV., accompanied by all his court, came there on the day of his abjuration, and gave thanks to God for his reconciliation to the Church.

Marie de Beauvilliers, the venerable Abbess of Montmartre, made, on that occasion, an appeal to the generosity of the monarch and the people of Paris, and obtained funds to rebuild the ancient edifice, which was falling into ruins. Her zeal was rewarded by a wonderful discovery. The workmen engaged in digging foundations for an addition to the building discovered a staircase leading to a crypt, where a very ancient altar was found, on which St. Denys must have said Mass. This was established beyond doubt by a careful investigation, and then a *procès-verbal* was drawn up containing these proofs. Mary of Medicis often drew after her to this shrine her courtiers, and all the devout people in Paris began to flock to it ; henceforward it was called the Cave of St. Denys, and a new impetus was given to the pilgrimages. It became the custom for the Papal Nuncios to visit this holy spot at their first arrival in Paris, and many Indulgences were attached to it by successive Popes.

Louis XIV. liberally contributed to the reconstruction of the old Abbey of Montmartre, which, in his time, had fallen into decay, and in 1686 the nuns again took possession of it.

Amongst the saints who, century after century, visited the Chapel of the Martyrs, are recorded St. Geneviève and St. Clothilde, St. Cloud, St. Germain, Bishop of Paris, his successors St. Ceran and St. Hugh, St. Gerard, St. Bernard on the 21st of April, 1147, and on the 15th October, a short time before his martyrdom, St. Thomas of Canterbury, also the saintly Archbishop of Bourges, William Berruyer, who died in 1209.

It likewise became in the seventeenth century the starting-point, so to speak, of innumerable religious institutes and great works, whose founders thus followed the example of St. Ignatius. In 1612, Cardinal de Bérulle consecrated there his new institute of Priests of the Oratory. St. Francis of Sales, who used to frequent it whilst he was pursuing his studies at the University of Paris, came there to recommend to God the foundation of the Visitation. St. Vincent of Paul never began any work of charity without first making a pilgrimage to the Chapel of the Martyrs. Later on, Father Eudes spent three months at Montmartre, and introduced there the devotion and the office of the Sacred Heart. M. Boudon, the eminent spiritual writer; Father Bagot, S.J., founder of the Seminary for Foreign Missions; M. Olier and his disciples, and a vast number of English religious exiles, swell the list of devout worshippers at this time-honoured sanctuary. Blessed Mary of the Incarnation (Madame Acarie) made a pilgrimage to Montmartre, before the foundation of the Carmelites at Paris and at Pontoise in 1604.

At the disastrous moment of the French Revolution, when so many religious monuments disappeared in France, Madame de Montmorency-Laval was Abbess of Montmartre. Dragged before the revolutionary tribunal, and, in spite of her advanced age and her blindness, sentenced to death, she expired on the scaffold with fifteen of her nuns.

In 1795, the purchasers of the abbey destroyed it entirely, and the ancient pilgrimage seemed doomed to disappear for ever; but the memory of it still remained in the minds and the hearts of many faithful servants of God. Holy priests were lamenting a state of things which did not allow the inhabitants of Paris to go and pray on the tomb of their great Patron Saint. At the time of the siege of Paris during the Franco-German War, a temporary Chapel of the Martyrs was erected by the Abbé le Rebours, Curé of the Madeleine, and, in the modest little sanctuary of No. 9 Rue Antoinette, Mass was said for the first time on the 3rd of January, 1871, the day of St. Geneviève's feast. Since then a pilgrimage has taken place every year, under the direction of the Curé de la Madeleine, at the period of the Feast and Octave of St. Denys; and many Parisians again find their way to the spot where their forefathers so often knelt.

The Abbé le Rebours and the Fathers of the Society of Jesus, to whom belonged the ground on which the ancient chapel stood, combined to place the pilgrimage on a surer foundation. They agreed to offer to the Helpers of the Holy Souls the site of the former chapel in the Rue Antoinette, with the temporary sanctuary. The Archbishop of Paris and his coadjutor sanctioned and encouraged this foundation, and the nuns took possession of it on the 9th of October, 1877. A convent of their Order therefore exists on the very spot where once stood the famous Abbey of Montmartre. It is an interesting fact that one of its former abbesses, the holy Mother Adeline, had been remarkable for her singular devotion to the Souls in Purgatory, and instituted a congregation for their especial assistance.

The Helpers of the Holy Souls at Montmartre are awaiting, with eager desire and hope, means for reorganising, in a worthy manner, the ancient pilgrimage once so dear to Christian France.

With regard to the community in London a change has lately taken place, which promises greatly to extend their work among the Protestant as well as the Catholic poor. The house which had been engaged for them in Queen Anne Street, Cavendish Square, for a term of nine years, by the late Dowager Marchioness of Lothian, was doomed to demolition, and at the end of that time it became necessary to find another not too distant from the first scene of their labours. Providential circumstances have attended this removal, and brought about what can now be considered a final settlement among us of the Helpers of the Holy Souls; for by means of some subscriptions from benefactors in England, and great sacrifices on the part of the mother-house in Paris, a house and garden, on freehold ground, have been purchased in the Regent's Park, near Gloucester Gate. There is room in the enclosure for the erection of a chapel, which would not only serve for the nuns, their devout associates, and the poor people they instruct and convert, but afford means of worship to a neighbourhood which has no church close at hand.

A heavy debt remains on the property, which will, no doubt, be paid off in time ; but for the present it sadly cripples the resources of the community. Providence, however, has so visibly smoothed away the difficulties attending the acquisition of Park House, and its capabilities for the development of every sort of good work are so remarkable, that there is every reason to hope that what has been so happily begun will be equally blessed in its progress. It is pleasant to observe how much the young girls employed in houses of business, who, as well as a number of children, assemble at Park House every Sunday for religious instruction, tea, and innocent amusement, delight in the garden, especially in the summer evenings. The influence the nuns exercise over the families, whose sick members they visit and nurse, enables them to bring about a number of conversions and returns to religion which have, in most cases, proved lasting and satisfactory. When one or two large rooms can be built, as well as the chapel, the apostolate carried on in that part of London will be furnished with all its needs. We can only hope and pray, for the sake of the many souls concerned, that our Lord will soon inspire those who could effect it with the desire to accomplish so good a work; for the Helpers of the Holy Souls may well be termed also helpers of every sinning and suffering soul within their reach.

Journal of the Last Year of

THE LIFE OF

MÈRE MARIE DE LA PROVIDENCE.

APPENDIX

TO THE LIFE OF

MÈRE MARIE DE LA PROVIDENCE.

[Those who not only appreciate the work of Mère Marie de la Providence, but who wish to study her spirit and the peculiar characteristics of her sanctity, will read with no common interest a record of the last year of her life, drawn up by one of her spiritual daughters, whose privilege it was to witness the daily details of that saintly existence, and who enjoyed the most intimate intercourse with her Mother in Christ.]

LAST YEAR OF THE LIFE OF OUR VENERATED MOTHER AND FOUNDRESS.

'I FEEL THIS YEAR WILL BE FOR ME A YEAR OF GREAT GRACES.'

ON the 1st of January, 1870, our Mother, after a night of severe suffering, and having dressed herself with difficulty, knelt down before her image of the Sacred Heart. I saw that she was weeping. 'Mother,' I said, 'what makes you sad?'

'I am thinking,' she answered, 'of the goodness of God, of His love for souls. I have no time to lose. O, let us make haste to love our Lord Jesus Christ.'

After another moment's silent prayer she rose quickly, and exclaimed, with that fervour so peculiar to her, 'Pray, O, pray, that I may be all on fire with Divine love. Would that I could die of love!'

After kissing her cross with passionate fervour, she went down to the chapel, which she expected to find beautifully decorated in honour of the feast. Having prayed a moment before the Tabernacle, she called the Sister Sacristan, and said, 'Why, Sister, where is your love for our Lord? Where are the outward symbols of the acts of virtue we are to practise during this year? Take away these faded flowers, and get the freshest and brightest you can find. Nothing is too good for our good God! O, that we had faith! Jesus in the Tabernacle! What a Divine mystery!'

Some one inquired that day what were her plans for some future occasions. 'Do not ask me,' she said, 'what I intend to do; I never know myself. As occasions arise, I do God's will as well as I can, and I never make any other plan; and it is curious how He almost always makes me do exactly the reverse of what I should wish, naturally speaking. Ever since 1867 I have felt impelled to pray for detachment—"O blessed detachment, lift up my heart into the Heart of my Divine Master!"' This was one of the favourite ejaculations of our dear Mother.

Early in that year she received the news of her father's alarming state of health. Her loving heart was deeply affected by the announcement. She had not seen that dear parent for six years, and was herself too ill to travel. 'God only knows,' she said, 'the acuteness of this trial; but let His holy will be done. My body, my soul, my heart are His property.'

It was at that time that she began to use what she called her 'spiritual chloroform': this was the constant repetition, on the beads of the Curé d'Ars, of the words, '*Fiat Jesus.*' We used to hear her continually reiterating this devotion. The spirit of her whole life was in that prayer.

Every day brought with it an increase of suffering for our poor Mother. Rapid were the strides of the terrible disease which was hurrying her to the grave. She kept it a secret as long as possible—only a few intimate friends knew of its existence. She used to call it her hidden treasure.

When the foundation of the house at Brussels was providentially brought about, she said to one of us, 'It will be a house of blessings. Who knows? We owe it, perhaps, to the numerous

prayers which have been made to the Blessed
Virgin for my cure. God knows what He is
doing. Whatever happens we shall always be
able, with the help of His grace, to say, " Thy
will be done." '

When the nuns were leaving for Brussels, our
Mother summoned up all her energy to control
the emotion which she felt in parting with her
children.

' Another parting ! ' she said. ' God knows
what it costs me, but His will is dearer to me
than all else ; and, after all, it is with eternity,
not time, that we are concerned. I feel this now
more than ever.'

She never liked the word ' Adieu.' ' Say
rather, *Au revoir,*' she used to answer. ' The
Helpers of the Holy Souls are never really
separated ; they meet in the Heart of Jesus.'

The example of her courage strengthened
us, but it was a terrible trial to lose such a
mother. We tried to accept it bravely, to be
faithful to our vocation. She was always trying
to soften to us the thought of this separation.
Her heart was that of a true mother. She
thought of us all with minute tenderness. She
foresaw and provided for everything.

It was on the 7th of January that the little
colony left us for Brussels. Our Mother went
with them to the door of the carriage.

' Come, my poor children,' she exclaimed ;

'we must be courageous; Jesus is with us. We must find our refuge in His Heart. Be always true religious. Live a life of self-sacrifice, which will make us saints.'

The following day our Mother was in bed, suffering severely, and deprived of Mass and Holy Communion.

'We cannot expect,' she said, 'to give birth to a new child without much suffering. It is quite right that I should pay for the foundation of Brussels. This wretched carcass must come to an end at last. My miserable body is rapidly decaying. This is as it should be. A Helper of the Holy Souls must reckon on suffering more than other people. She ought to wish it. O, what a noble vocation! I was thinking just now that we have, as it were, before our eyes every graveyard in the world. If we could only understand what God expects of us—if we had in our hearts but one spark of holy fire—what should we not be able to do! But we are cowards, arrant cowards; I, at any rate. It is dreadful!'

'Mother,' I said, 'God gives you a strange new year's gift. He lays you on this bed of suffering.'

'I remember little about the new year,' our Mother replied, with a smile. 'For my part, God's will is all that I think of. But, as you speak of new year's gifts, I can tell you that sufferings are indeed the chosen presents of God. O Jesus, my Master, give me Your love! I care not at what price.'

On Sunday, the 19th, she received letters from Brussels full of good news, and mentioning that the Archbishop had permitted the Blessed Sacrament to be reserved in the chapel of the house. 'O, what great mercies! what great mercies!' our venerable Mother exclaimed. 'Is it too much in return to suffer as I do? My God, how I thank Thee!'

In spite of weakness and pain, our Mother never lost her cheerfulness, which made her the life and joy of her community. She never would hear of our grieving about her.

'We belong to the other world,' she used to say. 'Let us live in Jesus, and let present things go on as they please. . . . I do not understand how any one can care about a wretched sinner like me, unless it is out of faith only. . . . God has vouchsafed to choose me because the depths of my unworthiness attracted His infinite mercies.'

Sometimes when her pains became excessive, she could not help exclaiming, 'O my God, how I suffer!' but she always reproached herself for it afterwards, as if it had been a complaint, and would beg pardon of all those whom she fancied it had disedified.

'It was sheer cowardice in a religious,' she

said, 'to complain of anything when her God is so often offended and outraged. It is difficult, no doubt, to bear very intense pain ; but it ought to be sweet too, when we can offer it up for the Holy Souls. Poor suffering Souls! our pains would seem slight to them if they could exchange them with their own.'

We heard her say to herself, 'How I thank You, my God, for this little share in Your Cross, and for the light You give me to see it! Detach me more and more from everything, and give me grace to accept joyfully my agonies and the sense of my entire helplessness.'

'You do more good lying still and suffering,' I said to her one day, 'than when you are working hard.'

'I make it a rule,' she answered, 'not to think of anything I have done. I can remember nothing but my sins, and that is why I say the *Miserere* every day.'

Although our Mother relied on Providence for everything temporal as well as spiritual, she expected each of us to help, as far as was possible, in supplying the pressing needs of the community. Following St. Ignatius's teaching, she used to tell us to exert ourselves as if there were no such thing as Providence; and, when we had done that, never to have a misgiving, but to say to ourselves, 'Jesus will see to it.'

On the last day of January she said, 'Another

month gone by; we are so much nearer eternity. What treasures of merit would be accumulated by sufferings if only one made good use of them!'

She had been ordered to take a drive, and complied in the spirit of obedience. Turning to her companion, she said, 'The sight of Paris makes me feel sad; let us say our beads for all those poor people who are hurrying to and fro without a thought of eternity.'

As we crossed the boulevards, our Mother sighed and exclaimed, 'O my God, how little Thou art loved! I am in great pain as it is, but I should wish to endure still more acute sufferings in order to make reparation for the outrages committed against Thee.'

When some fine new houses were pointed out to her she said, 'I can think only of the souls dead in sin who live in them.'

How can we describe her love for souls, her minute care to seize every opportunity of sanctifying those she could by any means approach? As to her purse, she called it God's purse, and herself His treasurer. She seemed always able to find means to give, but when asked to join in any new work she always begged not to be named.

'If we love our Lord,' she was wont to say, 'we shall seek only His glory; we shall win as many souls as we can for His sake, and hide ourselves in His Heart. The more we are ignored by man, the more we shall be known to God.'

She took no interest in politics and worldly affairs, except inasmuch as their results affected the Church.

'I do not know,' she used to say, 'whether it is from apathy produced by suffering, but I cannot concern myself with what goes on in the world. I feel sorry for those who agitate themselves as if God were not master of all.'

The Feast of the Purification had always inspired our Mother with special devotion. This year she made it a day of thanksgiving, and, looking upon her sufferings as a merciful means of purification, she blessed God for them with unspeakable fervour. A Jesuit Father preached in our chapel on the Gospel of the day, and, in reference to what he had said of the coming of our Lord to the Temple of Jerusalem, she exclaimed, 'O, let Him come, let Him come, that beloved Master! I am always expecting Him. O, why don't we die of love? We must empty our hearts,' she added, 'and it is a painful process. We feel a strange uneasiness till the void is made, and when that is achieved we suffer still, but it is a sweet suffering then. God is all we think of and long for.'

She remained that day a very long time before the Blessed Sacrament. When she was asked if she had been praying with any particular intention, her answer was, 'This is the anniversary of the day when I was made a child of Mary. I was thanking our good Lord for that mercy, but chiefly I blessed Him for the grace vouchsafed to-day to our dear house of Brussels. [The Holy Sacrifice of the Mass had been offered up there for the first time that morning.] It is the highest of all graces to have the Blessed Sacrament in the midst of us. What should we do without the Tabernacle?' and then she quoted the words in which St. Theresa expressed her joy when her Divine Master came to take possession of one of her new foundations.

On the 5th of February her pains were very acute. She was advised to shorten her meditation, and to withdraw to her room. 'O, do not ask me to do that!' she said; 'when I am dying it will be time enough to shorten my spiritual exercises. Remember the infinite value of each moment spent with God. If by our own fault we shorten by a minute the time we might have devoted to prayer, how can we make sure that it was not just during that particular instant that God intended to bestow on us some special grace? Of course, I am in great pain; but it is only by prayer that I can obtain a love for suffering, and that is the very grace I have most need of.'

As she was leaving the chapel our Mother

said again, ' All the time I was in prayer I could do nothing but ask for a love of suffering—of all the sufferings which it will please God to send me. I am sure some cross is at hand. Whatever it may be, *fiat*. My father has been in my thoughts all the morning.'

It soon appeared that an intimation had been thus given her of the sad news she was to receive that day—that of her father's dangerous illness.

' My God, Thy will be done,' she said, and then for a short time wept in silence. Determined to be always guided by obedience, she submitted to her director the ardent desire she felt to visit on his death-bed that beloved parent. He was of opinion that, in her precarious state of health, she would in so doing risk a life which was, humanly speaking, essential to the great work she had undertaken. So soon as he had given this opinion she submitted at once, and made a sacrifice only to be estimated by those who knew the strength of her filial affection.

' Thy will be done, my Divine Master,' she said, and then gave no other outward token of grief than frequently kissing her crucifix.

Words like the following often fell from the lips of our Mother, which showed what were the thoughts which sustained her in her torturing pains :

' Just before Mass to-day it seemed to me that

our Lord said to my soul, " I am going to be offered up for thee ; offer thyself up for Me." I should have thought it impossible a moment before to go down to the chapel ; but this gave me strength to do so, and at the moment of the Elevation I did offer myself up entirely, with all my sufferings, to our Divine Lord. Then I thought I heard Him say, " My love calls thee." '

She panted a moment, and then exclaimed, with indescribable fervour, ' O Jesus, would that I could feel that *my* love called *Thee*—that my entire detachment called Thee—that everything in me pined for Thee ! O Jesus, Jesus, convert my soul to Thee ! O my God, You alone have the power to change my heart ! '

During all the rest of the day those words, ' My love calls thee.' seemed to haunt our Mother. She kept repeating them over and over again, and wrote them on a paper which contained one of her favourite prayers. It was exactly on the anniversary of that day, the 7th February, that she died the following year.

On the 8th, though too ill even to hear Mass, or to receive Holy Communion, she summoned up all her strength to write a last letter to her dying father and to some of her afflicted relatives, to whom she had ever been an angel of consolation.

It was her habit when she had finished writing her letters, to lift up her heart to God and say, ' Bless these poor lines, my Lord, and bless those to whom they are addressed. I am good for nothing ; I can do nothing for others unless You choose to use me as Your instrument, and then there is nothing I may not be able to do.'

Often she exclaimed, ' Nothing seems to me to signify now. In all things I can only see God, and God alone ; and, after all, that is the only way to be happy. If once we begin to look at secondary causes there is an end to peace.'

' But,' some one observed. ' it is not so easy to arrive at that frame of mind.'

' If we love God it will be easy,' was her reply. ' If we are courageous, if we make sacrifices, there will be joy even in the midst of struggles and sufferings.'

On the following day, the 9th of February, it was thus that our dear Mother ended her meditation : ' Let us go and die with Him. This shall be my spiritual nosegay. I feel that God will soon call upon me to surrender my father. *Fiat, fiat.* My God, have pity on my weakness. All my trust is in Thee.'

These sad presentiments were realised. In the course of the day she received the news of that much loved parent's hopeless state, and whilst she was writing to her afflicted relatives another telegram arrived which announced his death. She kissed the crucifix and murmured,

' God's holy will be done ; ' then sat alone and in silence, whilst the whole community made the Way of the Cross in the chapel for the repose of the departed soul. Then, rousing herself resolutely from that profound abstraction, she went to her writing-table, and wrote in every direction for prayers for her dear father. ' This is the time to show my love for him,' she said.

The following day her pains were even more than usually severe. She rejoiced at it, and offered them up for the departed one, the thought of whom never left her for a moment.

On Septuagesima Sunday, after a terrible night, she made a great effort to rise and assist at Mass. She said to our Lord, as she went into the chapel, ' I do not ask to know my father's present state. No, my dear Lord, I like better to leave him to Thee.' As she was making that ejaculation she opened her Missal, and her eyes fell on the words of the Introit in the Mass for that day. They seemed like an answer to the cry of her heart :

' The groans of death surrounded me, and the sorrows of hell encompassed me ; and in my affliction I called on the Lord, and He heard my voice from His holy temple. I will love Thee, O Lord, my strength. The Lord is my firmament, my refuge, and my deliverer.'

She often spoke of the consolation these

words had afforded her. 'O, God is very good to those who seek Him!' she would exclaim, 'and He reveals Himself to us in all sorts of ways!' Her activity seemed to increase even whilst her physical strength diminished. She would write seven or eight letters running in an incredibly short space of time, although the act of writing had become very painful to her, from a want of power in her right arm. Often and often we used to tell her that she went beyond her strength. Her reply was, that if she stopped to think of her strength she would do nothing at all. 'But Jesus helps me,' she said; 'it is for Him I work. We must make our dear Master pleasing to others.' And when we asked what she meant by this expression she answered, 'Yes, we must do Him honour in the eyes of men. We must not let people think that because we are religious we have no regard for the courtesies of life. Letters should be answered, and we cannot take too much trouble to please those to whom we owe gratitude, or whom we wish to lead to God. What does it signify if we are tired? Suffering will pass away, and we shall have in eternity plenty of time to rest. O my Jesus, if I could only persuade others to love You!'

She never asked us to do anything for her which she could possibly do for herself, and was always exhorting us to make the most of time.

'Work whilst you are young and strong,' she would say. 'Youth is the time for labour and for prayer. You will one day find out how little one can do in illness.'

As far as she was concerned, we could never observe that she left anything undone on account of her sufferings. She planned, organised, and directed everything, and was at every one's service. Never did she cease to be the life and soul of her community, and the delight of her daughters' lives. Those of Nantes and Brussels were the constant objects of her solicitude ; and as to her dear Chinese missionaries, as she used to call them, they were the dearest, because the farthest removed, of her children. It was only during the blockade of Paris that she did not write by every mail a long letter to each of them, and that even at a time when to hold a pen gave her the greatest pain.

On the 18th of February, a Jesuit father, preaching in our chapel on the subject of our vocation, used the expression, ' For a Helper of the Holy Souls to be left without sufferings would be like the loss of her inheritance.' These words made a great impression on our Mother. She had that day, in addition to her habitual pains, a severe attack of neuralgia, which made her say, ' Thank God, I am not deprived of my inheritance.' And then she poured forth ardent prayers that she might understand more and more, and make others understand, the necessity of suffering for the Holy Souls.

' Let us feel that eternity is begun,' she was wont to say. 'Whatever pain we are going through, let us make joy out of that thought. Jesus is with us—Jesus is our all! O my Jesus, how I long to be with You, and to give You to others!'

Then, after a few moments' silence, she continued, 'We must keep up our courage by thinking of the Holy Souls, or we shall faint in the fight. They have a right to expect a great deal from us, for we have made them great promises. . . . I do not think it is quite as easy as people think to get into heaven. We say of persons that they were holy because they did some good actions during their lives. We forget that they have to expiate all the imperfections of those actions before they can enjoy their reward. As soon as they are dead we assume they are in heaven, and we leave off praying for them. O, let us love our dear vocation, and the more we suffer the more let us love it. If we do not want to suffer we have no business to be Helpers of the Holy Souls. Suffering is the key of heaven, and on the days we have nothing to suffer we have not opened its doors to the Holy Souls. Purgatory is a mystery of love and justice.'

Another time she said, ' The good God is our

supreme Master. Let us leave all to Him, but let us omit nothing on our side that we can possibly do.'

On Thursday, the 24th of February, our Mother suffered such intense pain in every part of her body that she said, in a moment of dejection, ' I cannot possibly live long, suffering as I do: I must prepare for death.' But she added, almost immediately, ' To live or to die, it is the same to me, provided God's will be done. And since, for the present, He wills that I should suffer, may His holy will be done.'

All day long her eyes were fixed on her dear crucifix. It was there that, in the midst of the greatest sufferings, she could find strength to bear her martyrdom. 'My sufferings are nothing compared to His,' she said. 'O my most patient Jesus, have mercy on me. Jesus, be my strength; Jesus, be my light, my joy, my consolation; Jesus, be my all.'

Some one once said to our Mother that her patience under suffering must be the means of delivering many Souls from Purgatory every day; but she answered quickly. ' Unless you wish to make me cry, do not talk about my patience. I have neither patience nor courage; I have only just strength to say *Fiat*, without so much as understanding what it means.'

The next day, Friday, brought an increase of suffering to our Mother, but she was as resigned as ever. 'Our good Lord knows very well what He is doing,' she said ; 'I have only to abandon myself to Him, and to be prepared for everything. Did not the Curé d'Ars tell me that I should have much to suffer? The will of God must be done in me.' After a few moments of silence she added, 'To think that God should make any use of such a nothing ! What a mystery of love ! What ingratitude on our part if we do not correspond with His designs! Give me, O my God, Thy love !'

Our Mother's only rest was in speaking of God. Her ardent love gave her strength to take part even in long conversations, provided their only end was the greater glory of God. After an interview with a person who had begged very earnestly to see her, some one asked her if she did not feel very tired. 'No, I am not tired,' she replied ; 'I could feel that God was in that person's soul, and when I can speak of eternity it refreshes me, instead of tiring me.'

The three days set aside for the devotion of the 'Quarant' Ore' in our chapel were days of special fervour with our Mother. She herself presided over the decoration of the chapel, and nothing seemed good enough to her for this purpose. On Sunday morning, after Mass, she arranged that six *prie-dieu* chairs should be placed before the altar, four of these being for the use of the religious, the other two for seculars, 'the angels of the mission,' who had been invited the evening before. In the middle of the day, seeing how pretty the chapel looked, she said brightly, 'Our Lord will, at any rate, know that it makes us happy to have Him among us.' In the afternoon, while engaged in some necessary letter-writing, which tired her the more that she was suffering intensely, she said, as her eyes wandered in the direction of the chapel, 'My God, I wish to be near You: let my sufferings and my fatigue tell You of my love.'

On Monday our Mother was quite prostrated, and for some time it was doubtful whether she would be able to hear Mass; but her ardent desire of receiving Holy Communion gave her strength to do so. As she came downstairs, leaning on the arm of one of her daughters, she said with inexpressible fervour, 'My God, give me the grace of a good death.' After Mass she said, 'I wish to love our Lord so much that, when the time comes, I may die of love.'

During the rest of the day, and in the night, her sufferings became agonising. On Tuesday morning she was unable to get up. Notwithstanding terrible fits of coughing, she had refused to take anything, hoping to communicate. This consolation, however, she was obliged to forego: the choking was too violent to allow of it. 'I really think,' she said, with a smile, 'that, instead of dying of love, I shall die of suffocation.' Then, pressing her crucifix to her heart, she added, ' O my kind Master, I say *Fiat* to this and all else.' In the evening our poor Mother was a little better, and kindly assisted at our extra recreation. She afterwards said a few touching words to us, in preparation for the ceremony of the next day, Ash Wednesday, and she ended with these words : ' To my mind to-morrow's festival is a grand one, which should send each and all of us down to our proper places. "Remember that thou art dust, and that unto dust thou shalt return." Too many lose sight of this truth ; let us now at least profit by it.'

This night was no better than the last ; nevertheless, our Mother insisted upon getting up. ' To stay in bed on the first day of Lent would indeed show want of courage,' she said. While dressing, her strength seemed to fail her, and she exclaimed, ' My God, uphold me ; I can do no more. Passion of my Jesus, strengthen me. O, I suffer indeed ; but what are my sufferings compared to what I have deserved—compared to Purgatory? O my God, how infinite are Thy mercies !'

Though quite exhausted, our Mother still found strength to perform her appointed round of duties, and Almighty God seemed to give her more to do every day, so that it was often very late before she finished her devotions.   But, even when she was most tired, she would never omit any of her prayers, and as it was now March, the Office of St. Joseph was added to the number.   On the first day of that month she was still up at ten at night, 'paying her debts to God,' for so she called the prayers which she had not been able to say earlier.   They begged her at all events to give up the Office of St. Joseph.

'You had better not interfere with my Father St. Joseph,' she answered quickly.   'I should never forgive myself if I omitted to do something special in his honour during this month.   I shall be none the worse to-morrow.   We have so much to ask him for, and he has given us so much already.'

On Thursday, the 3rd of March, thanks to our Mother's spirit of holy confidence, a very special mark of St. Joseph's protection was given to us.   A little before midday, the Superioress, speaking to our Mother of the necessity of having crosses made for the Ladies Associate, said, 'The goldsmith will only arrange to make them on condition that we pay him in advance, and we have not enough money ; they will cost 300 francs.'

'Well,' replied our Mother, 'have recourse to holy Providence.   Ask St. Joseph for the money : he will have no difficulty in getting it for us.'

Towards evening, two ladies, who had never

been to the convent before, came and begged to see the Mother-General. Our Mother was feeling so worn out that she excused herself, and sent some one in her stead : but the ladies redoubled their entreaties, giving as their reason for being so anxious to see her that they looked on her as a relic of Ars. The very mention of that name seemed to prevail with our Mother.

' My God, give me courage,' she said ; ' it may be that Thy Providence has something in store for me ; ' and, kissing her crucifix, she went down to the visitors.

Half an hour later she re-entered her room, saying, ' See the goodness of holy Providence ! We needed 300 francs, and those ladies put that sum into my hands before they went away. My God, I thank Thee.'

On Sunday, the 6th. our Mother was so prostrated by illness that the infirmarian advised her not to give us a spiritual conference, as she had intended to do. She had prepared it with great care the day before, saying, ' Shall I be able to speak to-morrow ? I cannot tell, but in my state one must do to-day's duties, and remember that to-morrow belongs to God.'

However, on Sunday morning she met the infirmarian's objections by saying, ' Our Lord will give me strength at the moment ; I think it is better to rely on Him than to be guided by my feelings.'

At the end of the conference she gave us a spiritual bouquet, which expressed most truly her thoughts—'Love can do all things, violence nothing.'

When we said to her, 'O Mother, you have done us all so much good,' she replied, with a look of joyful surprise, 'Thank God; if I have done you some little good, my fatigue will be better than rest.'

On the following day our Mother had a short time of relief: but suddenly she was seized with such intense pain that she cried out, in spite of herself, 'My God, my God, I can bear no more!' Scarcely had these words fallen from her lips, when, taking up her crucifix, she kissed it with inexpressible tenderness, and, some minutes later, when leaving the room, she said, 'I am going to the chapel to recover myself.'

What then passed between her soul and God is not known; but when she returned to her room our Mother sat down before her writing-table, opened her desk, and, pulling out one drawer after another, tore up a great many papers, smiling all the time, and often repeating, 'O Jesus, my eternal Love, what a happiness it will be to love Thee in heaven!'

'Mother,' some one said, 'why are you doing that?'

'Why!' she replied. 'Because I ought to put all my things in order, just as if I were going to die soon. Is it not so? Are we not all in the hands of God? To-morrow does not belong to us, and to my mind it is very consoling to be able to say that God is our Master.' But, seeing that we looked sad, she added, 'Do not distress yourselves. How can I tell that I shall die any more than that I shall live? I feel myself lost in the will of God, and have no other thought than to abandon myself to Him.'

That evening a novice, Sister St. Adrian, was taken ill, and never ceased to suffer till her death. Our Mother, who was herself very ill, entirely ignored her own sufferings, as she always did when there was occasion for the exercise of devoted unselfishness. She waited on the poor young Sister with assiduous tenderness, and scarcely once left her side that evening. The doctor having intimated that there was danger of death, our Mother prepared her for the last Sacraments, and induced her to make the sacrifice of her life to God.

On the following day the little novice had the consolation of receiving the Viaticum. Our Mother walked in the procession of the Blessed Sacrament, carrying a lighted taper.

After the ceremony, when some one asked her if she did not feel inspired to ask for a miracle, she replied, 'What I feel is that God must do as He wills.' Then for a moment she seemed absorbed in the thought of what had just taken place—Jesus leaving His Tabernacle at the invitation of a creature; and she repeated several times, 'Oh, what a mystery is the Holy Eucharist!'

On Wednesday, the 7th of March, our Mother reminded us of the beginning of a novena in preparation for the Feast of St. Joseph. It was thus that she took every opportunity of exciting her children to fervour and devotion. She bade us call to mind the many favours St. Joseph had obtained for us, adding that our gratitude should be in proportion to his benefits. 'You must ask,' she said, 'for all the temporal blessings the Order requires, and for yourselves ask what you please. As for me, I had much rather let Almighty God give me what He pleases, and then I feel sure that whatever comes, comes from Him.'

After prayers, when she had gone to her room, she gave some directions to one of the Sisters, and then added, 'To-morrow the novena begins, and I foresee for myself, in consequence, an increase of suffering.'

Our poor Mother was not mistaken. The next day was one of terrible trial, and it was only by a supreme effort that she forced herself to go to the Jesuit Church in the evening. She was in the habit of going there every Tuesday, to make her confession to Père Olivaint, her spiritual director. When she told him of her sufferings, he said. '*Dominus vobiscum!* Courage and confidence, my child ; your work is the work of the Cross, the work by which redemption came to us.'

The same evening our Mother said, 'O my God, make me understand that Thou hast a right to expect much of me, who have received everything from Thee. Give me wings ; detach me from everything that is not Thee ; raise me above nature, and make me suffer as if I loved to suffer for the love of Thee. I love one thing only—the love of God : to obtain that I will do anything. About the rest I will not bestir myself, but will let God do His work.'

To possess only God, and to belong to God alone, was our Mother's only ambition. How she must have suffered before arriving at feeling this ! How many times she must have sacrificed everything that is not God—how often died to herself before attaining to that happy state ! Our Mother understood the mysterious ways of suffering, and, casting off the human weakness under which she still laboured, she asked God every morning to have no regard to her tears and involuntary rebellion. 'All that I ask of Thee is that my heart may love Thee,' was her prayer ; and to us she would say, with a smile, 'Ought not the hearts of the Helpers of the Holy Souls to have no room in them for creatures, but be altogether filled with God?

We must ask for every one of our Sisters this happy state of detachment, for thus only shall we fulfil the end of our vocation, and do good to souls.'

A visitor having repeated to our Mother various remarks that had been made about her, she replied, with great sweetness and composure, 'Let people say what they please; of what value is the opinion of man? I care only to do the will of God. If He be with me, what can the whole world do against me? What is the world in God's eyes but a mere handful of dust? Ought such a small thing, then, to be able to vex me?'

One night, when our Mother could not sleep, her mind was much troubled by uncertainty as to the salvation of her father's soul; but next morning, at Holy Communion (as she told one of the Sisters with great simplicity), our Lord reproached her for this want of confidence; and, when she had humbled herself in His sight, there came to her the consoling thought that Jesus' Heart could not but be filled with tenderness for the father of His spouse. 'This thought,' she said, 'filled me with peace and joy. It seems to me now that God must give special help to the parents of religious when they are at the point of death.'

The many trials, vexations, and contradictions which are experienced every day of this our exile had never the effect of disturbing our Mother's serenity. 'I give up everything into God's hand,' she said, 'and do not trouble myself more than if I had nothing to occupy my mind. But you must pray for me, for I am overwhelmed with duties, and have great need of patience.'

On the 25th of March, our Mother's birthday, we all united in trying to show her our love, and to celebrate the day. When the Mother Superioress told her of all our good wishes, she replied, 'Thank you, my dear children, for all your affectionate and beautiful wishes. What deep meaning there is in those words, " the purgatory of love "! This blessed Feast of the Annunciation is the anniversary of days when I seemed to be on Calvary, and of others which I passed on Thabor. Pray for me that I may accept with joyful resignation the purgatory of love that you have wished me. St. Augustine says that those whose eyes are really open look upon sufferings as a means of getting quickly to heaven : pray that they may quickly carry me there. And, now that I have received your good wishes, I must make some for you in return. What shall they be ? A person who wished to bestow the highest praise on a Jesuit father said of him, " He is a man made up of heart." Well, I wish to each of you, then, a heart—yes, a heart burning with love of God and your neighbour. When iron is thrown into the fire it acquires all the properties of the fire ; and so, if we throw our hearts into the Heart of Jesus, they will be filled with humility, charity, and zeal. Humility will be the guardian of our offering and the pledge of our perseverance, charity will make of us all one spiritual family, and zeal will make us ready to do and suffer everything for the glory of God.' She shrank from none of the fatigues of the day, but cheerfully endured them, making herself all things to all.

On Passion Sunday our Mother heard that a precious relic of the Holy Table 'on which our Lord said the first Mass' was very soon to arrive. After telling us this good news, she asked us to begin a novena which would end on Holy Thursday. 'Try to find out,' she said, ' what there is that you can do for our Lord to make this novena successful.'

Our dear Mother did not speak of herself or her own cure, so earnestly desired by all, but told us that the intentions of the novena were the recovery of Mère de B—— (who did not herself wish for it) and the increase of postulants. 'For I must tell you,' said our Mother, ' that I will not consent to any foundation until at least twenty postulants shall have entered. It is not necessary that we should be spread abroad in every direction ; the important thing is that we should be good and religious. So make your novena well, keeping yourself in the presence of God; this will be a good preparation for our Easter duties.'

Our Mother received a visit from Père ——; their conversation was about eternity and suffering. The more she suffered the more her thoughts were centred on eternity. She seemed wrapped up in holy Providence, and her love of that Divine Providence seemed ever on the increase.

Writing to Père —— a few days later, she spoke of what had been her one desire during twenty years—to glorify God's holy Providence.

One morning, when she had received a telegram, she said, ' I do not feel at all frightened. I assure you that I do not mind it in the least. The only bad news to me is to hear that the will of God has not been done: the rest is nothing.'

Whenever the relic of the Holy Table was exposed, our Mother's love of Jesus in the Holy Eucharist seemed to increase. 'To think,' she said, with a holy fervour, 'that on this very table our Lord instituted the Holy Eucharist, the most touching pledge of His love for us, and our greatest consolation. If Jesus were not in the Tabernacle neither you nor I would be here. O, if only we had faith!' And here she broke off, her eyes remaining fixed on the relics, her

hands clasping her crucifix as she prayed for all
possible graces, but especially for love.

'O, implore for me the love of God!' she
said: 'for the rest I care nothing! My Jesus,
give me Thy love, that I may love Thee as
much as I wish to love Thee. Keep me in Thy
love.'

When her sufferings were at their height
she was often found in the chapel. There she
sought and obtained strength. Her faith made
her always look at things in their supernatural
aspect.

The reception into the Church of two poor
persons, in whose conversion one of our Sisters
had been instrumental, was to take place in the
chapel; and our Mother, besides overlooking
the arrangements, was brave enough to be present at the ceremony. In her eyes a soul was
not a thing of small value. But some hours
later she exclaimed, 'My God, give me strength,
or I can bear no more; give me courage and
patience. God knows that I suffer terribly. It
is His will, and to accomplish that is my only
consolation. In this matter only do I see my
way clearly—that I must do the will of God. I
suffer terribly,' she said: 'I can hide it from you
no longer. What I do, I do simply by the grace
of God, for I have no strength left.'

Having occasion to give some little admoni-
tion, she ended by saying, 'How shall we be

faithful to great things if we do not make small sacrifices? When I think about all that I have to do and to answer for, and about my present state, I say to myself that the only thing of real importance I have to think of is to obtain the love of God. What avails all the rest? Certainly there is one good thing about suffering— it detaches one's heart, and fixes it on God. Let us now go and visit Sister ——,' she added.

This religious was on her death-bed, and the sight of her sufferings affected our Mother deeply, though she concealed her grief that she might minister consolation to the dying Sister. 'You suffer,' she said, 'but Jesus suffers with you; you do not see Him, you only feel your own weakness; but He is none the less really near you. He takes count of everything. He will be your Cyrenian. Courage! this is the purgatory of deferred hope. Jesus will come to you; it is His love that makes Him leave you here to gain more merit; but He will come soon.'

After the Sister's death she prayed, and made others pray for her; for, while she had the greatest confidence in the mercy of God, she had at the same time so exalted an idea of His holiness that she had difficulty in believing a soul could go straight to heaven without passing through Purgatory. Purgatory was always in her thoughts. A short time before this she had arranged that the *De Profundis* should be said every day during the visit to the Blessed Sacrament, at half-past twelve o'clock, for such souls as had been recommended to our prayers since the preceding day.

Speaking to two seculars, our Mother said, 'Let us mount up higher and higher; let us mount up to God. We feel that we are not made for earthly things; let us seek better things. "*Sursum corda*"—let us lift our hearts higher and higher: "And I, if I be lifted up from the earth, will draw all things to Myself." These words of our Lord teach us what we must do: we must raise ourselves up to God if we wish to gain souls to God.'

Our Mother seemed to realise God's presence everywhere and at all times. 'When everything seems to be going against my wishes, it is as if our Lord said to me, "It is for Me that you are working," and this is most consoling when one has done one's best, but without success. We can all make sacrifices that are noticed, and admired, and praised; but to make sacrifices unknown to any one is by no means such an easy thing. And yet it is these last that touch the Heart of God.'

When some one asked her to describe her idea of heaven, 'You ask my idea of heaven,' she replied: 'it is love! love! love! On earth,' she added, 'we can love deeply, indeed, but our hearts are always crying out that they cannot love enough. In heaven it will not be so: our love will then be without limit, because we shall love God purely, and our hearts are made for Him.'

Our Mother said on another occasion, 'It is not for my own enjoyment that I desire heaven, but that I may for ever witness—that I may for ever revel in--the glory of God, without any of it reverting to me. If Almighty God should leave me quite in a corner in His kingdom, I should not care, provided that from that corner I might see the glory given to Him by the elect.'

Our Mother's sufferings were precious to her because they brought her ever nearer to God and His love. 'O Jesus,' she said one day after her meditation, 'give me Thy Spirit, the spirit of humility and charity. Transform me to Thy likeness in such a manner that I may love Thee only. How much I need the gift of fortitude!'

She said on Pentecost Sunday, 'I scarcely know whether I am living or already dead; and yet this must be nothing compared to Purgatory. O my God, how great is Thy mercy! Make me understand the greatness of the favour Thou conferrest on me by making me suffer in this way.'

In her greatest sufferings she used to say and repeat, '*Deo gratias;*' but, though she thanked God for thus accomplishing His will in her, she nevertheless admitted that at times her sufferings seemed unbearable. She must have needed very great energy to enable her to appear to take interest, from morning to night, in a variety of matters which, in reality, could only have added to the pains that never left her a moment's respite.

About the middle of July rumours of war arose, and these gave fresh occasion for the exercise of our Mother's spirit of faith. When she saw the world thus shaken, by the permission of Him who holds it in His hands, and can cause all human ambition to fall headlong to the ground, she did not conceal what she felt. 'It consoles me greatly,' she said, 'to see Almighty God reassume His rights, and prove to us that we are mere animated grains of dust.'

In a moment of great pain our Mother said, 'When I suffer most I console myself by fancying that I am dead, and that this is my Purgatory; and then, when I think of all those poor soldiers who will so soon appear before God, I say to myself that it is absolutely necessary that I should suffer. Now that we see all these people setting out to fight their earthly enemies, let us arm ourselves with courage that we may fight our interior enemies, and so gain heaven for ourselves, and for the poor Souls in Purgatory who expect so much from us.'

Our Mother could not understand how *self* could be any one's constant occupation. 'It makes me shudder.' she said, 'when I see any one wrapped up in her own little interests, in her own very trivial affairs, without caring for those around her. I beg of each one of you to wear herself out for others, if necessary. Is it possible that any one should remain buried in her own small range of ideas, in thoughts of herself and of her own sufferings, when we reflect on all that is happening—when one remembers the multitude of souls now appearing before God? Let us put self away ; let us enlarge our *ideas* and be generous.'

Our Mother kept secret her rich store of merit : God only knew what a martyrdom she endured. 'I place myself without reserve in the hands of God,' she said. 'Since I have chosen to be a victim for the Souls in Purgatory, it necessarily follows that I must allow Him to do with me what He pleases. God has no need of us ; it is of His pure mercy that He makes use of us in His service, for He could do very well without us. O, what a good thing it is to suffer, but how difficult to do so in a right way ! As for me, I do not know how to suffer. I am so convinced of this that no one could ever persuade me to the contrary. I may admire the charity of the person who tries to do so, but *my* conviction becomes firmer than ever. If only I had faith, how happy I should esteem myself, and how highly favoured! But I do not know how to suffer.' Often she would say, at the end of her meditation, ' I have done nothing but fight against pain.'

The terrible state of France and of Paris in the month of September, which added to our Mother's responsibilities and duties, served also to bring out more clearly the distinctive feature in her character—her complete resignation to the will of God. At the gloomiest times, words of confidence were ever on her lips. She seemed, however, to have a secret conviction that the end of the troubles was not yet at hand. 'O my God,' she said, ' Thou knowest what it is Thou doest. We have only to submit. Why should we be terrified by what is happening? Nothing can happen, except by the permission of God. He will watch over us now, as He has always done. He knows our situation. Let us rely on His all-powerful protection ; let us profit for our sanctification by this trial ; do not let us lose the fruit of it by undue disquietude.'

It was thus that our good Mother encouraged us all, but it was easy to see that she herself suffered terribly. In her state of illness, everything she had to do seemed to her difficult and complicated ; but though the future appeared all dark, she trusted in God, and in God alone, and hoped all things from His goodness. ' Let people say what they please,' she constantly said, 'and believe only in God;' and she often added, 'What account should we make of the opinion of a worm of the earth?'

Letters which came from China about this time confirmed her worst presentiments, and added to her sorrows. The revolt of the Chinese against the Europeans raised the gravest fears for the future, but our Mother's trust in God was never shaken. 'God knows it; God wills it.' These words told all that passed within her. Our Sisters had already left Sen-mou-ieu; after the Tien-tsin massacre, '*Fiat*' was the word that rose to our Mother's lips. 'If I did not know that the Heart of Jesus is watching over my scattered children, what would become of me? It is true that I suffer in body, in mind, and in my soul; but I abandon myself to our good Lord. He gave all, and He has no need of us; and, when He allows us to work for His glory by suffering, does He not show that He specially loves us? If I allowed myself to reflect on my position for only five minutes, I should be discouraged—I should despair. It is the grace of God that sustains me, and bids me live from each moment to the next. The will of God be done: that is all I can say. If I suffered in a right way, I ought to consider myself the happiest person in the world.'

In the midst of her own trials she never forgot others', but gave proofs to all of her motherly affection. One day, as she was wearing herself out writing a very long letter to China, some one remonstrated with her for thus overtiring herself. 'You may be right,' she replied; 'but, if I do not do it, who will? and what will become of our family spirit? Until my death I will do my utmost to keep it up.'

Her charity towards seculars was equally great. Some one advised her to let the poor creatures sent to us by the mayor do something towards their own support, that she might not have them entirely on her hands. 'But should we draw down the blessing of God on ourselves,' she replied, 'if we did not do to others what we should wish them to do to us? O, let us be charitable, for charity touches the Heart of God.'

Our Mother never missed an opportunity of inculcating this virtue—in her eyes the most important of all. 'Have we not all our faults?' she used to say. 'How can we expect others to be perfect whilst we are groaning under the weight of our own imperfections? It shows great good sense to be able to bear with the bad qualities of our neighbours' character, since we inflict the same discomfort on them. If we really loved God, we should have no difficulty in bearing with our neighbour; for love is blind, and charity, which is the love of God, covers a multitude of sins in our brethren. I cling to nothing now but the grace of God. I feel able to do nothing, yet still I do my work, for I know that God gives me His grace. I am so sure that it is His grace only which enables me to perform what I do, that nothing in the world is disagreeable to me except a compliment: to that I have an unbearable aversion.'

Our Mother used to welcome Père Olivaint as a messenger from God. He seemed to have received a special grace to help her, and uphold her at the foot of the Cross. He showed her the most fatherly goodness, understood her trials, and was able to sympathise with her the more truly that he himself was detached from all created things. 'Our good Lord performs a greater miracle by upholding you in your sufferings,' he said to her, 'than by curing you. You are suffering for the souls of men, and many sinners are returning to God.'

One day as our Mother was in still greater pain than usual, Père Olivaint came to see her; she received his visit as a special favour from Divine Providence. When he left her she seemed to be more absorbed in eternity than before. When one of the Sisters asked her what Père Olivaint's opinion was on the events that were taking place, she could not help laughing, and said, 'O, you have come to the wrong person if you want to hear news. What we talked about was the fruit of suffering when it is patiently endured: the rest we left in the hands of God.'

Our Mother did not suffer less after Père Olivaint had been with her, but she was morally refreshed.

Her own community and its secular friends pressed our Mother to leave Paris, the condition of the town becoming every day more alarming, but she wished only to obey, and allowed them to talk on.

'If God wishes me to go,' she said. 'He can easily make Père Olivaint and M. Roquette send me away. We shall stay here, and God will protect us. Let us trust in Him. After all, do we believe that God exists or not? Well, as we know He exists, we can be certain that He will watch over us. It may be His will to chastise us, and the chastisement may not be a light one. So be it! Let His justice be satisfied. I, for one, certainly have deserved to suffer. O, how suffering detaches one from all that is not God, and forces the soul to seek consolation far away from the things of this world! My God, give me grace to suffer! Nothing but the grace of God upholds me, and enables me to act, for I feel that I am a prodigy of weakness and misery.'

It was terrible to watch the progress of our Mother's malady, but we felt that God was thus daily placing before us an example of the most sublime virtue. And how little she ever dreamed that it was so! 'My theory is magnificent,' she used to say, 'but in practice no one is more backward. Virtue would make my condition bearable, but I have none, and so illness gets the better of me.' She herself was the only one who could not see those merits which filled us with admiration. Though she said that she was quite taken up with her own illness, she nevertheless paid as much attention to each one of us as if she had nothing else to do.

Amidst the many difficulties occasioned by the state of Paris, her motherly vigilance extended to the smallest details : she had scarcely recovered from one of her violent paroxysms of pain when she was to be found planning something for the general good. She had acquired the habit of seeing the will of God in all that happened, and therefore nothing ever disturbed her peace of mind. The remembrance of her children, now far away, always affected her ; but all she desired for them was that they might love God perfectly. And, when it was proposed that the Sisters should return from China if the persecution broke out at Shanghai, she said. 'They did not go to China only to live there, and I should not feel at all proud of them if they ran away from martyrdom.'

Thus were borne out the feelings which she had expressed after hearing Monseigneur

Fournier give an instruction on bearing witness to the faith by martyrdom.

'I think that I should die of joy,' she said, 'if any one were to come and tell me that one of my children had shed her blood for Jesus Christ. The thought of martyrdom, far from terrifying me, gives me great consolation. I profess to you solemnly that I had rather see all my children die than see them growing lax in God's service or leading selfish lives.'

Her own existence was a prolonged agony. The weaker her body became, the higher her soul seemed to rise above created things. Her faith made her see Jesus in the persons who approached her. Père Olivaint's visits were to her as visits from our Lord, and she always derived from them strength and courage.

During one terrible night, the long hours of which were hours of real agony, her thoughts were constantly fixed on heaven, as her words next day proved. 'I have spent the night on the Cross,' she said. 'God's will nailed me to it. Was I not in a happy position?'

When the doctor told her of the gravity of her illness, she said, 'I like to hear the truth, and this news does not at all distress me. Our good Lord knows very well what is best for me, and it is all His doing.'

When her sufferings forced her to inaction she would never let her crucifix be out of her hands : it became dearer to her every day. In her greatest pain no other cry than the name of Jesus escaped her. She once said, 'These words have just come into my mind—" My meat is to do the will of Him that sent me."' In a paroxysm of pain she exclaimed, 'I can bear no more ;' but, immediately recovering herself and kissing her crucifix, she said, 'Yes, I can bear still more, for I do not suffer as He did.'

Our Mother was no longer able, without great difficulty, to occupy herself about things of earth. 'I suffer too much,' she said, 'to desire anything.'

When some one asked her whether a visit from Père Olivaint would do her good, 'If God sends him to me,' she replied, 'I shall be very glad, for no one gives me courage as he does. I see Jesus in him more than in any one else.'

'Jesus! Jesus!' How often our Mother repeated that blessed word! She thought that she had not yet attained to the first degree of the love of God ; but those who knew her best were all of opinion that to love God was her one desire and her one prayer. Her trust in God was absolute. 'After I have prayed so earnestly to the Heart of Jesus,' she said, 'for my children in China, at Nantes, and at Brussels, I should be wounding His Heart and doubting His goodness if I gave way to disquietude.'

We never heard from her a word of complaint. We could see what efforts she made to overcome herself, and to fight against her illness. Her loving resignation never gave way for a moment. The sight of her calmness and recollection was very touching. When her pains became too violent, she would press her crucifix to her lips, and hold it so for some time without saying a word. It made us think of the silence of Calvary.

Every day her condition became more painful and more distressing. Nothing could be done to give her the least relief; but the love of God increased in her soul, and gave her strength to bear all, and even to love her sufferings. She would not admit that she had arrived at that, but her own words proved it. 'I have not courage,' she said, 'to ask for anything but what our Lord wills; it is such a grace to suffer, that I would not lose it through my own fault; and our Lord could not give me a more touching proof of His love than to fasten me thus with Himself to the Cross. I am nailed to it, and so cannot move. If I had but a little faith, a little love, how thankful I should be!'

These three words were always on her lips— 'Jesus! *Fiat! Magnificat!*'

The approach of the Feast of Blessed Margaret Mary Alacoque filled her with fresh devotion. On the morning of the previous day, during the recitation of the litanies, she knelt on her *prie-dieu*, shedding tears of love before the Tabernacle. In the afternoon she remained in the chapel from two until four. Though in dreadful pain, she seemed unable to tear herself away.

She superintended the decorations, and even helped in these herself. To look at her was at once painful and consoling. 'Last night,' she said, 'the thought came to me that our Lord loved me too much to take away my illness; and in reality He bestows a greater blessing on me by enabling me to bear my burden.' In honour of Blessed Margaret Mary's Feast, Père Olivaint came, according to his promise, to say Mass for the community, and he afterwards gave us a quarter of an hour's instruction. He took for his subject the Collect of the Feast, the Heart of Jesus as the perpetual dwelling-place of souls. He seemed on fire with the desire of saving souls. He spoke of the love of God in a way that seemed to transport us out of ourselves. Our Mother was enchanted. What he said of the life of the Saint whose Feast we were about to keep, and her devotion to the Sacred Heart, exactly answered to her own feelings. She had had the night before a dream which filled her with devotion. She dreamed that circumstances made it necessary the Sacred Species should be consumed. As she advanced to the holy table to communicate, instead of Hosts she saw in the ciborium grains of corn. The priest then said to her, 'Will you preserve the Blessed Sacrament?' She assented joyfully, and immediately she thought she had in her hands a golden heart, and that she held it out to the priest, who placed in it a number of the grains, but it seemed as though it could never be filled. She was joyfully holding her treasure when a person who stood by gave her a flower, saying, '*It is a myosotis.*' She put it into the heart, and, rising from the holy table, she saw our Blessed Lord appearing to St. Mary Magdalene.

Père Olivaint explained this dream in a very consoling way. 'The golden heart,' he said, 'is your heart.'

'O father! Mine a heart of gold?'

'A better one than that,' he replied: 'for our hearts can beat incessantly with love for our Lord. The grains of corn are the Souls which your prayers have released from Purgatory, and the flower is the offering of all your sufferings.'

Even her illness did not deter our Mother from visiting the 'ambulance.' At half-past one she went there for the second time, taking with her cigars and gingerbread to please the sufferers. She said a few words to each, and left them in high glee. This was a great feat for her.

By three o'clock she was quite exhausted, and unable to move.

Three gentlemen from the 'Mairie' came to visit her. The hope of doing some good gave her strength to see them. Later on, when she became unable to leave her cell, her charity still found room for action; and, with a little stove heated by a spirit-lamp, she used to make soup, which she sent to some of those whom she knew to be suffering most in those troubled times. One day she sent some to the parlour to a poor man belonging to the Garde Nationale, the father of a family, and who seemed to be almost starved to death. Her kindness made so great an impression upon him that he went to confession that very day.

Our Mother saw Jesus present in everything. Over and over again she used to say to us, 'If you would not lose your time, do all you can for Jesus.' After attending to some small household details, she often made the observation that it was her duty to work to the utmost as long as she had any strength left.

At the most painful moment of the day she was wont to exclaim, 'O Jesus, I thank Thee for this singular proof of Thy love!'

She had passed a very bad night, and while dressing next morning was attacked by violent pains, followed by hæmorrhage. She had great difficulty in reaching the chapel, but the thought that our Lord was waiting for her at the holy table gave her strength. After Mass she was quite worn out, but very calm and resigned. 'Our good God wills it,' she said; 'it is His good pleasure; we live here only that we may attain to true life in eternity. Life is but a day, and in heaven we shall neither suffer nor see others suffer, so that we ought not to complain as if our sufferings were not to have an end. To suffer is a great grace; so, courage! let us stand faithfully with St. John at the foot of the Cross.' And as she spoke she held tight her crucifix, which she never could bear to part with.

She was to see M. D——, a new doctor, that day, and she was asked whether she did not dislike the idea. She answered that obedience made her content with that, as with everything else. M. D—— was much astonished when he found out what was her disease, and declared that, looking at her, he should never have guessed it. 'She must have wonderful energy and power of endurance,' he observed. 'Hers is a most extraordinary state, and she must have wonderful graces to be what she is.'

Another time, when she had made a great effort over herself, our Mother said, 'In suffering one should always be ready to suffer still more, and something seems to say to me that the time is short. To-day is Friday; would that I had one spark of the fire which burned in the Heart of our Lord for men ! I always suffer more than usual on Friday : that is a great grace given to me by the Heart of Jesus. Purgatory is filling continually —no wonder that I suffer.'

Our Mother always longed to increase the love of God in the souls of those around her. She said one day to a person who had had a little dispute with another, ' I see that you were not in the wrong ; but do give way to her for the love of our Lord, and say five " Our Fathers " and " Hail Marys " for her before you go to bed. That is the way to make friends.'

When she saw any one acting impulsively, or showing the least temper, she never failed to take notice of it, and to exclaim with great earnestness, ' O, let us work for God, for His love, for Him only.'

Once, when she had put in order some community matters, she said, ' Let us now have recourse to our good God to obtain fresh strength, for I am suffering tortures, and it would never do if nature were to get the upper hand. See what a weight presses me down [alluding to her complaint] ; it reminds me of the heavy stone before the door of the sepulchre ; and I say with the holy women, " Who shall roll away the stone ? " O, Jesus, Jesus ! Thou art my only good ; be Thou my only strength. God's will is being accomplished in me. Is not that consoling ? *Deo gratias* for ever ! He that made me dissolves me. Has He not the right to do as He wills? What a grace this is ! . . . One would never have the courage to make oneself suffer like this—at least, I should not—and so our good God, who knows the value of suffering. metes it out to me like a true Father.'

Our Mother asked the Sisters to make a novena in their own hearts. to thank God for all the graces bestowed on her during the past seventeen years, but especially for this last grace of suffering, which nailed her, as it were. to the Cross. It was the seventeenth anniversary of the day on which she had for the first time thought of founding an Order of expiation for the Souls in Purgatory.

On November 2nd, 1870, the thought of the Holy Souls was never out of her mind. The clock having stopped. she said in the evening, thinking no doubt of the long sleepless night before her, 'How unfortunate! We shall not hear the hours strike, and shall not be reminded to make the sign of the Cross. I suffer for the Souls in Purgatory: that thought helps me to bear my illness. I can only satisfy my longing to help the Souls that God loves, by suffering for them. I believe that during seventeen years I have had no other thought than this. I love to help the Souls in Purgatory, for God's own glory is interested in their release. This is a time of grace,' she said, ' a time of expiation and of merit; we shall be very foolish if we let it pass without profiting by it—not for ourselves, but for the Souls who expect so much from us.'

On the 7th of November what she had to endure amounted to a sort of martyrdom; some one said to her that she ought not to be surprised at it, since this was the Octave of All Souls. 'O, I am not surprised,' our dear Mother answered: 'with me the Octave is never-ending. I must suffer, since God is the Master of my whole being, and I am His without reserve; and, though I sigh, I beg Him to be on no ceremony with me, and not to spare me.'

Convinced that she did not possess the love of God, and desiring to obtain it at any price, our Mother never ceased to pray for it, and to make others implore it for her. When she saw any one hesitate about making some little sacrifice, she would say, in a tone of entreaty, 'O, you must do it, to please our Lord, and to obtain for me the love of God. Would I could bear the name of Jesus engraven on my heart!' That morning our Mother kept silence, like Jesus on the Cross. To us her silence seemed eloquent, as she lay there perfectly still, with clasped hands, closed eyes, and the crucifix lying next her heart, while she suffered tortures in every part of her poor worn-out frame. Every now and then a word escaped, and told what was passing within. 'O, Jesus, my only true good, my eternal and only Master, uphold me by Thy grace;' and at another time, 'Do not talk about my merits,' she said, 'but of the Souls in Purgatory, for whom I am bound to suffer. Next to the grace of my vocation, God has given me none greater than this long course of pain. It is necessary for my sanctification that I should be purified by fire. This morning I was thinking that the three phases of our Lord's life were to be reproduced in me : the hidden life ; the public life—that is, the time of my labours ; and now the last, the life of suffering. O, that I could suffer like and with our Lord in His Passion!' 'And after that, Mother?' some one said. 'After that the resurrection,' she replied. 'But I shall not die yet ; I am not ready, and our Lord is too good to take me away just now. It is as if I were a piece of canvas stretched out before Him, on which He works with a sharp instrument, but the pattern is not yet completed.'

Another time she said, with a smile on her lips, 'How blessed is my state! My God, I thank Thee! O Jesus, Jesus, I thank Thee! Thou dost treat me as Thy servant ; give me courage to suffer as I ought, that I may know how to relieve and deliver the souls that Thou lovest. Thou didst love and desire only the Cross, O Jesus! Preserve me from the folly of desiring anything but this. I desire to suffer because Thou willest it ; I accept it ; I bless

Thee for it. . . . I have been asking myself whether on my cross I could say the seven last words of Jesus on the Cross; but I could never say with truth, " My God, why hast Thou forsaken me?" He never before showed me greater marks of His love; and when I am in any distress of mind, I think I hear Him saying, " Rely upon Me." '

At three o'clock at night she had not as yet had any sleep. ' I ought to say a *Te Deum*,' she said, ' because I have perhaps been able to give a little relief to the Holy Souls.' With her usual simplicity, our Mother told us that it seemed to her as if our Lord said to her that morning, ' The special love which you desire will be the reward of special sufferings;' and under this impression she said, ' O Thou that holdest the world in Thy hand, uphold me at the foot of Thy Cross. I can never suffer too much if I may thereby obtain Thy love.' She felt that her strength was growing less and less, but her confidence and her love supplied the strength that was wanting to her. She seemed quite wrapped up in thoughts of God; and when some one said as much to her, she answered, with a smile, ' Of whom would you have me speak and think, if not of God? We can never value enough the grace of suffering which makes us live for God only; our union with Him is ratified on the Cross. O Jesus!' she said, kissing her crucifix, 'Thou knowest how I long to love Thee above all things. . . . My pains are great indeed. . . . But I thank Thee, my good Jesus! I am as one dead, and in Thine infinitely great mercy Thou hast permitted me to go through my Purgatory here, in the midst of this little community, confided to Thy Sacred Heart. . . . I do not ask to be cured; that is not my business; it rests with God.' She understood the full meaning of what Père Olivaint had said to her a few days before: 'If you were cured, our Lord would not be so near you. When God does not take away our sufferings, it is often a proof that He accepts them.'

Time passed very slowly with her, confined as she always was to her room. 'Minutes seem to me ages,' she said one day; but she added, 'Our good God knows it; that is enough for me, and I say *Fiat.*' And again: 'Do not fancy I have courage; I have none. I never felt greater need of conversion. I do not know what it is to bear pain as I ought.'

Fighting was going on near Paris; the roaring of the cannon had not ceased all night, and had kept our Mother in a constant state of self-sacrifice for the Holy Souls. The protracted torture she suffered made her appear to live by faith rather than in a natural way.

'I am suffering for our Lord's intentions,' she said; 'I have no other myself. I suffer for the glory of God : I suffer for the Souls in Purgatory. Through them I ask for the graces which I desire. They are nearer to God than I am, and they know better how to pray. Our Lord loves them ; that is enough to make me offer myself up for them ; and I have no other wish, no other thought, than to relieve them for the love of Jesus Christ, whose friends they are.' In a moment of dreadful pain she said, ' This is the fire of Purgatory ; it is right that I should endure it, for, besides having deserved it myself, I am bound to offer it up for the Souls that are burning there. This is a grace which God gives me — a special grace. O, obtain for me the love of God ; obtain that I may have the folly of the Cross, the folly of love ! ' She became at last quite unable to move. ' God wills this,' she said, ' and I also will it for His greater glory. How can I be better employed ? What should I have done all the time of the siege if God had not thus appointed that which was good for me ? This state gives me a grand opportunity of obtaining the love of God— that love which I desire above all things.'

That morning she was not able to receive the Holy Communion ; and when one of us said to her that this must be a great sacrifice to her, she replied, ' Submission to the will of God is the best kind of union with Him, and if I were patient I might thus be united to His will a

hundred times a day. How backward I am!
Our Lord on the Cross had no one to console
Him, and can I complain who am surrounded
with comforts? O my God, forgive me! Jesus,
most patient, help me! I suffer so much that I
am almost overcome. My God, come to my
assistance; let Thy Divine arms uphold me lest
I fall.' Then she asked for her beads, and
recited what she called her *Fiat* Rosary. Every
now and then she would interrupt herself to say,
'O will of God, be thou blessed!'

Having had a very painful afternoon, in the
evening she asked for her crucifix, which she
kissed, saying, 'My God, I ask Thy pardon for
all my faults during the past day, and, in spite
of them, I offer it up to Thee for the Souls in
Purgatory.'

Our dear Mother constantly accused herself,
but no one else could help feeling admiration at
the sight of that lively ardent nature bearing
so resignedly the trials to which it was subjected. Her sufferings never abated: humanly
speaking, the case seemed desperate; but, in the
light of faith, all this was the greatest possible
blessing. Our Mother often repeated that it was
so; often, too, she would kiss her crucifix, and
say, from the bottom of her heart, 'O my Jesus,
it is for the love of Thee, it is for the Souls in
Purgatory!'

On the 1st of January, after a night of terrible pain, our Mother desired to see the community, and addressed to them a few words. 'Love the Cross,' she said; 'accept the Cross. *O Crux, ave! Spes unica!* Desire it at any price! *Fiat. Deo gratias.*'

Then she began to repeat an ejaculation inspired by her love of Jesus: 'O Jesus, eternal joy of the Saints!'

The dressing of the wound caused her great pain, but she was never heard to utter a word of complaint. Nothing that happened could disquiet her. When she heard the booming of cannon during the bombardment of Paris, she said, 'Jesus, my Master, protect us;' and, though she sympathised with those around her, she did not conceal her opinion that religious, above all, should trust themselves entirely to God, and should not be easily disquieted.

On the 6th of January, Père Olivaint came to see our Mother, and spoke to her of Extreme Unction. Two days later he called together the community, and told them that the Last Sacrament would be administered to her on the following day. Our Mother could not sleep that night. The thought of the Sacrament for which she was preparing did not leave her for a moment. She offered her sufferings in preparation. The thought of it filled her with emotion and thankfulness. Her eyes never wandered from her crucifix; she bewailed her weakness, which she called cowardice. 'O, if I had a little love,' she said, 'how sweet my sufferings would seem! O Jesus, be my strength, be my life! My God, I trust myself to Thee; I give up all solicitude; I have only strength to say, "My God, I love Thee!"'

For some days past this simple act of love had stood in the stead of all her religious exercises. 'Give me my crucifix,' she said; 'I must obey and make my meditation, as Père Olivaint told me to make it. Every one ought to acquire the virtue of obedience: it saves one from so many evils.'

When we had given her the crucifix, our poor Mother kissed it three times, saying, 'My God! I love Thee! This is my morning prayer.' And she did the same again as her meditation, and then, kissing the crucifix once more, she said, 'You will give it back to me for my examen of conscience. Père Olivaint told me to make my exercises so, for I have no longer strength to pray.'

On the 17th of January our Mother, in spite of her prostrate condition, called to mind all the circumstances connected with the foundation of the society, and said it was no wonder that she had so much to suffer, when God had showered down so many blessings on our congregation.

That night she was heard to say several times, 'I am going, I am going.'

Thinking that she was delirious, a Sister said, 'Where are you going, dear Mother?'

'Where God calls me,' she replied. 'His will is being accomplished; that is all that I understand.'

On the 6th of February our Mother communicated for the last time. Later in the day she fell into a kind of torpor. Letters having arrived, the first that we had had from Nantes and Brussels since the siege had been raised, her motherly affection gave her strength to hear them read, and she thanked God for the blessings He had granted to those houses. After a night of great pain and continual suffocation, towards morning our Mother fell into a kind of sleep. She thought she saw Mère du Sacré Cœur, and said, 'Why, there is Mère du Sacré Cœur; she must have returned. How good of her to come to see me! Père Basuiau must have sent her. I am very glad; but how can it all have happened? Our good God has done it all. I can do no more.'

On the very day of her death she inquired whether the Mère du Sacré Cœur had returned from China, and said, 'If she does not come soon, she will not find me here.'

THOUGHTS OF MÈRE MARIE DE LA PROVIDENCE.

LET us fight the battles of the Lord with that generosity which St. Ignatius speaks of when he tells us to go forward at any cost, in spite of all obstacles, never looking back, and each day learning a new lesson of sacrifice, until, if we practically love our Lord, the desire for it will become a burning thirst.

If we enter on the royal way of the Cross, each trial or sorrow will be a station, before which we shall kneel to adore the hand of Providence ; and the last station on that road will be the gate of heaven.

If we want to rouse ourselves to courage, we must look at that little door of the Tabernacle, out of which Jesus comes so lovingly to visit our hearts.

O, it is well to cherish an ever-increasing desire to live for God alone! Who but Jesus can satisfy these hungry hearts of ours, starving as they are for happiness ?

If we would thirst after God, we must thirst for everything that draws us closer to Him.

We say every day in our Office for the Dead, ' Sacrifice and oblation Thou wouldst not, but Thou hast given me a body. Then said I, " Behold, I come." ' Yes, let us repeat, ' Lo, I come to work all my life, by prayer, by suffering, and by action, for the deliverance of the Souls in Purgatory, and I come *for good and all.'*

The more we give ourselves to Jesus, the more He gives Himself to us ; and for the soul to which He gives Himself, Calvary becomes Thabor.

Let us receive our crucifix as a Divine legacy, which teaches us how to put our vow in practice, and shows us how complete must be our immolation for the Souls in Purgatory.

Let us make no other projects than to do God's will.

If the Souls in Purgatory could exchange places with us, how gladly they would suffer, and how slight would our sufferings seem to them !

Fear nothing but not to do perfectly God's will.

Let us never refuse to help any one if it is in our power to do so ; and depend upon it, we can do so much oftener than we suppose.

You feel as if you did nothing, knew nothing, and felt nothing. Never mind ; the good God will contrive to weave a crown for you out of all the nothings you have offered up for His love.

The Cross is at the foundation of every vocation.

Those who cannot suffer cannot love.

The true spirit of abandonment consists in keeping a tight hand over ourselves, and letting

God do with us as He pleases. ('Se laisser faire, et ne pas se laisser aller—c'est-là le véritable abandon à la Providence.')

It is only in sacrifice that a true religious can find joy.

Let us always remember that our vocation is an apostolate. We are bound to bring souls to our Lord, whether we find them upon earth or seek them in Purgatory.

We must never say, ' My sufferings are too great,' because it is not true. God measures exactly the sufferings that we can and must endure for the Souls in Purgatory.

We ought to say, ' I suffer—so much the better; I am exhausted—that is part of my business ; I am weary—so are others. I belong to the Lord. Jesus has chosen me to be His helper.' Let that thought be our strength in our labours, our consolation in sorrows, our hope in trials.

' *Sursum corda* '—is not that our badge? O, let us put on Jesus Christ; let us wear His livery with joy and love, and, thus clothed, descend continually into Purgatory, to give to the poor Souls, by our acts, our sufferings, and our prayers, all the hope and consolation expressed by the name of Jesus.

Personal sanctification is the first step towards apostleship. Before we can follow the martyrs to distant lands, we must vigorously accept the daily martyrdom of minute sacrifices.

God has chosen us for a special exercise of zeal. We must always bear in mind those words, ' The zeal of Thine house has eaten me up.'

Let us be docile instruments in God's hands. It is a marvellous mystery of love that He should make use of nothing to accomplish something.

Whenever anything happens, I say to myself, ' It *has* happened : and so it is God who allowed it to happen.' I will not puzzle myself any more with those two words, ' *why* ' and ' *how*.'

Let sacrifice be our special devotion. Let us ask God to teach us the art of making people lose sight of us and directing their attention to others.

We often make Acts of Faith, Hope, and Charity ; but it does not often occur to us to make Acts of Joy. And yet it would be very pleasing to God if, for instance, we sometimes said to Him, ' My God, how glad I am that I belong to You ! '

The Souls in Purgatory suffer without a moment's interruption. Their Helpers must never cease a moment to assist them. How could we think of rest on earth ?

THE END.

APPENDIX II.

Since this little volume was first published, the seed sown amidst the storms by Mère Marie de la Providence has pursued its quiet growth. As far back as 1878—only seven years after her death and twenty-two years after her humble beginnings in the Rue St. Martin— the work was already judged by the Holy See to have established its claims to a definitive approval, and to admission among the permanent institutions of the Catholic Church. Under such sanction from Leo XIII., in the first year of his Pontificate, it could continue its labours with renewed zeal and confidence.

Gathering up the further results attained during the new period thus commenced, we may note in the first place some new foundations. Among others, in France there have been such at Lourdes, and Versailles where one of the novitiates has been established ; in Italy at Turin and Florence ; and across the ocean at New York. This means that the work has now taken root in five countries, a serious consideration when one remembers how careful

young religious congregations have to be lest
by new foundations they should overtax their
strength. Still none have been undertaken
except with a deep sense of responsibility, and
in obedience to what in the judgment of ecclesi-
astical superiors has been a clear call from God ;
and God has certainly blessed them all in the
most striking manner.

To enter into a few details. At Montmartre,
the temporary sanctuary has been replaced by a
pretty Gothic chapel with side-altars dedicated
respectively to St. Denys and St. Ignatius of
Loyola. The object for which the care of this
sacred spot was entrusted to the Helpers—the
re-organisation of the ancient pilgrimages—has
been fully attained. The Octave of St. Denys
is now celebrated each year with great solemnity,
when the daily services in the chapel are crowded
with devout worshippers. Nor do the pilgrims
confine their visits to that particular season.
Throughout the year they come in a continuous
stream. Moreover, the Pilgrims' Book testifies to
the spread of the devotion by the signatures which
it contains of distinguished visitors—Cardinals,
Bishops, Heads of Religious Orders, Ecclesias-
tics of all degrees, Missionaries from East and
West, and devout lay-folk—who have come from
all parts of the world to seek a blessing on their
several works at this ancient sanctuary of Catholic France. The visit of one of these seems from

the circumstances to demand a special mention. In 1892 the Very Rev. Father Martin, the newly elected General of the Society of Jesus, came to this birthplace of his Society, that, in the very spot where St. Ignatius and his first companions had taken their vows, he might seek a blessing on his own future government.

It is not, however, solely in the happy success of these pilgrimages that the connection of the Helpers with Montmartre has been blessed. They have the daily consolation of receiving by hundreds the children of the *école communale* close by, who, humanly speaking, would otherwise grow up without any religious instruction. The struggle to start and maintain this work has been very great, but in view of the results so far attained it does not seem excessive to say that this Foundation is becoming a centre of Catholic life and labour, which may be destined gradually to transform an entire neighbourhood. No day, at all events, passes in which the Helpers have not been able to gather around them and catechise 500 children of both sexes, whilst on Sundays the number of these willing attendants at their classes usually reaches some 700. As early as 7 A.M. troops of boys arrive who are to be prepared for their first Communion, and one set succeeds another during the whole day, parents joining with children in their desire to learn. Thus, as may readily be

imagined, the way is prepared for the return of
many to the sacraments after the neglect of
years, for the rectification of marriage unions
on which the blessing of the Church had not
been sought, and for the baptism of those who
had been allowed to grow up for years unwashed
with the regenerating water.   Such, and so consoling, is the nature of a day's work at Montmartre, and the evening is usually far spent before
the last instruction is given.

The work originally contemplated, and still
assigned the first place among the works of
the Helpers, is the care of the sick poor, but
times and circumstances have led them into
other spheres of labour which seemed consonant
with the spirit of their institute.   One such is
that instruction of children and of the ignorant
now carried on in all the houses, of which the
results at Montmartre may be taken as a signal
specimen.   Another work is the *école professionelle*
('Technical School').   In these days, in Paris as
elsewhere the children of the working classes
leave school at a very early age, and it is then
that their most dangerous time, from a religious point of view, commences.   Too young
to do without the restraints suitable for childhood, and yet at the same time most anxious to
dispense with them, whilst, on the other hand,
there is so seldom in their homes the will or the
capacity to exercise over them a due supervision,

they are exposed to every possible temptation, and form habits most injurious alike to the Christian life, and to the acquirement of an honest living. It was to meet this difficulty in some measure, that at Paris in the Rue du Cherche Midi, a house adjoining the Mother House in the Rue de la Barouillère was taken in 1871. Here an *école professionelle* was started which is now much appreciated, and is doing valuable work. The girls number at the present time about 150, all engaged in learning some useful trade, such as dressmaking, millinery, artificial flower-making, etc., under the tuition of skilled work-women engaged by the religious, who of course have the government of the establishment. The children are day-pupils, living in their own homes, but spending the entire day in the school, where, besides studies useful for their respective trades, they can receive religious instruction from the nuns, who endeavour to cultivate in their young hearts and minds habits of piety and industry, simplicity and self-control. Nor are their bodily wants left without provision. There is a large play-ground for recreation and physical exercise, both of which are so important. Those who understand youth will realise the difficulties and anxieties of a work like this, but the Helpers have the consolation of knowing that through it they have been enabled to transform into good Catholics and useful citizens, not a few who might otherwise have fallen victims to the demoralisation of Parisian life.

From Paris let us pass to distant China and report the progress made by the little colony which Mgr. Languillat led out amidst so many prayers and hopes in 1867. The schools in the neighbourhood of Shanghai are flourishing, conversions are not unfrequently wrought, and the Helpers have even the consolation of seeing some of their children develop a religious vocation and pass either into their own ranks or into those of some other of the orders established in that vast empire. A new house has also been opened at Hong-Kew, principally for the use of the Portuguese and Japanese who congregate in that part of Shanghai, whilst at Zi-ka-wei, to the many promising works described in the body of this volume, another of great interest has been added. The number of deaf and dumb children brought to the orphanage made the nuns anxious to provide some means of instructing them. Accordingly the need was made known at the Mother House, and a nun specially trained for the work sailed from Marseilles in 1893. Seven pupils awaited her arrival, to which number others were soon added, including a few boys of the roughest and wildest Chinese type. The new teacher, having learnt the Chinese characters before her departure from Paris, was able at once to set to work, and before long her pupils were making good progress, learning at the rate of four fresh characters a day, learning, that is to say, not merely to read but to pronounce. When the school had been at work three months illustrious visitors of Church and State came to see how it was getting on. They were much touched and astonished when one of the pupils on being shown a picture of Our Blessed Lady said most distinctly: '*Sen-Mon-Mo-li-a*' ('Holy Mother Mary'). 'Do you love her?' asked the nun. '*Ai-mo-ke*' ('I love her') was the answer, no less distinctly given.

Every day the children learn a short lesson stenographically, and to impress it upon their minds they are also taught to draw the forms of the objects learnt. The sign of the cross was the one mastered first of all, so that it might be possible for them to join in the prayers before and after lessons, which they now do, not harmoniously it is true, but in such a manner as to affect deeply all who are present. The intelligence of a deaf child develops but slowly, and it may be imagined that the task of teaching the deaf and dumb is long and complicated. In China, too, it was complicated in the first instance by the necessity of adapting the stenography to the Chinese sounds, whilst simultaneously teaching the characters. The account given by the nun herself bears witness to the difficulty. Writing to the Mother House a report of her labour, she said : 'The fatigue is very great. It is a work of great responsibility and it is necessary to give oneself to it without counting the toil. The consolation, however, is great on seeing the happy effects produced on the minds of these little ones, especially when, for the first time, the countenance of a dumb child lights up with fresh life, as something new is understood, and eternal truths hitherto unknown dawn upon the intelligence.'

God's ways are not our ways, and in less than two years this first apostle to the deaf and dumb at Zi-ka-wei was struck down by a sharp attack of cholera. In less than twenty-four hours, the life which had been so devotedly given to God's children on earth was claimed by God for Himself. Nor was she the only one taken. Others of their number whom, judging by earthly reckonings, the little company of Helpers could ill afford to lose, were taken from them by the same disease. Still the seed had been sown, and others to whom the lost sister had been able to impart her talent were able to carry on her work, which still continues and prospers.

From the extreme East let us now pass to the extreme West. It was in the May of 1892 that the pioneers of the American foundation sailed for New York, whither the voice of Providence seemed to be clearly calling them. A small house in the southern part of the city (25 7th Avenue) was first taken, but the work grew so rapidly to their hand that it soon became necessary to move into larger quarters; and a commodious house was accordingly taken in October, 1894, at 114 East 86th Street. The character of the work in which the Helpers are engaged, is necessarily the same substantially in every large city; but there is this special about it in New York, that the numbers who have recourse to them are very large—fed too as they are by continuous accessions of newly arrived immigrants—and their variety is most perplexing. In Paris differences of nationality and religion are not sufficient to cause complications, and in London, though creeds vary, race remains more or less the same. But in New York not only every creed but every nationality is represented—Americans born, French, English, Irish, Spaniards, Italians, Turks, Chinese—and there is the further distinction of 'colour' with the strong prejudices which gather round it.

It is with this motley population that the sisters have to deal, with the consequent necessity of dividing their classes to meet the varying and incompatible requirements. However the commencements are full of promise. They have been able to attract a large number of children, boys and girls, who when released from the public schools, in whose teaching religion has no place, come regularly to the convent to be instructed and prepared for the sacraments. On Saturday, which there as in England is the weekly holiday, these same children have an opportunity of joining useful and pleasant classes, when the girls may learn needlework, and the boys the art of drawing. In the evenings, several days in the week, business girls who are employed during the day in the shops devote their free time to combined lessons in needlework and in Christian doctrine. Individual instruction of those who for one reason or another are not suited for classes, occupies intermediate hours of the day, and by this means, not to speak of Catholics brought back to the use of the sacraments, many consoling, because solid, conversions to the Catholic faith have been wrought, not merely from the various sects of Protestantism, but occasionally even from Judaism and Mahometanism. Of course the great day of all at the convent is the Sunday, when children, young girls, and grown-up women alike flock thither as to a house where they can be sure of a warm welcome and can spend some pleasant hours together. It is then too that they learn to love the Benediction of the Blessed Sacrament, which invariably ends their afternoons with its seal set upon their devotions, their instructions, and their amusements.

The work among the coloured people in this

New York settlement merits a special paragraph. American prejudice renders it absolutely necessary to deal with them separately, but they are well aware that they have as large a place in the hearts of the Helpers, and will receive as assiduous attention from them, as their more favoured brethren. It is the 'coloured,' in fact, in whom the Helpers recognise the choicest opportunity for the exercise of their zeal, and they are most anxious in every way to study their best interests, and to convince them that with our Lord there is no respect of persons. And the 'coloured' in their turn respond with all the confiding simplicity and affection of their race, and it is sweet indeed to see them flocking, old as well as young, to the convent doors as soon as they are opened to receive them. In particular, among the provisions made for their needs. the Mothers' Guild may be mentioned, which is under the patronage of St. Peter Claver, the 'Apostle of the Negroes'. It is attended very regularly by a goodly number of Protestant as well as Catholic women, who come regardless of weather—which in the coloured people is specially meritorious, as they are very sensitive to rain and snow. During their needlework they listen to reading, either pious or recreative, at the end of which they receive their religious instruction. Tea is then provided, after which hymns are sung until the hour for departure arrives, an hour

which is always protested against as unduly early.
During Lent special services are held for the
coloured people, and the tea, so much appreciated
at other times, is then suppressed in the spirit of
penance. The Protestant members of the Guild
were at first told that they need not join the
Catholics in this sacrifice, but they protested
their desire to make it with the rest, saying that
what they liked best of all was going to the
chapel for the sermon and benediction. Their
serious attitude too, whilst there, is continually
bearing witness to the thoroughness with which
they have learnt the lesson of our Lord's presence
in the Tabernacle. Of course this frequentation
of the Guild Meetings by Protestant coloured
women prepares the way for their conversion to
the faith which readily follows. Indeed it is
well known how comparatively easy it is to
convert the negroes, the great difficulty being to
preserve them in the faith when once converted,
so pliant is their nature to the persuasions of the
last comer. Here, however, the Helpers have an
advantage in the speciality of their vocation
which enables them to penetrate into places where
even the priest with all his zeal could not readily
find entrance. The sisters follow their converts
into their homes and endeavour, and will endeavour, to watch for a long time over their converts until the newly grasped truths have obtained
too firm a hold on the mind and heart to be easily

displaced. Among these house-to-house visits too we must not forget to include those paid to the sick, for the coloured people no less than the whites are taught to feel that they can summon the Helpers of the Holy Souls to the side of their sick beds.

It remains to record the progress made in the London foundation since the last edition of this account was published. The ' one or two large rooms,' the want of which was then felt, have now been satisfactorily provided, together with a devotional little chapel much appreciated by the different ' classes ' who attend it. Round this still small centre—small in the size of its buildings and yet smaller in the size of the community which administers it—it is really marvellous how much of busy life gathers. The Helpers are wont to employ the term ' conversion ' to designate cases both of Protestants brought into the Catholic Church and of Catholics recovered to the use of the Sacraments after long neglect. On such conversions they set great store, and they are consoled to know that their number amounts to something like one hundred each year. Surely this is in itself a striking evidence that God is blessing their work ; so at all events it is felt by priests, like the present writer, to whom from time to time these nuns bring souls thus won by their gentle and tactful zeal, or by whom other applicants for care and instruction are entrusted to them with the fullest confidence.

Of the guilds and other meetings the following particulars will be of interest. During the week there are the meetings of the Mothers' Guild, of the Destitute Children, and of the Children of the Rosary; on Sundays there are the Guild for young business girls with its threefold division, and the Guild of Our Lady of the Sacred Heart, established only in the present year.

The Mothers' Guild is for the wives of labouring men, who are invited to spend together a couple of hours at a time at the convent. They can bring with them their infants, whether in arms or too young for school, and these during the meeting are entrusted to the charge of one or more of the sisters in a room apart. The meeting combines work with instruction and recreation. Whilst the needles ply the nun in charge first reads aloud a pleasant story, then gives simple and practical instructions which are listened to with interest, and the fruits of which are not rarely seen in the improved character of the homes. The instruction over, hymns are sung and quiet conversation is encouraged. The needlework is regarded as, to some extent, a school ; it is for the purpose of learning, and useful progress in this respect is made. Many who on first joining the meetings could not make the simplest article of clothing, with the aid of a little steady teaching and practice become in time able to produce work that will bear inspection and criticism. To foster healthy emulation and thereby progress the following system has been found to answer. The work done at the meetings by its various members is allowed to accumulate until at the end of six months it has become a goodly pile of garments, quilts, etc. From this pile the members draw in turn according to the regularity of their attendance, and these days of distribution count as real red-letter days in their lives. At the Christmas distribution, moreover, to give it a further distinction, bags of grocery are distributed along with the garments to all who have attained a certain degree of regular attendance. None will be surprised to hear that, finding the benefit their wives derive from these meetings, husbands in their turn often become interested, and that in this manner the way is not seldom opened to much spiritual good. Books are asked for, the visits of the sisters are solicited in time of sickness, and, confidential relations being at length established, they find their opportunity of bringing in the priest—for in many of these houses, even when the inhabitants are Catholic, the priest's visits have not been hitherto welcomed, and besides it must be borne in mind that the membership of the Mothers' Guild is not restricted to Catholics.

The streets of London are filled with the children of destitute parents, who, either through necessity or through indolence, clothe them in little better than rags and allow them to run about half wild. Every evening some of these little unfortunates may be seen hurrying to the convent, where under the affectionate care of the nuns they are taught to clothe themselves with the work of their own hands—and not themselves only, for in the pleasing self-forgetfulness of childhood, a little tattered suppliant is not unfrequently heard asking: ' Please, sister, may I make an apron for mother ? ' or ' a shirt for father ? ' or ' a petticoat for my baby sister ? ' As with the adults, singing, reading aloud, and religious instruction accompany the sewing lessons, the capacities of tender age, and, indeed, of untrained natures, being of course considered. And here again experience shows how beneficial the work is. Not only are its effects visible in these poor children themselves, whose affections are soon enlisted to struggle with their wildness, but they are also visible in the parents whose gratitude leads them to desire visits from the sisters and to lend ready ears to their counsels.

The Association of Children of the Rosary is for children who, if poor, are not in want, and who come to the convent to work, not for themselves but for others. The clothes which they make at their class meetings are distributed at Christmas time to children poorer than themselves. Voluntarily for this purpose they give up two of their evenings each week, and it is gratifying to see the generous spirit which animates them. In this association also Protestants mingle with Catholics and imbibe the same spirit, joining with devotion in the Rosary and other prayers, and profiting by the catechetical instructions. Their work is appropriately consecrated to the Infant Jesus.

On Sunday afternoons, as has been said, the Girls' Guilds have their meetings, and it is then that the capacities of Park House are strained to the utmost. The principle of division between the three guilds is one of age, the Guild of the Guardian Angels being for children of school age ; that of Our Lady of Mercy for those who have left school but are still children ; that of Our Lady of Providence for those over eighteen. Such a division is necessary for obvious purposes, and the young people pass on from one to the other, the ambition of the younger being to enter in due course the Guild of Our Lady of Providence. Those who belong to this guild are mostly business girls, employed during the week in the large London houses. It is wonderful how good many girls of this class are, and when they join the guild they readily respond to the invitation to regard its title, ' Our Lady of Providence, Queen of Purgatory,' as having a real meaning for themselves.   They seriously unite with the religious in prayer and work for the Holy Souls, offering for this purpose the special devotions prescribed each Sunday, such as the Way of the Cross, and the Rosary, as well as the Hour of Recollection every month, not to speak of voluntary acts of self-denial which they take upon themselves, and the patient and at times even heroic bearing of troubles. It must not, however, be supposed that these pious exercises absorb all their time on the Sunday afternoons. If these girls are good they are also bright and know how to enjoy themselves in innocent conversation or employments either within the convent, or, when the weather permits, in its shady garden, where they delight to take the invariable tea which a kind benefactor always provides.

These girls are also energetic apostles. Their good example attracts the well disposed among their business companions, and it is perhaps chiefly through their influence exercised in this way, and through the simple explanations of the Catholic faith which they are able to give, that the Helpers obtain the ‘conversions’ which, as has been mentioned, are becoming really numerous.

The Guild of the Sacred Heart was established in the spring of the present year (1896) to meet a long-felt want. The destitute children who come for instruction in the week-day evenings are of school age and should be in some of the public elementary schools during the day. But when they pass out of school at the age of fourteen and go to work in the factories, or laundries, or, as they express it, to ' chare,' the dangerous age commences. What the nature of the danger is for the Catholic child in London may be gathered from the sort of answers the nuns so commonly get from the negligent Catholics whom they meet in their house-visiting expeditions. Not without a certain pride a woman of this class will say: ' Yes, indeed, sister, I was baptised a Catholic. But you see how it was. When I left school I had to go and work with Protestants. They did not care about going to mass and they never saw that I went—indeed, mostly they would not let me out at mass time ; so I got careless and grew out of the habit. Then when I grew up I met my present husband, who was an Englishman, and a bitter Protestant, and so when we were married for peace' sake I gave up all thought of practising my religion.' ' But are none of the children baptised then ? ' 'Well, the eldest one is, and the next two were christened in the Protestant Church, but the others have not been christened at all.' Such a dialogue, which might be repeated in a hundred cases, shows how danger began when the protection of school was withdrawn, and shows also how the danger increases with the subsequent generations. What chance after leaving school, even if by some happy accident they should have attended a Catholic school, for the children of such a mother?

Girls of this class are not admissible into the other sodalities, and some separate provision is required to attract them in from the streets where they will otherwise pass their Sundays idling on door-steps, or mixing with undesirable company. Hence the Guild of Our Lady of the Sacred Heart. This guild is in its infancy at present, and we must be content to anticipate instead of recording results, although it may at least be set down among results that some of these children have been prepared for the sacraments, which irregularity of attendance or other causes had rendered impossible during their school days. But there seems reasonable ground for hope that with the help of tea and games and suitable religious instruction, with the prospect of prizes at Christmas for good conduct and regular attendance, the meetings will be rendered attractive and useful to these not unwilling little victims of London life. If only they can be kept in hand till childhood is passed, and a riper age finds them in the confirmed possession of habits of piety and self-control, there is some prospect that they may become good Catholic wives and mothers.

It has already been stated how Protestants (with discretion) are admitted along with Catholics to the convent gatherings, but it may be noticed that the Guild of Our Lady of the Sacred Heart opens the door to a special class of Protestant children, those who, as so frequently happens, have been sent by their parents to Catholic schools. Such children are usually forbidden by their parents to become Catholics, but they often conceive the desire, and if the desire does not afterwards fructify it is in many cases merely because in quitting school they quit also their Catholic associations. Children of this sort have joined the Guild of the Sacred Heart, and a single instance of the results may be narrated as an illustration of what may easily happen again and often. A Protestant child followed some little Catholic friends, who had formerly been her school-fellows, to the guild and very soon after begged her parents' consent to be received into the Church. It was a bold step, for they had always been averse to her Catholic tendencies and had usually met her requests to go to Catholic churches with sharp reprimands. Still perseverance gained the day, and she was in due course received and made her first Communion with great fervour. The interest taken in his child touched the father's heart when he heard of it, and one evening he surprised the nuns by coming up himself to the convent, and saying : ' You can have the four younger ones whenever you like '. They were of course taken in hand at once, and the parents also became glad trophies of their child's piety and perseverance.

Just one single word remains to be said about the little boys, for it must not be supposed that they have no place at Park House. A noisy group congregates at the big gate of the yard every Saturday morning, and once inside quietly settles down to listen to catechism stories. Often these little lads are attendants at the Board schools, where they get no religious instruction. It is fortunate, therefore, for them that at these Saturday gatherings they have an opportunity in some degree of supplying the omission, and also of being prepared for their first Communions.

Here then this little chronicle of work done and hopes formed must terminate. Of course what have been set down have been the consoling successes which have been scored, and it would be a mistake if the reader were to suppose that all has been *couleur de rose*. There are disappointments also and many of them, and harassing anxieties as to whether work that seemed to be offering fair prospects of success is not destined after all to fall through. Then there are the varying moods of children in whom the gipsy element is so strong, very trying to the over-tasked nerves which have to bear with them. Still the Helpers encourage themselves by bearing constantly in mind, when the toils and even sufferings of apostolic work become their portion, that these at least offer them excellent opportunities of fulfilling what after all is the primary end of their institute—expiation for the Holy Souls in Purgatory.

S. F. S.